WHAT OTHERS ARE SAYING

"As a fan and author of true Christian fiction, I always love to find other authors who weave a spiritual message, lesson, into their books. Tanya Eavenson has done just that with *The Rescue*, a wonderful story of learning to trust God no matter the circumstance, to remember that He is always with you and will be your ever-present help in times of trouble. He is the ultimate Rescuer. Thank you, Tanya, for the reminder. I definitely recommend this this enjoyable page-turner to all those who relish a good western inspirational romance."

—CRYSTAL L BARNES,
AUTHOR OF THE MARRIAGE & MAYHEM SERIES.

"Ms. Eavenson writes a poignant tale filled with emotions. One can't help but feel for the characters as they battle an evil man intent on getting his way. A genteel lady and a gentleman cowboy on the race for their lives. This is a historical not to be missed!"
—LAURA V. HILTON, AUTHOR OF *MARRIED TO A STRANGER*
(WHITAKER HOUSE)

"Eavenson knows how to ratchet up the action and suspense, carried all the way through to the last chapter. Rosalind and Trent are endearing characters hounded by a villain that truly gave me chills, with a supporting cast as well-drawn as the hero and heroine. *The Rescue* will draw you in, pump you up, and touch your heart."
—CAROLE TOWRISS, AUTHOR OF *BY THE WATERS OF KADESH*

The

RESCUE

BOOKS BY TANYA EAVENSON

UNENDING LOVE SERIES

Unconditional
Restored

GAINING LOVE SERIES

To Gain a Mommy
To Gain a Valentine
To Gain a Bodyguard

The RESCUE

BOOK 1

TANYA EAVENSON

THE RESCUE

Published by All Roads Publishing

Copyright © 2019 by Tanya Eavenson

On file at the Library of Congress in Washington, DC.

ISBN 978-1-945981-03-6

Scripture quotations, whether quoted or paraphrased by the characters, are taken from the King James Version of the Bible.

Cover Design by Suzanne D. Williams, Graphic Design

"He delivereth and rescueth, and he worketh signs and wonders in heaven and in earth, who hath delivered Daniel from the power of the lions."
Daniel 6:27 (KJV)

CHAPTER ONE

Charlestown, Boston
May 1886

Rosalind Standford's heart thudded against her ribcage as she lifted her pale green ball gown and stepped into the foyer. *Where is he?* She stood on tiptoe and scanned the dinner guests, trying to catch a glimpse of Trenton Easton. Disappointment and the worry that had plagued her for the last few days clutched her. Was the gossip true?

Surely Trenton would have told her. Or her own mother, if she knew. Mother was the only person who encouraged Rosalind's feelings for her childhood best friend, feelings that had recently begun blooming toward something more.

Rosalind's stomach quivered at the thought. She ran her fingertips along silver threads and embroidered sequins at her waist. She'd picked this satin gown for Trenton, knowing it would accent her gray eyes, a trait he only last week said gave her a dove-like beauty.

Again she swept her gaze over the room, past her mother, her father—her gaze, unfortunately, snagging on that of Mr. Glover Richards, a man almost her father's age. He walked toward her, the click of his heels on the wooden floor lifting above the hum of scattered conversations and the hammering of her eardrums. She forced a smile and nodded, then turned to step away. His stiff, damp fingers slid around her upper arm, halting her movement.

A chill ran up her spine. "Mr. Richards." She pulled back.

His dark eyes narrowed, assessing. An amused smile twisted his lips. He bowed. "How are you this evening, Miss Standford?"

She trembled as her name slid past his thin lips with a hissing sound. It was silly, but she couldn't help herself. The man gave her the cold shivers. She didn't want to talk to him, let alone suffer his touch, though lately he'd spent so much time with their family he'd become hard to avoid. It was as if he and her father had become dearest friends. Manners demanded she give a polite response, but she couldn't bring herself to like the man. "Doing well, thank you. And you?"

"I'm grateful for your father's invitation to Mr. Easton's home."

"Being the bank's vice president has its advantages, does it not?" She folded her gloved hands and squeezed them together, wondering if Mother felt the same unease at Mr. Richards's constant presence.

"Indeed it does. It's my hope this new partnership between your father and me will secure more"—the corners of his mouth rose as if he enjoyed a private joke—"pleasant opportunities to come."

"I see," she answered, although she didn't understand his meaning. Father never spoke of business around her or her mother, but whatever the dealings, Mr. Richards seemed happy. "I hope you and my father have a great partnership."

Trenton descended the stairs, so handsome in his formal wear he took her breath away. He strolled past her, his jaw tense and his blond hair nearly touching his collar. Without looking to the right or left, he headed toward the dining room.

It's true. Trenton and his family were leaving Boston. The dinner was not a celebration but a final farewell. Tears stung her eyes. How could Trenton have kept this to himself? "If you will excuse me, Mr. Richards."

"Allow me?" He crooked his arm.

"Thank you, but no. My father is waiting." She hurried away before Mr. Richards could insist. Another minute with Mr. Richards might cause her to miss speaking to Trenton altogether.

She made her way across the crowded room, but the laughing, milling guests converging on the dining hall prevented her from reaching Trenton in time. Resigned, she joined her father and let him escort her into the dining hall. Music wafted in behind her while the spice of men's aftershave and the flowery scent of women's perfume clashed like cymbals. She reached the doorway and hesitated as dozens took their places in the wooden high-back chairs lining the tables. How many guests had been invited? She scanned the room. Fifty. Sixty. And they would all be finding out at the same time.

Her father escorted her to the table and selected for her the chair next to Mr. Richards. Mr. Richards stood, and his dark eyes met her father's with approval. Everything in her wanted to balk at not being seated next to Trenton, but her father's beaming smile gave her pause.

Throughout the meal, Rosalind pushed the roast lamb around her plate, glancing at Trenton from the opposite side of the table, hoping her imagination had gotten the better of her. When Trenton's father stood at the head of the table and clanked his knife against his water glass, a knot grew within her throat.

"Ladies and gentlemen, I want to thank you for attending our gathering this evening. It is an honor to have our friends here on this night. As some of you have heard, there is gossip circulating that we are moving." Mr. Easton glanced at his wife and then his son. Trenton frowned. "It's true. The Eastons are moving to Graham, Texas. We leave tomorrow."

A collective gasp rose from the guests.

Rosalind bit her lip and forced herself to stay seated, though every part of her wanted to drag Trenton outside and confront him for not telling her. She deserved to know the truth.

Mr. Easton's parting speech seemed endless, and through its entirety, Trenton steadfastly avoided her gaze.

After supper, Rosalind headed to the balcony. It was warmer than usual for the time of year, and the other guests had gone to the ballroom, giving her a few moments alone to compose herself. Instead, she paced, thinking. Was there no idea she could offer? No sound reason to discourage the move?

She could find none, except those growing in her heart.

Blinking back tears, she stopped at the rail and looked into the night sky; the stars, like her mood, seemed dim. Even the rose-scented breeze—her favorite—failed to bring comfort.

"Why are you upset, little girl?"

Her heart ached. She'd know Trenton's voice anywhere. She turned toward him, her chin raised. "I am not little."

"Are you not shorter than I? And are you not a girl?" A smile played on his lips.

How she would miss his teasing. How she would miss *him*. "I am shorter, but I'm a woman. I'm sixteen. Women my age are married, I'll have you know. And if I wanted to be married, I would be."

"And who would you marry, Rosalind?" His voice lowered as he took a step closer. "Who would be able to keep up with a wife who climbs trees and steals chocolate bars?"

She planted her palms on her hips. "I didn't steal them. You laid them down in plain sight, and besides, you said I could have them."

"Only because you left me none."

Rosalind giggled, then it hit her again. He was leaving. Her hands slipped from her waist. "I'll miss you."

Trenton stared at his feet. She studied the top of his blond head until he lifted his blue eyes to hers. "May I write to you, Rosalind?"

"Yes. You better."

A heart-stopping smile lit his features, and a dimple appeared in his right cheek, stealing her breath. Whether what she felt was a mere crush or whether she was in love … well, with time, she'd learn her true feelings. Either way, she would treasure his letters.

She took a deep breath. "I guess I should go. Papa said we were leaving soon, but I wanted to come out here one last time." She slowly turned, forcing herself to go.

Trenton reached out and took her hand. "Rosalind, wait."

From the lightest of touches, her fingers warmed. Though propriety dictated she move away, she let her hand linger in his for a moment. Mother had told her a woman's feelings sometimes grew in baby steps, other times in leaps and bounds. What did it mean that she wanted to lace her fingers with his and never let go?

"What was the matter earlier?" He regarded her, squeezing her hand slightly. "You seemed upset."

"How long have you known you'd be moving?"

"I heard the gossip like everyone else, but I thought it was only gossip." His gaze moved to their hands. "Mother told me tonight, right before everyone came for supper."

"I feared you knew but didn't tell me."

He ran his thumb over her fingers. "I would have told you."

Heavy footsteps sounded behind them, and her hand slipped from his. "We're going, Rosalind," her father said. "Your mother is waiting for you by the door. She's feeling a bit ill."

"Yes, Papa," she called, then blinked back tears. "Until I see you again, Trenton."

"Goodbye, Rose."

Her heart squeezed as she walked away and followed her father out the door. Trenton had never called her "Rose" before, and she liked the sound of it. How long would it be before she heard it again? Would she ever?

She heard sputtering and gagging even before she saw her mother standing outside by another's carriage, one hand gripping Mr. Richards's arm, the other covering her mouth, her eyes wide and frantic. Father rushed to her side. Mr. Richards yelled for his driver to bring his own carriage around.

"Father, what is happening?"

Her mother coughed violently as the carriage wheels crunched to a stop before them. Mr. Richards assisted her father, but as they lifted Mother inside, her hand fell from her lips, revealing bloody fingers.

"Mother?" Rosalind trembled. *Dear God, please ... What does the blood mean?*

Mr. Richards came to her side and placed a gentle hand on her elbow. "Come, Rosalind. We must go."

She nodded quickly and allowed him to assist her inside the carriage. Her mother had been feeling poorly for months now and had tried to hide it, but the coughing fits had worsened. *God, take care of my mother.*

The hacking cough increased, and her mother jerked and writhed.

"Father, can we do nothing?" Rosalind asked. "Mother?" She looked from one to the other, but they both looked afraid and lost, an expression she'd never before seen on either of their faces.

When they arrived at the house, Father instructed Mr. Richards to find the doctor, and only after several stumbles did they manage to get Mother inside. Mother's strength had simply vanished, leaving her pale and aged, too weak to even keep her eyes open as they helped her to bed.

It seemed a lifetime passed before the doctor arrived. During the examination, Mother lay still. Too still. Fear surged to Rosalind's core at Mother's motionless state. Then another cough raked through Mother's body, blood dripped from her nose, and Rosalind didn't know which was worse—watching Mother lie still as death or seeing the spasms and hearing the awful retching. Tears filled Rosalind's eyes as she stroked strands of soft brown hair from her mother's face and tucked them behind her ear.

"Do you know what's wrong with her, Doctor? Is it consumption?" her father asked.

Kneeling next to the bed, the physician wiped her mother's nose and folded the cloth. "Her coughing is worse. I'm afraid you are correct. She has tuberculosis."

Rosalind shook her head and ran from the room. She flew down the stairs, faltered into the stagnant night air, and stopped on the porch as reality weighed heavily on her shoulders. She swallowed down her screams. "God, are You listening? Don't You see? You must help my mother. Please don't take her. Don't …" She fell to her knees, sobbing into her palms.

Arms came around her shoulders, and she jerked back, biting back her tears. "Mr. Richards." She moved from him and stumbled on the hem of her gown but caught her balance.

"It's all right." He followed her. "I have your father's permission."

She wiped her cheek with the back of her hand. "What do you mean you have his permission?"

"We will be married."

Rosalind fought to understand what Mr. Richards was saying, but the words seemed scrambled, incomprehensible. Her mind a fog. "What do you mean, *married*?"

"Earlier tonight I asked permission to court you, but moments ago, he gave me his full blessing."

Surely she'd misheard him. "You asked for my hand in marriage now, while we're learning my mother is dying? My father is as distraught as I am."

"Perhaps the doctor's wrong," Mr. Richards whispered against her ear. "Perhaps she will recover. Nevertheless …"

"We shouldn't be … you shouldn't be alone with me here like this. Propriety …"

He dragged a fingertip along her jaw, then down her bare arm, his expression declaring ownership even as it dared her to argue.

Though her heart galloped, she fought her instincts to flinch. Glover Richards was a very powerful man, she'd overheard her father saying once, powerful enough to harm his enemies. Father must need the man's friendship, otherwise he would never have agreed. "Why? Why me?"

"I will court you as your father wishes." A slow smile slid up one side of his face. "And at nineteen you will be my bride."

Rosalind's pulse pounded in her ears. None of this made sense. If only Mother were well. She'd never let Father agree to this marriage, and he would listen to her.

She balled her hands into fists at her waist, squeezing the satin lace crisscrossing there—satin meant to draw Trenton's eye. Yet Trenton was packing his trunk for Texas, even as Mr. Richards's gaze roamed her hair, her face and throat, and her bodice and cinched gown.

"We don't have to announce our betrothal … yet," he said as if the deed was done.

She swallowed, meeting Mr. Richards's stare.

He took her hand and slid it through the crook of his arm. "Let's get you back inside, shall we?"

She let him lead her, but her heart recoiled, and she threw a desperate prayer toward heaven. *Lord, You must heal my mother and rescue me. Save us.*

CHAPTER TWO

Graham, Texas
June 1888

The work never ends here ... but I wouldn't have it any other way.

Outside his two-story home, Trent pulled a bandana from his back pocket and wiped the sweat from his forehead. The midafternoon sun pressed down as if branding his scalp. He'd put away his parents' wagon, now neatly stored in the barn. He'd chopped wood, with the logs stacked four and five high along the kitchen wall. After grabbing his canteen by the barn, he took several gulps.

"Trent!" The back door opened, and his mother peeked out. "Isn't that enough for the day?"

"Plenty of daylight left," he answered, pouring the rest of the cool water over his face and shirt. "And I promised Father I'd see to the fence." They couldn't afford to lose another longhorn.

"A body ought to rest now and then. Though I suppose you'll sleep well enough tonight."

"Yes, ma'am," he said as she closed the door. And he hoped

she was right. Last night he'd dreamed of Boston. The busy streets and crowded buildings. The parties and … Rosalind.

He swiped his Stetson from a tree stump and settled it on his head. With a sigh, he swung into the saddle, then rode back to the western edge of their property. This was the land he loved, the place where the Lord seemed to meet him. Wind breezed past his ears as he smiled at the cattle egret that crossed his path. Orange and pink streaked the distant sky. *From whence cometh my help? My help cometh from the Lord, which made heaven and earth.* God was his helper and provider at all times.

God had been good to his family over the past two years. Ranching was hard work and a hard life. But Trent had learned the ways and the whys, the how-tos and the how-not-tos, while memories of Boston traveled farther and farther away. He never wanted to leave the land God had given him here, let alone return to his old hometown. He missed none of what was before— except Rosalind.

A longing he couldn't quite shake squeezed his heart once again. Yet the more he thought of her, the more questions he had. Always questions and never answers for why she had stopped responding to his letters. He hadn't heard from her in well over a year. Had he misinterpreted her feelings and their discussions of the future? Maybe, in an effort to be kind, she had chosen not to respond rather than hurting a childhood friend.

With a deep breath, Trent dismounted and approached the broken fence line. He and Matthew, his best ranch hand, had made significant progress patching the breach that morning. Only a dozen or so posts still needed to be set, and the two remaining rolls of barbed wire lying on the ground would surely do the trick.

He measured for spacing between each post, marking the ground with the edge of his boot. His already tired muscles tightened in protest when he grabbed a shovel and started digging the holes deep, to the exact width he and Matthew had done this morning. Trent dropped in the first post and began refilling the hole.

Mending fences. A far easier task than dealing with women and their fickle hearts.

He worked alone as the sun dropped to eye level. Hooves pounded toward him—someone was in a hurry. Securing the wire, Trent reached for the bandana in his pocket, then wiped the back of his neck. He shielded his eyes as Matthew came to an abrupt halt.

"Your father sent me. You're needed at the house."

"Is everything all right?"

"I'm not sure. All I know is your mother is crying. Go. I'll finish."

Trent ran for his horse and leapt into the saddle. He goaded the animal to a full gallop and strained forward as if doing so would quicken his arrival. Mother seldom cried. Was she hurt? Had something happened to one of the cowhands? *Dear God, give me strength to face whatever's come our way.*

He jumped from the saddle before his horse came to a stop, rushed up onto the porch, and blasted through the front door. "Father?"

"I'm here, son." Solemn faced, his father exited the kitchen into the living room. Sounds of his mother's hiccups reached Trent's ears.

"Why is Mother crying?"

"She received a letter from Boston. You remember the Standfords?"

He nodded. Of course he remembered them. One in particular.

"There's been a death."

Trent's legs wobbled. He steadied himself against the back of a chair, his rough callouses pressing against the wood as fear clawed its way up his throat. "Rosalind?"

His father's brows furrowed. "No. Her mother … Sarah. Apparently, she was buried almost a year ago. I'm not sure why the letter took so long getting here, maybe it got lost, but I received word in the mail today from Mr. Standford. Your mother knew Sarah was ill, but not like this. She died of consumption."

Mrs. Standford dead these last twelve months—she'd been a second mother to him during his childhood—and not one letter, not one word from Rosalind. Not for over a year now. He'd proposed marriage, and then, silence. Had she stopped writing because of her mother's passing? Or had she found someone else? "How is everyone?" He cleared his throat. "How's Rosalind?"

"I'm not sure. Roger didn't say, but your mother has expressed a desire to return to Boston and see how Rosalind is managing. You know Rosalind's sister was married and had her own life even before we left. Your mother is set on visiting, so I'll accompany her. Would you care to join us? We'd like for you to, but the choice is yours. I believe Matthew can handle the ranch while we're gone."

Hadn't Trent just told himself he never wanted to go back? The last time he'd seen Rosalind, she'd looked so lovely in the moonlight. He'd taken her hand before she'd turned to leave, and the warmth had left him tingling long after she'd gone. The smell of roses would always remind him of her.

He clasped his hands on the back of the chair. His sandpaper callouses weren't the only reasons he no longer belonged in Boston, but they were evidence enough of the unmistakable changes inside him. Never again would he fit in, mingling with high society and attending endless parties. He belonged with the bluebonnets and longhorns on his ranch, where working hard and getting his hands dirty brought a satisfaction he'd never dreamed of while growing up in the city.

Trent wasn't the only one in the family who'd changed. Back in Boston, his father had owned one of the largest banks in the city, a position which commanded respect but also left little time for family. Although the move to Graham had fulfilled his father's dream of being a rancher, Trent had also found his place in this world. And he'd gained a father.

He met his father's gaze. "If I join you, I'll need to be back in time to drive the herd to market."

"I'll make sure of it."

"I'll go. You need me. I'll go."

A whimper came from the kitchen, and both men followed the sound. His mother stood, holding a tissue to her cheek, then dabbed her eyes. "She's gone."

His father wrapped his arms around her and pulled her to his chest, kissing the top of her hairline. "Shhh. Rest, my love. Know the Good Shepherd has called His lamb home where there are no more tears or pain, only love and peace."

Trent left them alone, making his way back to the front of the house. Was Rosalind all right? Did she still mourn the loss of her mother?

He cared about her grief, of course. But what he desired most was to cuddle her in his arms as his father had done with his mother. If Trent had stayed in Boston, would Rose have allowed him to hold her?

Trent shook his head. He dreamed of her often, the way her gray eyes shone in candlelight. Even when meeting other girls here in Graham, he always compared them to Rosalind.

He ran a hand across the scruff along his jaw. She might not even recognize him. He'd left Boston as Trenton, a well-groomed boy unsure of his future. Now, he was Trent, a man, a rancher. Working his own land.

As he closed the front door, it gave its typical squeal and bang. Matthew caught up with him on the porch. "Is everything all right?" he asked, lifting the brim of his cowboy hat from his eyes.

"Mother's not doing so good." They headed for the horses. "Friends of ours in Boston had a death in the family. Mom and Dad are going there for a visit."

"Are you going with them?"

"Probably. Yeah. Think you could handle things around here?"

Matthew shot him a look.

"Had to ask." Trent smiled as he mounted his stallion. "Were you and Blake able to find where the longhorn strayed after the storm?"

Matthew swung onto his horse. "I'm thinkin' he tried to find shelter but found the fence torn down instead and escaped. We tracked him to the brook behind the west edge of the property, but beyond there the trail disappears. Blake thinks it might have something to do with the longhorns that went missing on the east side of town."

Trent looked west where rippling heat waves obscured the horizon. A bead of sweat ran down his collar, tickling his neck. Could rustlers be stealing his cattle, as Blake believed? "Time to buckle down if I plan to go to Boston."

Matthew nodded.

As they rode, Trent's stomach clenched—but why? Over fear of rustlers? Or the prospect of seeing Rosalind again?

Daylight was breaking when Trent rose to the smell of coffee, but he knew enjoying the dark brew would have to wait until he'd completed the milking.

With a pail in hand, he sat on the three-legged stool next to one of the cows. "Good morning, Rose." He placed his cheek against her side and began their morning routine while the musty scent of cow flesh and sweet hay worked to ease the tension in his shoulders.

After a few minutes, Blake entered, grabbed his own pail, and began milking.

Blake cleared his throat. "Do you mind if Grace starts comin' around? I mean, Ella will be here with Matthew."

Trent released the warm teat between his fingers. "I had no idea you and Grace were courting."

Silence.

"Sure, she can come out too. I'll tell Martin to make extra for dinner on Saturdays while we're gone." Trent resumed his work, glad to know someone had taken an interest in Blake. The ragged scar across his cheek kept most women away, almost gave him a fierce look. Trent caught a glimpse of Blake with his head against the cow's side. Nothing could be further from the truth.

Matthew strolled in, whistling. "So … you ready to see Rosalind?" He hoisted a bag of feed to his shoulder.

"I'm accompanying my parents to Boston," Trent answered over the rhythmic pings of milk landing in his bucket.

Matthew chuckled. "Sure, nothing to do with Rosalind whatsoever."

Annoying though it was, the man had a point. Trent wanted to be there for Rosalind if she needed him. And he needed to know why she'd stopped writing. Not that Trent would admit it to Matthew. "Watch yourself." He squirted a jet of milk onto his friend's boot.

Grinning, Matthew backed up, hands held up in a gesture of surrender. "All right, all right. Well, the sows need my attention, but I'll be back. Mornin', Blake."

Blake stood with his pail and nodded. "Mornin'." He eyed Trent for a brief moment, poured the milk into a can, then moved to the next cow, questions shining in his eyes. "Rosalind, huh?"

"Matthew talks too much."

After the animals were fed and tended to, Trent climbed the stairs to the porch at the back of the house. He swung open the door, and the aroma of coffee met him. Inhaling, he took a cup from the counter and poured what his taste buds had yearned for the past two hours.

Trent scooped up the plate from the stove where Martin had left it warming. The cook fed both Trent's family and the ranch hands. Although Martin tended to wear a scowl, one bite of his eggs, perfectly seasoned, reminded Trent the man was worth his weight in gold.

He pulled out a chair to sit, the wooden legs scraping against the floor. He hadn't seen his parents this morning but knew they were awake, readying themselves for their long journey. Just thinking about the carriage ride to the railroad, the ride on the rails to Boston, the time he'd spend away from his land, stole his appetite. He pushed his uneaten food away.

With one last sip, Trent left his dishes and headed outside to hitch the wagon, but Matthew had beaten him to it. "Are you trying to get rid of me?"

"You know the real reason you're goin'." Matthew stroked the horse's mane but looked at Trent. "She must mean somethin', the way you've steered clear of all the beautiful women around here who throw themselves at you." Matthew took off his Stetson and slapped it against his leg. "Yep, Rosalind means somethin', all right. You've only talked about her a few times, but if you ask me, you owe it to yourself to find out exactly where you stand with her. If not for your sake, for mine, so Ella will stop askin' me to set you up with her friends."

"Just help me tote down my mother's trunk."

Matthew secured his hat on his head with two hands. "You're not backing out, are ya?"

"I'm going, but I'm itching to change my mind," Trent said and led Matthew into the house.

CHAPTER THREE

"Rosalind." Her father knocked on her bedroom door. "Are you up? Glover's here to see you."

"Yes. I'll be down in a moment." She swiped at the tears before they fell, protecting the worn pages of her mother's Bible as she read aloud. *"Bow down thine ear to me; deliver me speedily: be thou my strong rock, for a house of defence to save me. For thou art my rock and my fortress; therefore for thy name's sake lead me, and guide me."* She fought back a sob. *"Pull me out of the net that they have laid privily for me: for thou art my strength."*

Oh, Lord, please help me. Free me from this marriage.

She rose and stood in front of her vanity. Puffy eyes gazed back. She brushed a finger across her reddened skin and inhaled, trying to steady herself and erase evidence she'd been crying. "That's the best I can do." She took a deeper breath, exhaled, then left the sanctuary of her room. As she descended the stairs, arguing voices rose to meet her.

"You have no choice, Roger. Now that she's back from your mother's home, you will not send Rosalind away again. Do you hear me?"

The last step creaked, and her father appeared in the parlor doorway. "I thought I heard you." He took her elbow and smiled, but it didn't reach his eyes.

Glover approached and gave a half bow. His dark hair fell over one eye, but it didn't prevent his gaze from roaming over every inch of her form before stopping at her chest. "How are you this evening, my dear?"

"Fine," she whispered the lie through dry lips.

Glover's gaze met hers. He pushed her father aside and came to stand directly in front of her. "How are you truly?"

She straightened under his scrutiny. "I am well enough."

"You are *not* well." He gently cupped her cheek, and her body trembled against his touch. "Was your trip not satisfactory?"

"It was, indeed. I'm rather exhausted from the journey, as you might expect."

"Yes, well, you won't be taking another trip." His hand dropped to his side. "I've spoken with your father, and I have his word on the matter. From now on, you will be where I can find you."

She clamped together her shaking hands as fear and the reality she'd never be free of him crept through her.

Glover yanked a wad of bills from his jacket pocket. "See to it she eats. And rehire that cook."

"Doris?"

"If she's the one. Rosalind is becoming too thin." He counted off ten bills, handed them to her father, then pocketed the rest. "I shall see you both for supper."

Her father quickly counted the bills. "What time shall we expect you? I'll make sure the cook serves something to your liking."

Glover placed a firm hand on his shoulder. "Do I need to remind you how this money should be spent?"

"No." Her father flushed as he lowered his head. "I won't forget."

Glover turned and sought her lips. Rosalind fought the bile climbing her throat as his hands roamed her back. "Until tonight, my dear."

She shivered at his promised words as her father followed Glover to the front porch. After hurrying upstairs, she closed her bedroom door and sought to keep her mind from the memory of Glover's touch. Staring at the sparse furnishings, only her vanity, armoire, and bed remained. Even the jewelry box that had once rested on her dresser, her special place for a gift from her mother—a diamond necklace—had vanished. She glanced at her right hand, a thin line etched her skin where a ring once adorned her finger. She clenched her hands at her sides.

Gone. Sold.

Three taps sounded at her door. "Rosalind, may I come in?"

She sat on her bed, resisting the urge to say no, as her fingernails dug into her palms. "Yes."

Her father entered, shoulders slumped, hands stuffed in his pockets. "Was Glover right? You're not well?"

"How could a man like Glover know my condition better than my own father?" It crushed her to say the words, but the truth was hard to deny. When had he stopped caring, loving her?

He stared at her. "I have something I must discuss with you. It's important." He withdrew his hands from his pockets and sat on the edge of her bed. "We will have company soon."

"Company? We've had no company since mother was alive. Who's coming?"

"The Eastons."

Panic rose within her at the sound of their name. *Trenton*

and his family, here? She blinked back moisture filling her eyes at the thought of their return and how long she'd waited, but it mattered little now. They mustn't come. "Why visit after all this time? What purpose could they have?"

"When Sarah passed, I sent word to them in Texas. It seems they didn't receive my letter until recently. A telegram came for me several days ago. The Eastons should arrive within the week."

"They cannot come." She rose, her voice wavering. "You must send word before it's too late."

He looked away. "It is too late. They are on their way as we speak. It's only proper that I invite them to stay with us."

She knelt at his feet and grasped his hands. "No. Please, Father. I beg you. Send them away. They can't stay here. I couldn't bear it if—"

"I have no choice. I need to at least make the offer. While the Eastons are here, nothing can seem amiss. If they ever found out what I've done—the gambling or about Glover—we'd both be in danger."

She stood and began to pace, desperate not to allow fear to overtake her. How could this be happening? She'd given up hope of ever seeing Trenton again. But now, how could she do so with Glover near? Freezing, she turned her gaze to her father. "Have you told Glover?"

"I've been waiting for the right moment, but he's been so angry about you visiting my mother, there hasn't been a right time. This is why I need your help. We need to keep Glover happy and the Eastons in the dark. Do you think you can manage it while they're in town?"

"You mean as you've asked me to do with my own sister?"

Her father moved to the door and stopped. "What choice do we have?" He spoke over his shoulder. "Are you willing to put

Sydney's or her twin infants' lives in danger along with ours?"

"I wish you had thought of the consequences before you gambled our lives away."

"What's done is done, Rosalind. All we can do now is survive."

Survive. She gritted her teeth. "I have done nothing else since I learned of Mother's consumption. I spent days, weeks, months nursing her, watching her die before my eyes, never able to tell her about my betrothal to Glover. When she was alive, I dreamt of marrying for love, then she died, and my dreams died with her. Your actions give me no choice but to marry Glover. So, yes, Father, I know how to stay alive—I appease the man who holds our lives in his hands."

He didn't answer but paused before closing the door behind him as he left.

The squeal of the train's brakes jerked Trent upright in bed, heart pounding. Sweat moistened his brow. He glanced around his small sleeping compartment and drew a shuddering breath. His dream, what did it mean?

Sheep grazing in an open pasture. A woman, her face blurred, sat within the sheepfold. And wolves … three—no, four—but one's eyes were aflame. With teeth as long as spears, the wolf with the blazing eyes caught and devoured a lamb, then the entire image dissolved in fire.

Not knowing the hour, he drew back the window curtain and stared outside. The sun highlighted the dormant fields with a golden hue. He focused closer to the tracks, then the scene blurred as the train passed through a stand of trees. Within the blur, he thought he saw the woman from his dream.

He shook his head of the image, released the curtain, and ran his fingers through his damp hair. One of the hardest feats he'd managed was leaving his Stetson behind. He slid from the bed, glanced down at his worn leather boots, and smiled as he pulled them on. The train jerked again and then slowly rolled to a stop. He grabbed the handle of his bag.

Boston.

Five minutes later, he followed his parents onto the station platform. Black smoke billowed from the smokestack and formed a gray cloud, obscuring his path. His steps grew heavy. He had tried to bury his feelings for the girl who rejected him, and now, behind this cloud was a hope he never wanted to die.

The whistle blew once more, startling his heart to gallop as a skittish colt. A gentle breeze blew the smoke aside, and he caught himself scanning the passersby, looking for Rosalind. Father said he'd wired the Standfords regarding their visit. Would she even care to see him? The weight of the past two years struck him between the eyes. Had she already given her heart to someone else?

With a calming breath, he roped in his weary nerves and glanced around. A wagon filled with cargo passed across the street. He turned to ask his father about his wire to the Standfords when a black carriage stopped directly in front of them. A man wearing a bowler hat stepped out.

Rosalind's father. Mr. Standford approached, seemingly thinner and shorter than Trent remembered. Lines creased the corners of his eyes. "It's been a long time." Mr. Standford smiled at them, shaking their hands and hugging his mother. "Let's get your trunks." He hurried down the platform.

While Trent stood aside, Father helped Mother climb into the carriage.

Mr. Standford handed their trunks to the driver, who heaved

them onto the top. Luckily, they hadn't brought much. Their Texas-style garments were so different from those of Bostonians. If they hoped to fit in to society here, they'd need new clothing. Trent climbed into the carriage behind Mr. Standford, who took a seat closest to the door.

"I'm sorry for your loss, Roger." His father spoke as Trent wedged into the small space between his parents and the door. "How have you been?"

"It's been hard." Mr. Standford closed the door curtains, plunging the carriage interior into darkness. The carriage jerked, then took to the road.

Trent's eyes took a moment to adjust, frustrating him as he strained to see the woman sitting beside Mr. Standford. Her face was hidden by a fashionable hat as she bent to whisper to the two tiny children bundled against her chest.

Mother leaned forward and covered the woman's hand. She turned, revealing her face.

His heart stopped and his gut clenched. *Rosalind. With children.*

Her brown hair cascaded over her shoulders. He stared—he couldn't help himself—and her gray eyes peered back at him through long lashes. Their gazes locked for a moment before she looked away. She was breathtaking … and obviously married. He forced a smile as he studied the infants in her arms. Motherhood suited her well, and somewhere deep within, he mourned that the children weren't his.

"We didn't come to inconvenience you, Roger." His father's voice brought him back to the present. "We'll be happy to stay at our old home, but we had to come after receiving your letter. I'm sorry we didn't receive it sooner."

"Nonsense. You will stay with us until your house is in order. I insist."

His father glanced at his mother. "We'll be your guests under one condition. We will purchase our provisions while we're here."

Mr. Standford raised an eyebrow. "You're welcome to stay as long as you like, but there's no need to worry about—"

"We won't be a burden. No arguments, Roger."

"All right. You win." Mr. Standford smiled. "I hope you don't mind, but we're dropping Rosalind off before heading to the house."

His mother inched to the edge of the seat and touched the finger of one of the infants. "How old are they, dear? Twins?"

"They are." Rosalind's face brightened, and pride showed on her lovely face. "This is William in the blue gown, and Anna is in the yellow. They'll be two months old next week. We were afraid William wouldn't make it, but he's grown wonderfully."

"Yes, he has. They're both beautiful."

"I couldn't agree more," his father said, and the two men began discussing recent banking trends and ranching.

As the carriage clattered along, Trent struggled not to gawk at Rosalind but failed miserably. He wanted to stare, not only stare but touch. It was wrong of him to think such things, but she was no longer in his dreams. Now she was before him in the flesh.

When the carriage finally slowed to a stop, he snuck one last look. She handed her father one of the babies. Mr. Standford climbed from the carriage and assisted his daughter out. Trent wanted to follow but held himself in place.

Up the steps to the house, Mr. Standford opened the door for Rosalind. They spoke a few words. Rosalind's brows dipped slightly before she nodded, took her other child from his arms, and entered the house.

Mr. Standford returned quickly. "Shall we?" He closed the

door as the carriage once again jerked forward.

Trent's mother exhaled, folding her hands in her lap. "She has turned into a lovely young woman, Roger. You must be so proud. And those grandchildren …"

"Oh yes, they are the center of this old man's heart. And my daughters … one can only hope and pray that God has them both in the palm of His hands."

"Hey, now." Trent's father sat up straight and tall. "If you're old, what am I? I have you by two years."

"I rest my case."

Laughter billowed from everyone except Trent. Rosalind was married. Why hadn't she told him, instead of not responding to his marriage proposal? He'd waited, but after months of no correspondence, he'd given up hope they might have a future.

Now he knew why.

Rosalind laid the babies side by side in the crib, then spread a small yellow quilt over them. She kissed their soft cheeks and quietly left their room. How wonderful it would be to one day have children of her own.

She forced the thought away and plopped onto her sister's couch, blowing hair from her eyes and tucking a rebel strand behind her ear. Trenton had never looked more handsome. He needed a haircut, but the way his blond hair turned slightly, touching his tan skin, made her heart jump. Although he hadn't recognized her right away, he'd stolen her breath. Even now, her heart hammered just thinking of him being so near.

She rose. She'd find a way to hide her feelings from Trenton. She couldn't let anyone else know of them. But would it be so wrong to pretend that he still cared for her?

Careful not to wake the sleeping infants, she wandered to her sister's closet. She pulled out a brown silk dress she favored over all the others and ran a fingertip across the gold metal adorning the waist. When Father had dropped Rosalind off, he told her to find something of her sister's to wear for the evening. Would Sydney mind? And what if she asked why Rosalind needed to borrow a gown? She couldn't very well tell Sydney about Father's financial condition.

The front door slammed closed, and Rosalind jumped at the sound. She stuffed the dress back into the closet and rushed into the hall to meet her sister.

"How are they?" Sydney peered around the tower of boxes in her arms. Wisps of brown hair escaped her hat.

"They're asleep. Did you have fun shopping? What did you buy?"

"Come. I have a surprise for you."

Rosalind followed her back into the bedroom, glancing around to make sure she'd left nothing amiss.

"I bought you a few things. I wanted to thank you for all your help with the children since our move. With Joshua stationed at the naval base, I couldn't have survived without you." Sydney let the boxes tumble from her arms onto the bed. She picked out three and stacked them in front of Rosalind.

"Oh, sis." Her eyes widened. "I don't know what to say. You really didn't have to—"

"I wanted to. Now open your presents." Sydney sat on the bed, tugged off her gloves, then unpinned her hat.

Thrilled, Rosalind lifted the lid of the first box and pulled out a gown of the palest blue. Tassels and flowers gathered on the sides. She held the dress against her frame. It appeared to be a perfect fit.

She met her sister's gaze. "This is the most elegant gown

…" Tears filled her eyes. She hadn't worn something new since, well, she couldn't remember when. Most of her dresses had been patched and re-patched. They were wearing thin. Even her shoes …

She grabbed another box and removed the lid. *Shoes!* One by one, tears rolled down her cheeks.

Her sister smiled up at her from the bed. "Don't thank me yet. You still have another box to open."

Rosalind threw aside the last round lid. Lovely undergarments filled the box.

"I haven't seen you wear anything new recently and figured you might need undergarments as well. They are a bit harder to request from a father than a mother, and my guess is you haven't had new ones since Mom passed."

Rosalind hugged her sister and held on. "Thank you."

"You're so welcome. Now, I bought three new dresses for myself, and I need to make room in the closest. Are there three dresses of mine you'd like to have?"

She released her. "I couldn't. You've done too much."

"Nonsense. I haven't done near enough, and now with a certain gentleman staying at the house, you might want to catch his eye. And honestly, I'm not sure it would be too difficult, considering …"

Rosalind tilted her head. "Considering what?"

"He's come back."

Rosalind fingered the hem on her new gown. "He didn't come back for me, Sydney. He came back because of his family."

"But don't you see? He's old enough to make his own decisions. He could have stayed behind, but he didn't. And I think I know why." She wiggled her brows.

Rosalind turned away, fighting the emotions swirling in her

heart. Oh, how she wanted it to be true. To know Trenton still loved her, desired their union. But it wasn't to be, no matter how much she wished it. "Sorry, sis, but I have to disagree. I'm not the reason he came back."

"How do you know?"

"I just do." She walked over to the window.

Sydney's arm wrapped around her waist. "I know you're betrothed to Glover, but he's too possessive of you. Joshua agrees with me on this. He's wrong for you, Rosalind. Why father gave his …" She bit her lip. "It doesn't matter any longer. I have a feeling God brought Trenton here."

Rosalind shook her head against thoughts of Glover. And God? He'd not healed their mother, not kept her father from making awful choices for himself and her.

"You'll see I'm right," Sydney said and gave her a small squeeze. "Three dresses. You'll need to hurry before dinner. How I wish I could attend, but Joshua's coming home for the evening. I have an idea!" She clapped her hands together. "Dress here. I'll have my carriage take you home. That way I can do your hair. What do you say?"

Rosalind forced a smile. "How can I say no?"

And more important, how was she going to hide her feelings for Trenton during dinner?

Rosalind pressed a hand to her heart and stared at her reflection. Sydney had indeed styled Rosalind's hair, sweeping it up high on her head, bangs feathered across her forehead. The pastel blue dress accented her small waist, and the bodice … She felt like a woman, and so wished her mother was here to see.

"Oh, Sydney, I look—"

"Like a princess." She turned Rosalind to face her. "You have a wonderful time tonight, but you need to hurry or you'll be late." She pushed her through the door to the waiting carriage. "And don't forget to tell Trenton hello for me." Sydney smiled and waved before reentering the house.

Rosalind's heart pounded during the short ride. What would Trenton see tonight when he looked at her? The little girl he'd left behind, or the woman she'd become? She had never stopped hoping this day would come—a day he'd return home—but she couldn't let him know of her feelings. She couldn't let *anyone* know.

She touched the sides of her face and felt the heat against her palms. There was no need to pinch her cheeks to feign a blush.

The wheels slowed to a stop, and the carriage door opened. A hand reached in to help her out, but she recognized it as Glover's. Fighting the urge to recoil, she extended her hand.

The corners of his mouth lifted into a smug grin, and he maintained his hold as they entered the house. "You look ravishing tonight, my dear."

"There you are." Her father regarded her, then Glover. "Please, come in."

"I must say,"—Glover raised Rosalind's gloved hand to his lips and kissed her knuckles before releasing her—"I wouldn't have missed it for the world."

She drew a deep breath and discreetly wiped her glove against her dress. Her stomach clenched, and nausea bubbled up her throat. In moments she'd be in the same room with two men—one who'd won her heart and didn't know it, the other who was trying to steal her very soul.

With a few steps more, they entered the dining area.

Father cleared his throat, and everyone seated along the

oblong table eyed them. "You know my youngest daughter, Rosalind, and Mr. Glover Richards," her father said, introducing them. Glover placed a hand on the small of her back and guided her toward the seat beside his.

She clutched the back of the chair as heat once again flooded to her cheeks at Glover's incessant possessiveness. Lately his boldness had increased, and she'd resorted to desperate maneuvering to avoid being alone with him, simply to avoid being ogled and touched in ways just short of unacceptable. Unbidden, her gaze went to Trenton.

She'd loved him, she realized—when he left, during that first year when his letters were plentiful, and even after she never answered his proposal. She loved him still.

He looked only at the empty plate before him.

CHAPTER FOUR

She'd married *him*?

Trent wouldn't have believed it if he hadn't heard Mr. Easton introduce them in such a way, if he hadn't seen the proof with his own eyes. Sadness sent shockwaves reaching to the depths of his soul. All the hopes and endless dreams he'd held close over the last two years … He felt his heart tear in two. He didn't dare look at her, afraid of what his eyes might reveal. What had gone wrong between him and Rosalind? *God, I don't understand.*

"Trent owns the west property that backs up to ours," his father was saying to all seated at the table. "It's about fifteen hundred acres."

"That's a lot of responsibility for a man your age." Mr. Standford leaned forward. "How old are you now, son?"

Trent felt Mr. Richards's curiosity as the man angled his body toward him, but he chose to look directly at Mr. Standford. "I turned twenty-one this past winter, sir." He wanted to say more, but his emotions stole his voice. Trent recalled the older man from the night of his father's announcement, their move to

Texas. Rosalind shouldn't have married Glover Richards. What did she see in him? He was much too old for her. What eighteen-year-old woman wanted a man in his late-forties? *Obviously she did.*

Trent swallowed past the sorrow burning in his throat. "I run the ranches with the help of my trusted hands."

Mr. Standford smiled and nodded. "Let's eat." He lifted a silver bell. The ring brought two women from the kitchen. They hovered over each plate, adding chicken and boiled potatoes.

Trent eyed his host a moment longer, then glanced at Rosalind and Glover. Glover smirked and leaned over, whispering close to Rosalind's ear.

Trent had to stay seated and keep a tight rein on his emotions, so he counted to ten, then to thirty. The conversations around the table continued, as did his counting. He thought of his land, the wide-open spaces. Ending his count at ninety, he stood. "If you'll excuse me." He strode out into the garden to clear his head, but memories met him there. He and Rosalind playing hide-and-seek when they were children. The time he'd chased her, causing her to fall and skin her knee. He'd gently wiped her tears then, heartbroken he'd hurt her. Her fourteenth birthday, when he'd plucked a pink rose from a bush in this very garden and slid it into her hair just above her ear, his thumb grazing her soft forehead.

He glanced around and made his way to the pink rose bush, near the center of the garden. Smiling, he held a petal between his fingers as he had back then, imagining how lovely she'd look now with a fresh bud in her hair, how soft her cheek would feel.

His hand fell. He shouldn't think such things. Yet tonight, with her hair piled on top of her head, exposing the curve of her slender neck. Her rosy lips …

"Hello, Trenton."

He paused before turning at the sound of Rosalind's voice. "How long have you been standing there?" Yet his tone rang of bitterness, and he hated himself for it, for the way it made her flinch.

She gave a weak smile. "Not long. You've been gone from the table for some time."

"Only for a spell." He glanced around, seeing nothing but the truth staring him in the face. "Where's your husband?"

"Husband," she said tightly. "I'm not married."

Rosalind drew his gaze as he recalled their ride in the carriage. How she spoke of the children. "The little ones in your arms. William and Anna. You're not married?"

"No. I am not." She looked away, then moved farther into the garden. He followed as twilight began to fall. How could he not? He needed answers. He needed the truth.

Rounding several plants and a bed of red roses, she made her way to a bench and sat, her gown covering the surface. "Do you remember my sister, Sydney?"

"I do." He hesitated, hanging on to her every word while a small flame of hope ignited inside him. "She married and moved away several months before we left."

"Well, she lives here now with her husband, Joshua. They transferred him to the navy base in Charleston. I help care for my niece and nephew."

"I see." Although he didn't know who Mr. Richards was to her, his heart and hopes soared, giving her no indication of what he felt as he searched her gray eyes.

She bit her lip and turned away. Silence spread between them.

What had he seen? Sadness? Pain? He had so many questions mixed with *whys* and *what-ifs*. But no matter how much he needed to know, he was more frightened of what he felt at this moment, standing before the woman he loved. He loved her. He simply loved her, and he couldn't stand to see her in pain.

"How are you, Rosalind … since your mother's passing?"

She sniffled softly but didn't speak.

"I'm terribly sorry for your loss. If I'd known, I'd have been here for you."

"I …"

Anguish whispered passed her lips, causing him to step toward her. "Rose."

"I never thought you'd return."

"I never stopped caring. Never stopped—"

"Maybe it would have been best if you had."

Stunned, searching for something to say, he could barely breathe as his mind told him to retreat, but his heart told him to stay and fight. "I will always care. What we've meant to each other …"

"We're not the same people that we once were. Everything changed when Mother died. I've moved on. And so should you."

How many times did she need to reject him before he'd accept the truth? He didn't belong here, reminding her of the past—a future she wanted no part of.

She didn't need him. Didn't want him.

"I'm sorry." He reached to tip his Stetson and realized it wasn't there. "Excuse me."

Trent found the way back through the garden and into the house. Everyone had moved into the parlor. He knew the protocol. It had been engraved in him as a child, but he was no longer a child, nor a resident of Boston.

If his parents wanted to stay in Boston, so be it. He'd make his own plans. By week's end, he was going home.

When Trent left the garden, Rosalind stared after him. *He would have been here?* She stood from the bench and felt the blood drain from her face.

He would have been here.

To hold me.

To love me.

Oh, God … why did You take him from me when I needed him the most? Why have You abandoned me? What have I done to deserve this?

But just like when she'd prayed for her mother's life to be spared, tonight she heard no answers.

She dragged herself through the garden and entered the house, fighting against the questions and the turmoil churning her insides. At the top of the stairs, she hesitated, unable to take another step, though she should rejoin Glover and her father's guests.

"Rosalind."

She jumped at Trenton's voice and quickly placed a palm against her chest. She spotted him coming toward her from his room down the hall. "I didn't see you there."

"I was waiting for you." He glanced over the rail and down to the first floor, then at her. He ran his fingers through his hair. "I don't know how much time we have to talk in private, but I must apologize. In the garden … I didn't mean to hurt you when I spoke of your mother or when I brought up the past. I came to Boston for many reasons, and one was to see how you are. As a friend. Not to disturb your life."

"Friends?"

"Yes. After everything, Rosalind, we are friends. I care about you and your well-being. Don't ever doubt that."

She met the sincerity of his gaze, and the color of ocean blue stared back. She wanted to stay there and drown in the pools of his eyes.

He stepped toward her and lightly rubbed his index finger over the bridge of her nose and forehead. At first she didn't realize what he was doing, but then the pleasure of a childhood memory seeped through. The need to be near him, to feel his touch, held her in place. Her skin tingled.

"See now, the wrinkles are gone, as is the worry."

Heat rose to her cheeks. "You still seem to have a way of making things better."

His eyes gleamed with pleasure, and the corners of his mouth lifted into a smile.

"Thank you," she said finally, taking a step back. She'd missed this—their friendship, his teasing, his smile. Opening her bedroom door, she glanced back at him. "Good night, cowboy."

"You're welcome, ma'am." He nodded and turned toward his room.

A shadow over the banister caught her attention and her body stiffened. Her gaze shifted to the darkened first floor and she listened for a moment but heard nothing.

Rosalind hurried into her room and closed the door. Moments later, three taps rapped against the wood. "Father." She shut her eyes and took a heavy breath, wishing him away.

He barreled in and then closed the door behind him, his lips pressed into a fine line. "What on earth were you doing out in the hall with Trenton?"

She stood ramrod straight and pulled at the tips of her gloves, yanking them off. "Speaking to one another. We do share a hall to our rooms."

"I thought I made myself clear before they arrived. If Glover had seen the two of you just now …"

Her eyes grew wide. "He didn't. Please, Father, tell me he didn't."

He came to her and gently placed his hands on her shoulders. "No, but I did. Glover's testing you to see where your heart and loyalties lie. He knows of Trenton's proposal."

She frowned. "I don't understand. How would he know?" Something passed over her father's eyes. "You didn't tell him, did you?"

Her father didn't pause or even blink. "Yes. Some time ago."

"Why? Why would you put his or the Eastons' lives at risk with such a move? Did you think it would benefit you?" When her father averted her gaze, she knew her answer. "So it did."

"I never thought they'd return. What harm would it have done?"

"Plenty. How could you?" She began to pace, fear mounting in her chest.

"Rosalind, you cannot let yourself love him." He stepped in her path. "You will be married to Glover soon."

She shook her head and backed away. "It's too late. I never stopped loving him."

"But I thought over time …"

"You never understood. I pleaded. You wouldn't allow me to answer Trenton's proposal. I loved him. I could have been married now with a family of my own. Happy."

His eyes reflected concern. "I can't undo what I've done, but you need to be careful, Rosalind. Glover won't tolerate another man giving you attention."

"There's no need to concern yourself. I have it on great authority Trenton cares for me only as a friend."

"And whose great authority are you claiming?"

Her heart ached at the thought, but to voice those words … "From Trenton himself. He cares for me as a friend and nothing more." She lifted her chin as if the words hadn't affected her, yet they had—deeply.

"Then he is a fool, but I'm glad." Her father headed to the door. "Now, rest. Glover plans to pick you up early. You're spending the day with him away from the house. I will see you in the morning." He left, closing the door behind him.

Rosalind dropped onto the bed and laid her gloves beside her. Having collected her resolve, she urged her thoughts to what was expected, yet her heart rebelled. How could she marry a man she could never love and would always fear?

Chapter Five

Being near Rosalind these last few days and two doors down from where she slept was driving Trent mad. He rarely had a moment to speak with her. Glover was always close, dropping by throughout the day, every day, flaunting her in front of him at every turn.

He'd tell his parents that he simply *must* leave. But not today.

Trent climbed into the waiting carriage, where Rosalind was seated inside. They were going to church together, and he might get the chance to speak with her, unless of course Glover would be joining them. Trent sunk to the bench next to her.

"I'm glad your mother asked about attending church before I left," Rosalind said, twisting her reticule strap around her gloved fingers. "A few minutes more and I'd have been gone."

"Will Mr. Richards be joining us?" he asked.

"No. He doesn't attend and neither does Father." Her gaze slid to the carriage door. "My mother would want me to go, so I go alone."

Something in her tone hinted at a deeper meaning, and Trent

was curious to discover what it could be. Did Rosalind feel alone? She never cared to be alone. The thought dared Trent to reach for her hand and draw her close. Instead, he held himself in place. "It was nice of you to wait on our account."

"Why wouldn't I?" Rosalind looked to him. "You and your family mean the world to me."

Again, there it was. Something seemed to pass between them and skirted over her eyes. From the moment he'd stepped into the carriage, everything was familiar but so different. And almost every word she spoke seemed cryptic. He wished for an opportunity to ask but held his tongue as his parents climbed into the carriage and sat across from them. The door closed, and within seconds they were moving.

"Thank you for allowing us to accompany you, Rosalind," his mother said, tucking a few strands of hair under her hat.

"Glad to have the company." Rosalind now followed his mother's primping and adjusted her hat, elbowing Trent in the process. "I'm dreadfully sorry." She squeezed her arms in close. "I didn't mean …" Her cheeks turned a dark pink against her green dress. She dropped her hands to her lap and glanced away.

Trent chuckled, drawing back to regard her profile. Wisps of brown hair graced her ear and cheek. "You may need to be careful in the future, Rosalind. I'd hate to have to retaliate."

She turned to him with wide eyes, and he smiled. "You're teasing me, Trenton."

"Yes, ma'am. If I do it again, don't be surprised."

"And why is that?" She sat taller, biting her lip.

Trent had always loved teasing her, even more now. "Knowing I can make you blush after all these years is satisfying." He reclined in his seat, catching his father's stare. Yes, Rosalind was to be married to another man, and although Trent still loved her, he must keep his true feelings to himself.

Yet, they were always playful growing up—climbing trees, teasing—and once, not so long ago, she was his. He wasn't willing to give her up so easily, but what choice did he have?

Trent turned his attention out the window, intent on the passing city. He tugged on the collar of his white shirt, feeling the black carriage constrict around him. How could he walk this line of friendship when she held his heart?

A few minutes later they slowed to a stop in front of the church. Trent glanced at Rosalind, ready to assist her from the carriage, when the driver opened the door and reached in to help the women out. Trent stepped from the carriage and noted the gothic cathedral looked more worn then he remembered, but its scent of seasoned wood and musty books greeted him as they entered. High ceilings pointed skyward over the altar, the same altar where he gave his life to Jesus as a young boy. He smiled inwardly while his eyes scanned the wooden pews for a place to sit. Most were full, but Trent led Rosalind to a small opening while his parents found seats a few aisles over.

"Do you attend church where you live now?" Rosalind folded her gloved hands in her lap and faced forward.

"The church meets twice a month when the preacher comes to town. Less often during the harvest months or cattle drives, when men gather and work together to help families in the community."

"Do you go as well? Travel, I mean. To help others?"

"I try to live the second commandment. 'Love your neighbor as yourself'… and maybe help sheep in my spare time."

She turned those beautiful gray eyes on him, brows furrowed. "Sheep? I thought you raise longhorns?"

Trent laughed and leaned in slightly, inhaling her light rose scent. How easy it would be *not* to walk the line of friendship. He inhaled her scent one final time and sat upright before he did something he couldn't take back. "I've had a dream about sheep." He shrugged his shoulders. "Perhaps soon I'll start tending sheep."

Later, as they traveled back to the Standford home, Trent considered the Scripture the preacher had read. Jesus asked Peter three times if he loved him, then said to feed his sheep. And the other verses about sheep in the book of Peter. That the shepherd, in times of suffering, would tend to his flock, feed them with God's Word, and protect them. Did either passage have a connection to his dream? The sheep and the wolves?

"Son."

Trent focused on his father. "Yes, sir?"

"Take your mother and Rosalind to the door, then meet me out front. I feel like a walk."

Trent glanced out the carriage window in disbelief. He'd wasted his opportunity to speak with Rosalind. The driver opened the door, and Trent climbed out first. After helping his mother down, he reached for Rosalind's gloved hand. Her light fingers rested in his palm. He wanted to keep her hand in his but released her and escorted them to the front door.

"Thank you, son." His mother smiled and unpinned her feathered hat as she entered.

Rosalind hesitated at the door. "Did you enjoy the service?"

More than you know. "I did. Hadn't expected that message."

"About sheep? God must be telling you something. When you figure it out, let me know." She grinned. Her gaze roamed beyond his shoulder, and her smile disappeared. "I must go."

Trent nodded but didn't understand the hurry until he rounded the carriage. Glover stood beside his father.

"You remember Mr. Richards," his father said, top hat in hand.

Saying it was nice to see him again would be a lie, but

manners and the Great Commandment demanded he be kind. "Yes, I do. Hello." He turned to his father. "Are you ready for our walk?"

"Mr. Richards, I hope you don't think us rude, but we had planned to see the monument."

"No, not at all. Please, enjoy yourselves." Glover offered a stiff smile, then headed toward the house.

Trent took a deep breath. The man raked on his every last nerve, and yes, Rosalind was the cause, but there was something else—an uneasiness about the man Trent couldn't quite shake.

They took several steps. "How are you doing?" his father asked as two boys scampered by at a fast pace, lobbing a ball back and forth.

On the corner ahead, a horse-drawn wagon clattered past. Maybe his father could help him reason through his problem. "It hurts to see Rosalind with Glover, but she must love him if they plan to marry. She deserves happiness after everything she's been through." Trent inhaled, missing Rosalind's sweet scent as rising dust filled his nostrils. "I'm ready to go home. I don't belong in Boston."

"Your words to Rosalind while we were in the carriage … I see the way you watch her. I fear Glover notices as well. Maybe it's for the best."

Had Glover seen his feelings for her, as his father said? Trent slowed his steps. "She's still grieving her mother's death."

"Has she spoken to you about it?"

He didn't answer immediately. "No, but I can tell. I've always been able to tell when she's hurting."

"I believe she is." He pointed to the Bunker Hill Monument. "Let's go."

Trent glanced toward the house one final time, praying Glover would truly make her happy.

"Do you hear me, Rosalind?" Glover whispered against her cheek. "I do not want to see you and Trenton alone again." His fingers wrapped around Rosalind's wrist so tightly that the veins in his hand rose to the surface. His knuckles turned white.

"Please, Glover, you're hurting me." She tried to pull away, bumping her arm against a living room chair. "We were childhood friends. We're still friends but that's all. I promise."

He twisted her arm, and her legs almost buckled. She opened her mouth to plead with him again, but his piercing look stopped her. Tears sprang to her eyes at his expression. He meant to break her spirit, to make her compliant.

He released her and her legs finally gave way, but he caught her by the elbow. "Stand and look at me," he said. "I mean no harm, only to teach you what is expected."

Tears filled her eyes as she simply stood there, cradling her arm.

He wiped her tears with a gentle finger, then raised her chin. "I never want to hurt you, but my anger and passion rages for you, Rosalind. I'm not responsible for my actions. This is your father's doing. I've waited much too long to take you as my wife."

"Rosalind. Where are you?" Trenton's mother called.

His expression grew hard again. He ground his teeth, and she knew—as soon as the Eastons left, what little freedom she now enjoyed would be lost forever. She couldn't afford to anger him further, but …

Rosalind looked up at him. "She's all I have left of my mother. Please don't keep me from her. I need the connection."

"She's not the Easton I'm concerned about." The harsh planes of his face smoothed and were replaced by a practiced smile. "Answer her. It's all right." He kissed her cheek.

She shuddered.

Another instant switch. How could a man be so violent one moment, so seemingly gentle the next? Rosalind's heart pounded in her chest. "We're in Father's office," she called. Her voice broke as she tucked her arm against her side.

"Oh, there you are," Mrs. Easton said. "I don't mean to interrupt."

Glover cleared his throat. "Not at all, Mrs. Easton. We were discussing … wedding arrangements."

"How nice. Rosalind, when you have a moment, I'd love information about any new shops in town."

"I'd be happy to help." Rosalind slipped past Glover, keeping her attention on Mrs. Easton. "There's one in particular Sydney loves." She fled the room, lacing her injured arm through Mrs. Easton's arm.

Mr. Easton and Trenton entered the house, discussing something about horses. As they climbed the stairs, Rosalind looked over her shoulder at them.

Behind her, Glover cleared his throat. Reluctantly she turned. Fear coursed through her at seeing the anger in his eyes.

CHAPTER SIX

Trent's internal clock awoke him to begin his daily chores—chores Matthew would be doing right at that moment.

With a huff, he threw back his covers and strolled to the window. Darkness shrouded the Bunker Hill Monument in Monument Square. He'd enjoyed spending time with his father yesterday, but it made him eager to leave. He'd never suspected one could hurt so badly while loving another. Trent was beaten down, his heart tattered in ways he never knew he could feel.

He ran his fingers through his hair. Coffee. He needed coffee.

Trent dressed in the dark, put on his boots, then headed downstairs to the kitchen. Back home, the cook would have already prepared his coffee. Here, it seemed there was never a cook on hand until supper. Odd. He rubbed his chin, the stubble reminding him he needed to shave before going to buy his ticket home.

He found a box of matches and struck one. Fire sparked, casting shadows and illuminating a candle on the table. He lit it.

"Trenton?"

He turned at Rosalind's voice. The fire burned up the matchstick, searing his finger. He waved his hand, extinguished the match, then threw it on the table and glanced at his fingers.

"Were you burned?" Rosalind took his hand in hers and held it near the candlelight.

"You surprised me is all. I'm fine." Her breath grazed his cheek. He hadn't realized how close their faces were, their lips only inches apart. He couldn't move. Nor did she.

Then Glover's hard face flashed across Trent's mind. He reluctantly pulled his hand away and searched through a cabinet.

"What are you looking for?" She spoke softly behind him.

He almost paused at the lovely sound of her voice, her nearness, and the ache to feel her touching him once again only grew. "Coffee. I usually start my day with a cup." He yanked another cabinet open.

"We're out, but I can buy some. I had already planned to shop today after I pick up my sister's children." She withdrew a cup from the cabinet.

Trent turned to leave the kitchen and the house, knowing he couldn't stay with her any longer.

"Trenton, is there anything else you need?" she asked.

He stopped in the doorway and turned to her. "Trent. I go by Trent now."

A brow rose. "Trent." She said his name as if trying it out for the first time. And he loved how it sounded. He wanted her to say it again. Instead she gave him the sweetest of smiles.

He'd made an idiot of himself by loving a woman who would never love him in return, and if he didn't leave this house now, he'd say or do something that proved it to Rosalind.

"Nothing, thank you." He walked out the door, fighting the urge to go back to the house. Maybe by the time he walked through town, he'd have enough courage to buy his ticket or send a telegram to Texas, forcing himself to leave the woman he loved behind.

Rosalind leaned against her bedroom door and closed her eyes. In the short moment she'd run her fingers over Trenton's palm, she'd discovered calluses. Still, that simple touch made her feel … warm, safe. She'd forgotten what it felt like. "Mother," she whispered, her voice cracking. "Every minute that ticks puts me closer to a marriage prison. I can't even tell Sydney. I'm keeping secrets from her as you said not to, but what choice do I have? None. Only isolation."

She could have been loved and protected.

She thought about Trenton and how he'd left as a boy, and yes, she'd cared for him then. But now he was all man and—she had to admit—everything about him intrigued her. *Trent.* Her thoughts turned to his broad shoulders and tanned skin, his callused hands and the scruff along his jaw. He wasn't clean-shaven as the men in Boston. He was like no one in Boston. Most definitely not. Trent was now a Texan. And he would eventually return with his family to the town and land he loved.

With a breath, Rosalind righted herself, running a hand down her dress. She collected the money Glover had given her father and stuffed it in her reticule, then rushed out, unable to stand being in the house that was once a home. Sydney's federal-style house came into view as Rosalind hurried down the cobblestone street. Her sister waited in the doorway.

She frowned and quickened her steps. "Am I late?"

"No. I'm just excited to see Joshua." She smiled. "William and Anna are in the carriage, ready for their walk." Her sister rushed into the house, then slowly rolled the pram out. They lifted it down the steps. "I'll be back after a while." Sydney hugged her quickly and scurried off to her carriage.

Rosalind glanced down at the infants in the stroller. "Your parents are so blessed to have each other. Come on, you two, before these disobedient tears of mine fall once again." She ambled down the sidewalk, her fingers flexing on the carriage handle. Children. She wanted them. Had always wanted them.

Her blood ran cold at the thought, and she almost doubled over with certainty. Glover would want children right away. To further bind her to himself. To own her.

She reached the general store but didn't want to enter and risk seeing someone she knew—someone who might see her, recognize her distress, and question her. Possibly report back to Glover. She continued to the post office, to return later.

Rosalind approached the post office, and just as the door opened, Trent stepped out of the building. "Trent?"

He met her gaze and smiled. "Rosalind." He grabbed the door and held it open for her. "I was heading to the general store, but I can wait. Can I keep the children for you while you go in?"

She glanced down the street toward the entrance of the bank. Although she couldn't see it from where she stood, she knew Glover would be there. "I won't be long." She left him with the carriage and two sleeping babies and hurried inside.

"Hello, Miss Standford. What can I do for you today?" The older man's lips rose almost hidden within his graying beard.

She smiled in return. "Well, hello to you, Mr. Brown." What would it be like to truly be so happy that a smile could be that contagious? "I came to pick up Father's mail."

"A letter came for Mr. Standford just yesterday." He pulled an envelope from a slot in the wall and handed it to her.

"It's a shame that young fellow, Trenton Easton, is leaving so soon. I remember him when he was waist high and you two were running around here like a bunch of Indians, claiming you were going to skin us alive." He chuckled.

Her breath caught. "He's leaving? When?"

"Oh, I think the telegram said Tuesday. Yep, if I'm not mistaken, he'd be on the train by Tuesday."

He was leaving. And so quickly. Was it because she told him to leave? Now she regretted the words. With the letter in hand, she said goodbye to Mr. Brown and exited the post office. Trent was cooing at the twins when she approached. "Thanks for watching them." She squeezed the carriage handle, her voice unsteady.

Trent's eyes narrowed at her in question.

She looked away. "Thank you, Trenton," she said again more controlled. She didn't want him to leave, leave her, not again, no matter what she said in the garden. She loved him to the depths of her soul. But she wouldn't beg him to stay. Her life had been bargained away, and her heart had no say in the matter.

"You on your way to the store?"

She nodded.

"I'll walk you then."

She shouldn't. She knew she shouldn't. If Glover saw them…

Although Glover had meetings today throughout the afternoon and evening, he'd not be visiting her until tomorrow. And she wouldn't be alone with Trenton. Not exactly. But would it be worth his wrath if he found out? Without accepting or declining his offer, she started walking, and he fell into step beside her. She wouldn't think about it. Obviously, these moments would be her last with Trenton. With each step they took, her heart sank further to the pit of her stomach.

"Can I push?"

She looked at him. "And why would you want to push a

baby carriage?"

"To know what it feels like. I know what it feels like to lasso a wild stallion and pull a calf from its mother, but I've never pushed a carriage." He winked.

"I've never seen those things done. But this has to be much easier. Take over when you're ready."

Without stopping, Trent placed his hands next to hers. "You should come to Texas."

She released her hold of the carriage. "So, you're leaving Tuesday."

Trent slowed in front of the general store and nodded. Several children ran across the street. His gaze trailed them as they ran behind the building. "I bought a train ticket for Monday, but my mother told me today that Father is throwing a party in my honor on Monday evening. I purchased another ticket for Tuesday. So, yes, I'm leaving Tuesday morning. I planned to tell you. It's time for me to head home."

The thought of him leaving was still a shock, but knowing she was bound to a loveless marriage with Glover made her shudder. There was no way out. No one to trust. "I'll take the children."

"I'll get the door." He held it open so she could enter with the carriage.

"You need coffee. It's this way." She pointed to a tall shelf at the back of the store. "I'll get the flour and sugar I need."

A display of lace-trimmed handkerchiefs caught her attention. She ran her finger along the edge of one, a lovely white linen waiting for a woman's embroidered initials. Her mother had owned several like these—special, elegant pieces just like Mother. A passage in Psalms her mother often read to her sprang to mind. *"Trust in the LORD, and do good; so shalt thou dwell in the land, and verily thou shalt be fed. Delight thyself also in the LORD; and he shall give thee the desires of thine heart. Commit thy way unto the LORD; trust also in him; and he shall bring it to pass. And he shall bring forth thy righteousness as the light, and thy judgment as the noonday."*

Rosalind gazed at the sleeping babies. Yes, their small forms dwelled in the land and safe pasture. She wanted to believe the words were true for her, but God never answered her prayers. Her noonday sun was never coming. God had left her long ago to be hunted, then captured by a wolf.

Trent neared, breaking into her whirling thoughts. "I hope you don't mind. I bought what you needed. I'll carry the items back to the house. Are you on your way there now, or do you have other things to do in town?"

It took her a moment to come out of her chaotic reverie. "Uh. No. I need to take the little ones home now."

"Shall we?"

She opened her mouth to tell him no, that she could manage the rest of the way on her own, but the temptation to spend just one last precious hour in his company was more than she could bear. "Yes."

CHAPTER SEVEN

How dare he?

From the window of his rented carriage, Glover eyed Trenton and Rosalind leaving the general store. She pushed her sister's stroller and smiled and laughed, obviously enjoying herself. Any casual onlooker might assume them a family.

He'd known Trenton wouldn't keep his distance from Rosalind. Known Trenton would pounce on the first opportunity to spend time alone with her. Glover had purposely led her to believe he'd be busy elsewhere, just to present the opportunity to watch.

He nudged the curtain open a little more, following their progress down the street.

"Driver, back to the bank." He reclined and folded his arms against his chest. Since the Eastons arrived, Trenton had been an aggravating thorn, possibly influencing Rosalind at every turn. If Roger hadn't insisted on her being nineteen before marriage, she would already be his wife. Yes, he was almost old enough to be her father, but he wanted her, and he *would* have her.

Glover pushed his way through the bank's heavy double

doors. His secretary—the bank president's babbling idiot son—hurried to his side and followed him down the hallway. "Your one o'clock appointment is here, sir."

He stopped abruptly at his office doorway and barely refrained from sneering at the sniveling boy. "Does my one o'clock have a name?"

The young man stared down at the pad in his quivering hands. "A Mr. Easton. Isn't his portrait hanging in the foyer? As one of the bank's founders? My father knows him."

"The very same." What could Easton want? The man had suddenly resigned his position and left Boston under suspicious circumstances. Glover hadn't ever been able to uncover anything, but something had driven the man west. Of that he was certain. Pity he didn't know what it was, or he could use it against Easton. "Give me a minute, then send him in."

"Yes—"

Glover entered his office and slammed the door in the young man's face. Personal files lay on his desk. No doubt if he left them out, Mr. Easton would poke his nose where it didn't belong. He stuffed them in the top drawer just as a knock sounded and his door opened.

"Mr. Richards."

"Mr. Easton." Glover walked over, shook his hand, and ushered him inside. "What a pleasant surprise. What brings you by?" *Tell me you and that son of yours are going back to Texas.*

"My son, Trent, has decided to return to Texas. We had planned to throw him a dinner later in the month, but with his change of plans, the dinner will be held on Monday, before he leaves on Tuesday's train. We would like you to attend."

Perfect. "I'd be honored. I'll tell Rosalind so she may accompany me."

"There is another reason I came to see you. I asked Roger

about your relationship with Miss Standford."

Did he now. "I'm sure he told you we're betrothed. My feelings for her run deep."

"I'm sure they do. As you know, prior to our move to Texas we were rather close with the Standfords. Trent and Rosalind grew up together, so much so that we still consider Rosalind like a daughter. I've come to ask your permission to allow Rosalind to dance freely with Trent that night if she so desires. I'm sure you understand."

Although it galled him to admit, agreement would further his plan far better than a refusal. Roger must have kept secret how he acquired Rosalind's hand—good boy—or Easton wouldn't be here asking permission as a gentleman. After they left, he'd immediately marry Rosalind.

"Thank you, Mr. Easton. I appreciate your concern for my feelings in this matter. You and your family have my consent."

Mr. Easton offered his hand. "Thank you, Mr. Richards. You don't know how much this means to us."

Glover accepted and gave a cordial smile. "Until the party then."

He'd monitor Rosalind's every moment, especially when in Trenton's company. Any fool could see the man still had feelings for her.

And Glover was no fool. If Trenton Easton tried to steal Rosalind away, he'd pay with his life.

With Rosalind next to him, Trent strolled down the boardwalk contentedly, keeping a lazy pace with the baby buggy. This felt so much like what he wanted—to have Rosalind as his wife and raise a family with her.

But she didn't want him that way. Yet, by looking at her and Glover together, her heart didn't seem to belong to him either.

The road curved between the buildings, and people bustled in every direction. An acrid smell seeped through the still air. Trent exhaled. He missed his home, the quietness, working the land and riding through the clear night air. Soon he'd be there and find contentment again, but alone.

"What's wrong?" Her gray eyes met his.

"I miss home."

She faced the street suddenly. "Boston is a wonderful place to live."

"Maybe for some. It feels like such a long time since I lived here."

"I remember everything from our childhood."

He smiled, recalling how she'd sneak his chocolate bars and how he'd eventually given them to her. "Tell me. What do you remember most?"

She stayed silent for a while, then a tiny smile flitted across her face. "You mean like the day in church when someone kept pulling on my hair and got me in trouble? I couldn't help but squeal. You pulled it so hard."

Trent stifled his laugh. He had forgotten until now, and how her high-pitched cry carried. "Was that me?"

She stopped. "Now you know it was you, Trenton Easton. You were the only one who ever messed with my hair."

He couldn't deny it. He took a few steps ahead of her and turned, still carrying the bag of dry goods. She stood with one hand on her hip, the other on the carriage, her foot tapping the ground.

"Well, what was I supposed to do?" he asked, eyes wide with mock innocence. "I couldn't let that Michael Davenport keep hanging around. I had to do something. And it worked. His parents never let him come back to your house after you screamed like *that*."

"You listen to me, Trenton." She pointed a finger at his chest and forced a seriousness in her tone, but the lift of her lips said otherwise. His heart leapt as her gray eyes sparkled. "Do you know because of you I got a scolding after church?"

"I hope your father wasn't too harsh." They continued their stroll down the street, Sydney's brick house coming into view.

"He wasn't harsh then, loving really."

The emotion in her words drew his gaze. The sparkle in her eyes had faded. A fierce urge to comfort her within his arms took form—and the thought raised the beating of his heart. Before she made it to the front steps, he reached for her hand and squeezed. "I'm sorry."

She took a breath and glanced toward the house. "I should go inside. The children will need tending to very shortly."

One of the babies squalled.

She bent to the crying child. "I know, William. It's time, isn't it?"

He didn't know what time it was, but as Rosalind lifted one child from the carriage, the other one starting crying, her wails rivaling her brother's. Trent set down the bag and lifted the baby. "I'll help you inside." Clutching Anna against his chest with one arm, he pulled the carriage to the porch and followed Rosalind into the house.

"What can I do to help?" He glanced around and spotted a plum-colored high-back chair. He lowered himself, gently cradling the back of the squalling child's head. When he looked up, Rosalind left with William to another room.

The little girl sniffled and snuggled against his chest, her tiny hands clenched into small fists. Trent traced his finger on the soft skin, and her hand opened as she fell back asleep. A longing to have Rosalind as his wife, to have a family with her, washed over him again, and a gut-wrenching pain took its place. She was marrying another man.

The comfort she felt from the touch of Trent's hand still warmed her. How could a sense of peace settle around her like a soft blanket on a cold day? She still wanted him to love her, to take her in his arms and hold her there for all eternity. She could even imagine how wonderful being kissed by him would feel.

No. She must stop such thoughts. What she wanted didn't matter, *couldn't matter*, she reminded herself as she fed William his bottle. Yet, the longer she stood around the corner watching Trenton with Anna, the more her heart ached for what she could have had, should've had. She finished feeding William, then laid him down in the children's room and returned to the living room where Trenton sat.

"I can take her so you can leave." She reached down for her sleeping niece.

"Actually, I'm enjoying this. I have always wanted children, but I didn't know how much until now." He smiled as he studied Anna, then looked back at Rosalind.

Her heart broke—she felt it crack down the center. Again.

The grandfather clock chimed. "I need to start dinner for Sydney. Are you sure you're fine?"

"Yes. Do you want me to feed Anna?"

"Give her a few more minutes to sleep. I'll bring a bottle to you soon."

Rosalind hurried into the kitchen and pulled out the flour canister. She scooped out just enough to make biscuits. She'd halve the flour they'd bought, which was still outside on the porch, with her sister after she rolled out the dough.

Rosalind pulled a bowl from the cupboard as tiny cries sounded from the other room. As the cries grew more intense, she left the biscuits to prepare Anna's bottle.

"I'm coming!" Maybe the sound of her voice would quiet Anna some. She didn't want Trenton to regret holding the child or staying. His presence in the next room comforted her.

She wiped down the bottle and spun, almost colliding with Trenton. He stood before her, patting Anna's bottom as he held her against his chest. The sight of him doing so stirred her heart. "I was coming." She held out the bottle.

Trent slipped it from her hand. "I can feed her. It can't be that hard since she's so hungry." He bounced the child in his arms, placing the bottle at Anna's mouth. She latched on and immediately her cries ceased. He smiled. "I'm a natural."

"I guess you are." She smiled up at him, engraining this moment in her memory.

"I'm home." Sydney's call came from the foyer. "Look who I found outside."

She turned. "Glover." Her month went dry as his eyes narrowed at her, then he glared at Trenton.

"What a lovely picture." The clinch of Glover's jaw sent a shudder down her spine.

Sydney eased past Glover and deposited on the counter the dry goods they'd left outside. "Since you're all here, I want to share my news. Joshua's coming home."

"Oh, Sydney, I'm so happy for you." Rosalind hugged her sister, then held her away. "How long will he be able to stay this time?"

"He's been reassigned to a desk job. His stints at sea will be few and far between now. I'm happy for me too." Sydney beamed as tears formed in her hazel eyes. "Thank you, Trenton."

She collected Anna and held her close. "Daddy's coming home soon, Anna-bug. Daddy's coming home."

Rosalind watched her sister say goodbye and ascend the stairs.

Trenton nodded. "I should be going."

The front door no sooner closed behind him than a python-like grip seized her wrist. Glover twisted her arm behind her back and shoved. Her cheek hit the kitchen wall. She squeezed her eyes against the pain. *Oh, God, I'd rather faint than suffer Glover's wrath.*

"Do not think I am so naïve, Rosalind." He pressed his mouth to her ear, his hot breath seemed to sting her skin. "I will not be played a fool," he whispered. "Do you hear me?"

Eyes still shut, she nodded, hoping he'd do nothing else to her.

CHAPTER EIGHT

I shouldn't have left her. Trent sat at the dining table with his family, swallowing back the unease he'd felt since leaving Rosalind with Glover at Sydney's home. He wasn't a man who carried his gun belt unless he felt the need, but right now he wished for the pressure against his hip. Was that rage he'd witnessed in Glover's eyes? If it had been, when he blinked it was gone. Whether Trent had seen it or not, he sensed something that provoked an urge in him to protect Rosalind and Sydney.

"Trent, are you all right?" his mother asked.

He stopped shuffling his food around his plate and set his fork down. "Things on my mind."

His father glanced from around his newspaper. "Excited about returning home?"

"It will be good to get back." But the thought of leaving Rosalind caused a knot in the pit of his stomach. A blurred outline of a woman running flashed through his mind. He reached for her in his thoughts and she vanished, only for the wolf to appear. *My dream.*

Trent grasped his cup to remind himself it was only a dream, but the fear for the woman rose like the tide, pulling him in. A muscle twitched in his jaw.

"I spoke with Glover Richards today about your party Monday night." His father folded the paper in two and set it on the table.

Heat climbed through Trent's veins at the sound of the man's name. His father lifted the napkin from his lap, set it on his plate, and leaned back in his chair.

"Well, dear, don't keep us in suspense." His mother's eyes widened. "Did he agree or not?"

"Am I missing something here?" Trent glanced to his mother. When she said nothing further, his focus trained on his father.

"Trent, I know this trip has been a little more than difficult for you, and with you leaving so soon, your mother and I thought this would give you and Rosalind a proper chance to say goodbye after these many years of friendship."

More than friendship, Father. Trent lifted his watch from his pocket and assessed the time. After five and still no sign of Rosalind.

His mother touched his arm. "Trent, your father is speaking to you. He's done you and Rosalind a great service." She searched his eyes. "Is everything all right?"

Trent glanced toward the door and snapped his watch closed. "What time do you expect Rosalind?"

Her brows furrowed. "I'm not sure. She never mentioned a time she'd be returning."

The heat he felt moments ago flamed to his feet. He stood with an immediate need to find Rosalind.

"Trent," his father said. "You're still in love with her."

He paused, stared at his father, and swallowed. It wasn't a question, and he had no reason to ask his meaning. "I never stopped loving her, but she's set her sights on someone else."

"I see."

Trent sat back on his chair. "I—I can't stay here. When we're together ..." He met his father's gaze again. "I ..." Could he tell his father that he couldn't keep from thinking about her, that the thought of losing her to another man tied him up in knots so bad he was going crazy? He wanted to sweep her into his arms and kiss her lips, jaw, cheek ...

Dear God, what am I doing? She isn't mine, but my heart can't let her go. Why, Lord? I'm fearful for her ... and this dream that haunts me day and night ...

The front door slammed.

Trent quickly rose from his chair, his father beside him.

Rosalind ran up the stairs with Glover close behind.

A nerve pulsed in his jaw.

"Mariam," his father called, but his mother had already moved toward the stairwell. "Where is Roger?" A look of concern rested on his father's face, but there was something else he didn't recognize. What was his father not telling him?

"I don't know." She paused on the step before following Rosalind and Glover up the stairwell.

Help me, Lord. Rosalind ran up the stairs toward her bedroom, intent on locking herself inside where she'd be alone, safe.

Glover's hard fingers caught the door, and he followed her inside, pushing the door shut. With an ominous click, he locked the door behind him and stepped to her like a lion ready to pounce. If possible, her blood turned even colder than it had when he'd pinned her to the wall just minutes ago. *Is he simply going to kill me now?*

She'd fight, scream. She opened her mouth, but Glover cupped her cry with his firm grip.

"Shhh," he whispered close to her ear. "You hold too many lives in your hand. I'd hate to see harm fall upon the Eastons or Sydney's sweet little twins."

Her body trembled, and she couldn't breathe. She tried to pull away, but his grip only tightened. She saw it then, held within his gaze. He controlled her, owned her. Her body went limp.

The corner of his mouth rose. "Good girl." He slowly removed his hand, then gently wiped her tears.

She heard footsteps on the stairs, saw in his eyes that he heard them too. He unlocked and opened the door as Mariam reached her doorway. Her gaze flicked between them.

"Rosalind. What happened?" Mariam rushed to her side and cupped her bruised cheek.

Rosalind winced as she searched for a reasonable excuse to what was going on.

"I'm to blame for the mishap, Mrs. Easton," Glover said. "Rosalind mentioned how much she loved Boston this time of year and asked if I would take her for a walk. I agreed. I should have insisted we take the carriage. If I had, she wouldn't have fallen. But what man could deny a fiancée as lovely as Rosalind. I confess, I succumb to her every whim."

How can anyone lie with such ease? Such conviction? Rosalind swallowed hard and looked away. "I need to sit down."

"Yes, of course." Mariam guided her to the bed. "Thank you, Mr. Richards, for bringing her home. I assure you, I will take great care of her. We need to call the doctor."

"I wholeheartedly agree with you, Mrs. Easton, but Rosalind will have none of it." Glover gave Mariam a sheepish look. "I admit, before we entered the house, Rosalind and I argued over her refusal to see the doctor." He strolled over to the bed, collected Rosalind's hand, and pressed his lips against her knuckles. "Although I heartily disagree, I accept her wishes." Glover's fingers squeezed around her shaking palm.

Play your part, Rosalind. You have no choice. "I'm a little bruised is all. I'm fine. No doctor."

"Rosalind, I have a late meeting, but it seems I'm leaving you in capable hands. Mrs. Easton, if I can be of service, please don't hesitate to send for me. Good night, dear." He kissed the top of her head, then left.

"Good night, Mr. Richards." Mariam glanced at him as he left, then embraced Rosalind.

She pulled back, studying her face. "Are you sure, Rosalind? I think a doctor—"

"No doctor." Rosalind's head pounded. She wiped her face with the back of her hand and flinched, careful not to show the depth of her pain, then leaned against Mariam's side.

Mr. Easton came into the room, forehead creased. "Are you all right, Rosalind?"

Seeing the concern on Mr. Easton's face, love she missed from her own father, Rosalind inhaled a deep breath. "I'm sorry to worry you both."

"Nonsense. No need for that." He gently lifted her chin with his finger, then scanned her eyes and face. "I will be back with some ice. You rest." His gaze landed on his wife for the briefest of moments, then he turned and left.

Mariam held her close. "We are here for you. In fact, you're the reason we traveled to Boston. When I received your father's letter, I was heartbroken by the news, but also that I wasn't here for you. We love you, Rosalind."

"I'm glad you came." Her voice quivered. Steps sounded in the hall, and she straightened at the thought of Glover's return.

She wouldn't put it past him to make sure she remained silent, but it was Mr. Easton, who'd returned with Trent on his heels.

Mr. Easton extended his hand, placing the ice on her cheek. "Doris brought in the dry store goods."

"Thank you." Rosalind held it in place.

Heat rose in her cheeks at their attention. What were they thinking? Did they suspect Glover in any way for her "accident"? It was possible, but she hoped Mariam believed Glover's explanation of what happened. She'd share Glover's story with Mr. Easton and Trent, and all would be well. She tried to reassure herself, but fear gnawed in the pit of her stomach. Or was it Trent's presence? Or both? She had yet to look at Trent, but she felt it in her body, the burn of his gaze.

"How are you, Rosalind?"

She lifted her gaze to him, and the blue in his eyes had turned frightfully dark. A storm of emotions raged and pinned her. She wished to look away, to answer, but she was powerless. She didn't want to lie to him, but she needed to protect him, his family, and her sister. She'd do anything. "I'll be fine. Once I rest—"

"Your cheek …" He knelt before her and lowered her hand, exposing her injury. "I'm sorry you're hurt."

"Nothing a little chocolate won't cure." She forced a smile to her lips. What she wouldn't give for her words to be true.

"We aren't children any longer, Rosalind. Chocolate won't cure everything. Especially this." He ran his fingers through his hair and took a long breath. "When Glover left, I saw Doris. She looked frightened, and when I questioned her, she clammed up."

Doris not only disliked Glover, but also feared him. She, like Rosalind, could see past his calm demeanor and sense his displeasure or when his anger tilted to rage. Certainly she witnessed it now. "She doesn't care for Glover." She spoke quickly, perhaps too quickly, judging by Trent's narrowing eyes.

"She mentioned to me yesterday that you haven't eaten chocolate for some time, since your mother's passing. That Glover doesn't allow it. Why is it a man who claims to love you won't allow you this simple pleasure?"

Her mouth gaped and she closed it quickly. "Doris isn't aware of what Glover does or doesn't do for me."

"Then it's not true?"

Rosalind thought for a moment, trying to find the correct words.

Mariam's hand settled on hers. "It's true … isn't it? Why, dear? Why would he deny you something you enjoy when moments ago he said he gives in to your every whim?"

"I don't ask," she said, recalling Glover's words. *You shall refrain from chocolates until we wed, then after, you may have your fill. But if I learn my money has been spent against my terms, you both shall go hungry.* Another one of his controlling demands to keep her under his cruel thumb. A ridiculous demand they had no choice but to abide. "Father and I have been poor for some time, but Glover has provided for us nicely. I couldn't ask for more." Rosalind touched Mariam's hand. "Mrs. Easton, I think I should rest for a bit."

"Come, son." Mr. Easton cupped Trent's shoulder. "I think the rest will do Rosalind good." He escorted Trent and Mariam from the room, but not before Trent pierced her with one final look.

Rosalind lay down and rolled over to her side. "God, please take this love from me. I can't love him. Trent and his family need to be safe. William and Anna need to be safe. Protect them from Glover. Oh, God, show me the way to escape."

But as the words whispered through her lips, she believed no answer would come.

In the middle of the night, Rosalind's skull throbbed, waking her from a dull sleep. She winced as she sat up, tenderly touching her sore cheek.

Glover. He'd hurt her worse this time than before. And the snarl on his face, the coldness in his eyes as he'd shoved her face against the wall. If she'd screamed, begged for mercy, still he wouldn't have stopped. Once they married, he could do anything he wanted to her.

A light tap sounded at the door, and when she didn't answer, it creaked open. She clenched her covers to her chest. A dark form moved toward her. She gasped. "Glover?"

"It's me, Rosalind. Are you all right?"

Her heart pounded in her chest, but relief weaved through her middle at the gentle sound of his voice. "Trent, what are you doing here?"

"I know Mother will check on you through the night, but I had to see you with my own eyes, hear your voice."

"You shouldn't be here with your mother gone."

"She knows I'm here. She's talking with my father for a second. I … I couldn't sleep. I had to know if you were all right. I prayed that God would lessen my worry and fear for you, but I had to see you."

"You shouldn't be here," she repeated.

"Yes, I know."

Silence stretched between them, but it was a comforting silence. She rested in the knowledge he was near. "You said you pray. Do you think God hears? Your prayers, I mean?"

Trent turned and, where he stood, the moon shone through the curtains, casting light on his handsome face. "I do. It might not be my timing, or the way I like, but He does answer them.

Would you like me to pray with you?"

"That won't be necessary, but will you say a prayer for me?"

"Of course. What is your prayer?"

"From what my mother told me, God already knows my prayer. But maybe if you prayed … maybe if He heard you …"

Trent left the moon's glow and stood before her. Two heartbeats passed before he lightly palmed her cheek. "If I could promise you anything in this world, Rose, it would be that God does indeed hear your prayers. Let me pray with you now."

She nodded. Tired and weary, she rested her face in his large hand as he prayed over her, for her health, and for God to reveal Himself in her life.

After the "amen" was said, Trent said goodnight and left the room, but the hole in her heart grew.

CHAPTER NINE

Trent exited the kitchen into the dining room and slowed at the sound of hushed, angry voices. He cocked his head, straining to hear, and took quiet steps toward the entryway. Roger and Glover—both men's fists clenched, their faces red with anger. Trent stopped and backed up slightly.

Glover shoved a finger into Roger's chest, then glared up the stairs. "You have no right to stop me from seeing her."

"Mariam is with her now, serving her breakfast upstairs."

"Did you tell her I'm here?"

"She's not coming down."

Rosalind. Trent retreated farther into the dining room. They were arguing over Rosalind.

A vicious hiss and something akin to a growl rumbled through the doorway. Trent squared his shoulders. If Glover lay anything more than a finger on Roger—

The front door opened and closed, then Roger passed by the dining room, his shoulders slumped.

Should he go after Mr. Standford, see if he could offer any help? But he'd been waiting all morning for word on Rosalind's condition.

His mother sniffled her way down the stairs, and her steps paused. Trent could envision her wiping her eyes with a handkerchief and stuffing it into her dress pocket.

Dread rose in Trent's stomach, but he made himself return to the kitchen. Maybe staying out of the way was best for the moment.

His mother stopped when she entered the kitchen. "I didn't realize you were in here." Avoiding eye contact, she prepared a glass of juice.

"How is she? When do you think she'll be coming down?"

His mother took several sips from her glass.

"Mother?"

She placed a hand on his arm and gazed into his eyes. They held moisture, but what else did he see there?

"She's been through so much. If only we'd known." His mother squeezed his arm and placed her glass in the sink. "Has your father returned?"

"Not yet."

"I gather he will be out for a while. I have something for you to do, though. I need you to go shopping for the clothes we talked about. Since we've been here, you've worn your ranching clothes or your Sunday best. You can't wear those for the party."

She laid the chocolate bar he'd bought Rosalind on the table. "Doris found this in the sack you brought from the general store. After yesterday's conversation, I think you should give it to her." His mother gave a small smile. "Go now before anyone sees."

Trent lifted the candy from the table, struggling over wanting to show kindness yet understanding his undeniable love for this woman could blur that line. Could he give her the chocolate posing simply as a friend? Without demanding answers he was sure she was hiding. Without showing his growing uneasiness and, yes, dislike of Glover.

He took the steps two at a time. *Dear God, give me the answers to my questions, and help me walk away without regret when the time comes.*

He reached Rosalind's door and knocked.

A loud knock rattled Rosalind's bedroom door, and her stomach clenched. She'd known Glover cared little about the Eastons' requests to return tomorrow, but with the them here, she had hoped it made a difference.

With trembling hands, she slipped on her robe and answered the door. Trent stood across the threshold. "Trent." His eyes fell to her bruised cheek.

She avoided his stare, glancing at the floor. Her unbound hair fell across her face.

"How are you?"

Unwilling to meet his gaze, she pushed back her hair slightly, noticing his scuffed boots. "I'm fine. Did you need something?"

Trent lifted her chin with his finger and ran his thumb gently along her bruised cheek before clenching his hand and shoving his fist into his pocket. "I bought this yesterday when we were at the general store. I thought you might like it." He slipped out a chocolate bar and handed it to her. His eyes lightened as his face took on a warm glow.

Rosalind recalled the times Trenton brought her chocolates as a child, and the affection she'd felt then with the simple offering. She felt it now, acutely aware of her affections and how deeply they'd nestled within her heart. Why did he have to be so kind, so gentle? She squeezed her eyes closed. The longer she loved him, the greater the danger she brought upon him and his family.

Rosalind startled at her father's voice downstairs, and Trent, brow lowering at her hiss of fear, pressed the bar into her hand. "Perhaps chocolate can fix everything. I want to believe it can."

She pulled the candy to her chest and willed steadiness into her voice despite the tremble of her jaw. "Now, you must go."

When she began to pull the door closed, he blocked it with his boot and leaned toward her, looking as though he would deny her retreat. Instead, after a lengthy intense pause, he whispered, "I'm here for you, Rosalind."

Once inside her room, with the door closed and locked, she sprang to her bed and opened the candy. She savored a piece, listening for steps on the stairs and glancing at the door. When they were younger, Trent had often said if Rosalind owned all the chocolate in town, she wouldn't share. She placed another morsel in her mouth.

Rosalind broke the remaining chocolate into sections and stuffed all but one into her mouth. She smiled. How ridiculous she must look. She licked her lips and swallowed, inhaling the delicious scent.

"Rosalind," Mariam called from outside the door.

She wrapped the last piece in the brown paper, placed it under her pillow, and hurried to open the door.

Mariam glanced around, her brows dipped slightly. "Is Trent here?"

"No. But he came to see me."

Mariam smiled. "Good." She strolled to Rosalind's armoire and inspected the few dresses hanging there.

"Mrs. Easton?"

"We have a party to attend, and you will need proper attire." She closed the armoire. "I'm taking you shopping, and I won't take no for an answer. Tomorrow.”

She tensed. “But Glover … He’ll expect—”

Mariam waved her hand. “Oh, don’t worry. I’ll explain to the men. Mr. Richards can accompany us if he chooses, but I believe he will decide not to join us.” She turned to leave.

“Mariam?”

She paused at the door and sent her a warm smile. “Yes, dear?”

“Thank you.”

If only Trent knew what to do. He ran his fingers through his hair and closed his bedroom door. He’d spent most of the day shopping for clothes for the party and wrestling with how to help Rosalind, yet came up blank, besides kidnaping her for a few hours and making her talk. He drew in a frustrated breath, sat on the bed, and had begun to pray when his father entered his room and gently shut the door.

“Son, you’re not thinking straight.”

Trent was in no mood for riddles. “I have no idea what you’re talking about.”

“I saw Roger in town this afternoon. He said you were standing in Rosalind’s doorway, alone, while she was wearing only a robe. He saw you leave her.”

He met his father’s solemn gaze. “Well … yes.” She was everything to him, and he couldn’t bear to see her hurt. If chocolate could help in some way, he’d give it.

“Should I be concerned?” His father paced away, then back when a knock sounded at the door.

“Thomas.” His mother’s whisper came from the other side. His father opened the door and ushered her in, closing it behind her.

"Son, what if Glover had come up the stairs and found you both? Then what?"

He gave his father a sideways glance. "He'd never know."

His mother lowered to the bed and covered his hand. "I'm sorry I hadn't realized earlier, before this trip, that you still love her."

Trent gave a nod. "I never stopped."

His father palmed his shoulder. "This isn't about you, Trent."

"I'll have to disagree. This has everything to do with me." Didn't his father understand that his love bound them regardless of his future with her?

His mother clucked her tongue. "Thomas, this concerns him and Rosalind and Mr. Richards. You know I care for Rosalind as if she were our own daughter, and quite frankly, there's something about Mr. Richards I *don't* care for."

His father's hand slipped from his shoulder. "Son, I guess what I'm trying to say is, don't let your feelings for Rosalind blind you to what is in front of your face. You need to protect yourself. There are wolves dressed in sheep's clothing here. Be on your guard."

He frowned. *Wolves?* The dream he'd had on the train. Wolves among sheep. He'd awoke just as one wolf—eyes like flames and teeth like spears—caught the woman in his grasp ...

His mother sighed. "Thomas, what do you mean? Stop being so cryptic."

"I mean exactly that. Never be alone with the man. I don't trust Mr. Richards. I believe he's dangerous."

His mother quickly stood. "Then we must tell Roger. Has he returned? Rosalind is set to marry the man."

"I suspect Roger knows, Mother, and so does Rosalind."

Trent exhaled a long breath and the room turned deathly quiet. He took over his father's pacing. "What else would explain her odd behavior?"

"Impossible," Mother voiced, troubled. "Roger wouldn't allow his daughter to marry someone as you're suggesting."

"Let me explain." Father stood alongside Mother and wrapped his arms around her shoulders, as if his words would soon tear her apart. "Roger gambles."

"What?" Trent halted his pacing and whirled toward his father.

Father scowled. "He came to me one night before we moved to Texas. He asked for money." His gaze flashed reliving the memory. "He didn't say why he needed it, and I didn't ask. I should have."

Trent closed his eyes. He knew. He already knew what his father was about to say.

Father continued. "Several weeks later, he asked for money again. This time I did ask. He told me he'd lost everything—everything he and Sarah owned. He asked again for help, and when I again refused, he said he'd find another way. A week later in the office, he handed me something to sign. I was hurrying to a meeting. I signed without looking. He stole thousands of dollars from the bank and used me to get it. With my signature on the transfer, I had no proof of what he'd done. I replaced the money from our personal account so no one would know. I was afraid, Mariam. Roger might have destroyed our lives."

"Oh, Thomas." She placed her head against his chest, and they held each other in a loving embrace. "That's why we left so abruptly? You could have told me."

"How could you not have told *us*? We moved because of fear?" Hurt and frustration clipped Trent's words. He was led to believe they'd moved because it was his father's dream to ranch.

Isn't that what his mother told him the night of their farewell party, words that crushed him, having to leave everything he'd ever known, his friends, his dreams, his *Rosalind* behind? But it seemed even now his mother had known it to be nothing but the truth. "Father, have you ever dreamed of ranching?"

"Yes. But if it hadn't been for Roger, I wouldn't have sought after the dream."

Trent couldn't believe what he was hearing, yet hadn't his family grown close? Hadn't he thanked God more than once for the move and having a father for the first time in his life? Trent took a calming breath.

Father set Mother at arm's length and met her gaze. "I'm sorry, Mariam. Trent." He looked over her shoulder to him. "I should have shared this with you, but I hated myself for being tricked and not confronting Roger. Maybe if I had, I could have helped him and things would be different now, and Glover wouldn't have manipulated the situation. I'll never know."

Trent swallowed hard at the sound of Glover's name. "Father, how is he tied to this?"

"I've done some investigating since we arrived, and only today have I learned that Mr. Richards cleared Roger of all debts in exchange for Rosalind's hand. Roger's stipulation was they wait until she's nineteen to give the impression they were actually courting."

His mother gasped. "Thomas, you can't be serious. Rosalind's birthday is less than two weeks away."

"I paid handsomely for this information, and the source can be trusted."

Trent groaned in disgust. How could a father sell his daughter to pay off gambling debts?

He looked at his father. As a thought took hold, Trent knew it, felt it deep within his soul before he even spoke the words.

"She's in grave danger."

His father cleared his throat. "I believe so."

Trent struggled to keep his voice down. "Mother, did Rosalind tell you how she got those bruises? I noticed one on her upper left arm."

"You don't think …"

"It's a distinct possibility." His father's words hung in the air, and though no one said anything further, Trent would do anything to protect the woman he loved.

Father took Mother by the waist. "We shall all keep an eye on Rosalind and pray for wisdom." He opened the bedroom door and gave him a reassuring smile. "God will help us. Now get some rest." The door clicked closed behind his parents as they left the room.

Rosalind awoke to voices in the hall, one of them being Trent's father. Perhaps he was speaking with Trent. She threw her robe on the chair, dressed, and pressed her ear against the door. Nothing. She vowed to speak with Trent for the way she closed the door in his face earlier and to offer him the last piece of chocolate.

Trent still loved her. She'd sensed it, but it hadn't become clear until he touched her cheek last night and prayed over her. She needed just a few minutes with him, and maybe it would be enough.

She reached under her pillow and pulled out the wrapped chocolate, then made her way to Trent's room. At the door, her hands trembled, but she pressed forward and knocked. The door opened, and their gazes met. She couldn't help but notice the way his blond hair was tousled, or how several of the buttons from his white shirt were undone, revealing tan skin, or how she stood dumbfounded before him.

"Rosalind?" He stared at her, his voice breaking through her daze.

"Thank you." She held out the chocolate as if a peace offering. "I need to speak with you." She wasn't sure what she saw in his blue eyes. Worry? Confusion? Maybe both.

"Is everything all right?"

She hadn't planned on entering his room, but now that she was here, she couldn't help herself. She stepped inside and closed the door. They stood mere feet apart, so close she found it difficult to breathe. What was she doing? This was a mistake. She stepped away and grabbed the back of the chair near the hearth.

He came to her quickly, brow furrowed, eyes searching. "Are you dizzy? Do you need to sit?"

Although she shook her head, he gently grasped her elbow and directed her to sit.

He knelt before her. "If you're feeling ill, please tell me. I'll do whatever I can to help you."

She did feel ill. Not because of anything Glover had done, but because she'd soon be forced into a loveless marriage. The man she truly loved peered into her eyes, begging for answers. What could she tell him?

She held out the chocolate again. "For you."

Trent continued to search her eyes as a small smile lit his face. He cupped her hand within his and unwrapped the candy. "I think this is the largest piece you've ever given me."

If only she could give him more. "Oh, Trent …" Her gaze fell to his lips, even as she felt her own part. How she loved him. If only she had one chance to feel love.

Leaning forward, she brushed her lips against his. A soft

moan escaped his throat, and electric jolts surged through her. He had yet to kiss her in return, but heaven help her, she wanted this.

"Oh, Rose." He stood, pulling her into his arms and kissing her gently, reverently as if it was a privilege, lingering. "What am I going to do?"

She bit her bottom lip to keep from crying and pressed her cheek against his chest. She closed her eyes against her life—her future—and instead inhaled his clean soap scent. How safe and warm she felt in his arms. How perfectly she fit there.

"Can I see you tomorrow?" He kissed the top of her head.

"I'll be shopping with your mother for your party."

"She's ordered me to buy something too, more formal than my 'Sunday best,' as they say in Texas. It's what I've been doing since I saw you last, but I'd be happy to join you."

The pain from his closeness, his gentle touches, his endless love, and the fact she would never be his wife crushed her. The last shred of hope to be free to love him in return was slipping through her fingers. "Glover might join us on our shopping trip. I don't think it would be a good idea if you're there too."

Trent loosened his hold, but she held tighter. She'd pay the price if Glover found out, but she couldn't let Trent go. Not yet.

"Do you still plan to marry Glover?" His voice rose in disbelief, but he clung to her now, reality of the situation hitting them both.

She couldn't answer. Bile rose in her throat.

"I can make you happy, Rose. I'll be true to you, care for you, protect you. You'll never want for anything. I'll make sure of it."

Her heart wrenched. "I should go."

"Please don't leave."

"I can't stay. I shouldn't have come." He released her then, and her heart broke at the emptiness his touch left behind. "I'm sorry."

"Why did you come to me?"

"To give you the candy. To tell you thank you."

He gathered her once again within his arms, and she went willingly. "You came to tear my heart out? To make me suffer?"

She shook her head against his chest. "No … I …"

"I've missed you, Rose. Longed for you. Day. Night. In every sunset, you were there. My thoughts. My prayers. There is nowhere I can go that my love for you isn't." He cupped her cheek. "I love you."

"You can't." Her words came out weak.

Trent tilted his head, softly brushed his lips against hers, and whispered, "I do."

"You can't." She swallowed back tears. "I can't. You don't understand." She moved from his embrace and turned around, covering her face with her hands. She sensed him close behind her. What had she done?

"You kissed me, Rose. You came because you love me."

He touched her arm and she flinched, spinning to face him. "Please …" She groaned. "It was a mistake. I shouldn't have come … the kiss. I'm to wed Glover—"

"But you don't love him. I can feel it in your touch, your kiss—"

"And I was a fool. I'm marrying Glover, and if you care for me as you say you do, I beg you not to say anything further about what just happened. It's for the best. Please, Trent. Give me your word?"

Moisture filled his eyes and his jaw clenched. He blinked hard and turned away from her. "This is what you want?"

No! "It is." She fought to keep from going to him.

"I'm sorry, Rosalind. I can't make that promise."

How she found her way to her room, Rosalind was unsure. Exhaustion pulled at her as she sat on the edge of her bed. She felt something in her pocket. The chocolate.

She slid the wrapper out and threw the chocolate against the wall.

Trent sat in the chair Rosalind had just occupied and took off his boots. The faint smell of her rose-scented perfume lingered in the air, torturing him, as did her kisses.

He still couldn't believe she had kissed him. He'd imagined their first kiss countless times, but never with the possibility of her marrying another man. The impact of her declaration of marrying Glover, after all he learned and after kissing him, was complete and utter torture. But Trent knew the truth now about Glover, her father's debt, and their upcoming marriage. He'd hold his tongue until he found a way for Rosalind to be free of Glover. If not, God would provide a way of rescue, of that he was sure.

Hours later as sleep proved impossible, Trent heard a noise outside his room. He climbed out of bed and cracked the door. Mr. Standford stumbled toward his room.

CHAPTER TEN

Trent woke Sunday before dawn. He tossed and turned, replaying in his mind what he'd learned the day before. Mr. Standford had indeed allowed his own greed and selfishness to control him, to ruin his life and Rosalind's. What horrible consequences for an innocent daughter to face. Trent had seen so little joy in her since he'd arrived. Now he understood why, and he was almost certain the reason Rosalind had never answered his proposal was her father's doing. She loved him still. Otherwise she wouldn't have kissed him the way she had.

He dressed for church—knowing Glover wouldn't accompany them offered little ease—and made his way downstairs with his Bible in hand. Pushing through the kitchen door, he found Doris pouring a cup of coffee. He inhaled the rich aroma and smiled at her. "Good morning."

"It's good to see someone's happy. Let me fix you a cup." Doris pulled another cup from the cabinet, poured, then gave it to him. "Be careful. It's hot."

"Thank you for agreeing to stay on while we're here."

"Reminds me of old times when the missus was alive. I'm

glad to serve your family."

Trent took a warm gulp and enjoyed the brew. "How would you feel about attending church with Rosalind and me? My parents have been asked to attend a friend's church later this morning, so there will be plenty of room in the carriage if you'd like to join us."

Her brows rose. "That's very kind of you, Mr. Easton, but I've already made plans to attend with my children. If that's all, I'll go now and return for lunch."

"Of course. And thank you for the coffee." He took another swallow. "If I didn't have a cook back home, I'd be offering you a job."

Doris chuckled. "You're welcome, Mr. Easton." She placed her apron on a hook next to the icebox and left through the back door.

Trent crossed the room to the round table by the window, set down his Bible, and sank into a chair. A wide oak tree stood beyond the glass, stretching toward a bluebird sky. He closed his eyes, envisioning the wide-open spaces of his ranch back in Texas. The tree at the property line. He'd carved his and Rosalind's names in the bark when he thought they'd marry. It was his way of giving her everything he had from the land, right down to the roots that dug in the soil.

He never had the strength to scratch out their names, and they still remained there today. Would Rosalind ever get to see the tree, the sunflowers he planted for her, or the house he'd built with her in mind? Every detail had been for her, and now he understood why she didn't answer his proposal.

Trent heard the front door slam. He jumped up and raced outside just in time to see Rosalind duck as she climbed into the carriage.

"Are you leaving so soon?" he called out.

She looked out from the carriage. "I assumed you'd be with your parents, visiting friends."

Lord, lead me. Thank you for the few moments alone with her. "No. I'm going with you."

The ride to church passed with agonizing slowness. With Trent sitting on one side of the carriage, and Rosalind on the other, evading his gaze. Not a word had been spoken. And she preferred it. It was better to avoid conversation altogether, no matter how much her heart ached at his nearness. She deserved the pain, selfishly indulging on a whim of a kiss. What had she done? She put everyone's life in danger for a passing moment of pleasure she now regretted. The fear of Glover learning of her indiscretion gripped tightly around her neck. She touched the collar of her dress.

"Rosalind?" Trent slid alongside her. "Your face has turned pale. Speak to me."

"I can't," she managed to say just above a whisper, nestling her hands in her lap. She stared out the carriage window at the passing landscape to avoid his scrutiny. Trent covered her hands with his own, but only for a moment before he returned to his seat. Instantly she grew cold.

Arriving at the church, Rosalind seized the opportunity to separate herself from Trent among people, in hopes he'd find another pew to sit in. After an instant, she found her usual spot and scooted toward the middle. Trent followed, and his arm grazed her shoulder as he sat and reached for a hymnal. He stretched out his legs, and she inched away to avoid further contact.

The pastor asked the congregation to join him in song, and

everyone stood. Trent held the hymnal for them to share. At his nearness, Glover came to mind. Once again, her throat constricted. She glanced at the doors through which she'd entered.

After the singing, Pastor John motioned for everyone to sit. He took his Bible from the wooden stand and instructed everyone to turn to Exodus chapter seven and read along.

She touched the thick binding of her Bible. Her mother had given it to her. She flipped open the hard brown cover. *Translated out of the original tongues ... New York: American Bible Society. 1872.* There it was. Her mother's script.

To my darling daughter,

The words in this book will quench any need or thirst you may have in this life and guide you to know the power of God and His will. Take hold of God's words and grasp them to your heart. Tie them around your neck and never depart from them. May God be a lamp and a light to your path as He directs your future which He has prepared in advance for you. Never forget how much you are loved and treasured, but most importantly, I pray you will know how deep and wide your Heavenly Father's love is for you.

With much affection,

Your mother

Her heart hammered, and her pulse raced as she clasped the Bible in her grip. *What lamp, Mother? What path? There's no light, only darkness. I can't see. God abandoned me. He lied. I'm not loved as you claimed—for you lied to me as well.* Tears blurred her vision, and her hands shook the pages.

She blinked, fighting back the moisture, but tears rolled down her face.

Pastor John looked toward her, and she swallowed. Could he see her distress? She rested her back against the pew and bowed her head. He continued, "God had a plan to free His people from slavery, teach them who He was by having a relationship with them. And that plan included one man, a shepherd by the name of Moses."

From the corner of her eye, Rosalind caught Trent shuffle in his seat. He seemed uncomfortable all of a sudden.

Pastor John's voice rose. "God uses us as His instruments to help rescue people from bondage. Don't ever doubt, beloved, like the Israelites, for they wandered in the desert for forty years because of their unbelief in their Creator's promises."

Rosalind felt like she was in the desert—unable to walk another step, thirsty—and all she wanted to do was give up. She was tired and her heart weighed heavily, even more so since Trent arrived in Boston. She closed her eyes, fatigue settling all around her body and mind.

Near the end of the invitation, she'd give anything to know God still thought of her, loved her, even for a moment.

Pray. A soft voice filtered through her heart.

She ached for God's presence. *Please, God* ... Until that very moment, she'd never felt so empty and alone. Her mother was gone. Her father had given her away. And God abandoned her when she needed Him to love her as her mother had inscribed in her Bible. Unable to stay seated a moment longer, she stood and hurried down the aisle and out the door.

"Rosalind!" Trent called once her feet reached the sidewalk. "Wait."

She climbed into the carriage and closed the door, fighting back tears and the urge to run far away. But there was nowhere to go, no one to help her.

Trent yanked open the door and sat across from her. "Talk

to me. Tell me what's wrong."

She let out a breath and stared out the window. "I need to go home."

"Why did you leave?"

She glanced at him, but the worry etched on his face broke her heart. "You ask too many questions."

"And you give little to no answers."

"You're leaving, so what does it matter to you?"

"I'll stay, Rosalind. For you."

"No." Her breath caught in her throat. She dropped her reticule, then snatched it from the carriage floor. "I'm getting married tomorrow." And she couldn't endure being this close to him another minute. "Go home to Texas. There's nothing for you in Boston." She exited the carriage and rushed down the sidewalk, tears streaming down her cheeks. Her body shook.

I'll stay … for you. The words rang clear in her heart and mind as if Trent had spoken them behind her. She glanced back over her shoulder but saw no one. As she left the sidewalk and cut through a cobbled street near her sister's, she knew she couldn't return home. Not with Trent there. The pull to him was too great. If she could no longer hide her true feelings for him, Glover would see how deep they ran.

She jerked to a halt. He'd threatened Sydney and the babies. He'd have no qualms about harming Trent. Because of her, Trent was now in danger.

Rosalind made her way to Sydney's home. To keep from being seen, she sneaked in a back way through a narrow fence. She'd send word to Glover that she was visiting her sister. He'd probably be happier with that than the idea of her being home alone with Trent. And Trent would be kept out of harm's way.

Tomorrow's party would be the last time she'd see Trent. Hiding her true feelings and facing both men while being in the

Eastons' company would be a horrible challenge. But she'd do it if she had to, to protect those she loved.

CHAPTER ELEVEN

"I know I asked yesterday, but I wish you would tell me what's going on." Sydney rocked a swaddled William in the chair beside the fireplace.

"Do you ever wonder why William shivers so?" Rosalind asked with all the nonchalance she could muster. Keeping secrets from her sister was both tricky and dire. "What will happen to him when winter comes?"

"I believe since William was much smaller and had more difficulties, his body chills easily. But I pray when the colder temperatures come, he'll be old enough to handle them." She ran her fingers over his bald head. "Rosalind, you changed the subject again. Something about Glover isn't right, and I don't like the way he obsesses over you. Like yesterday, I could tell he wasn't happy when he found out you were here. I'm your sister, Rosalind."

"He was concerned over my well-being is all. After we had a chance to speak, he warmed to the idea of me staying with you."

She snorted. "I'm sure he did. Trenton wasn't anywhere

around. Are you here because of Trenton? His care for you is obvious. Why, if *I* had a choice, I'd marry Trenton instead of Glover."

"Marrying Trenton isn't a possibility for me. He's leaving."

Sydney stopped rocking, her brows furrowed. "Leaving? Are you sure?"

What other option did she have but to send him away? "Tonight is the last time I'll see him." She rose from the couch, twisting her fingers. "Would you be willing to collect my dress from home? It seems I have none of my things for the party."

"I don't understand you, Rosalind." Her gaze fell to Rosalind's hands. "Look at how upset you are. I can tell you wish to see Trenton. If only you'd encourage him to stay, I'm sure he would."

She dropped her hands. "Please, Sydney. I don't want to talk about this." And yet her heart rebelled within her chest.

Sydney rose and slowly slid William into Rosalind's arms. "Then I shall go now, as Anna is still asleep in her crib." She hurried up the stairs and minutes later returned with a large bag in hand. "I love you, my sister. Don't fault me because I care about your happiness."

"I do not fault you. Just please, trust me. I know what's best for everyone, including my future."

She gave a slight nod of acceptance. "Is there anything else you need from home?"

"My cream slippers in the bottom of the armoire, and there's a bow in the top drawer on the left. Select anything else you think I might need." She looked down at her nephew, then back at her sister. "May I stay longer, until Joshua comes home?"

Her sister smiled then. "You may stay as long as you like. I love having you here with me."

Rosalind chuckled at the excitement in her eyes. "Please

bring whatever you think I'll need to stay."

"How wonderful." Sydney kissed William's cheek, then headed for the entryway. "I'll bring Doris. She'll watch the children tonight so we may attend Trent's party together. I won't be long."

Rosalind moved to the rocking chair and set it in motion, recalling Glover's words. With a sneer, he had shared with her Mr. Easton's request regarding the party. Glover made sure to let her know he granted the request—which had delighted her—then informed her they would marry tonight, right after Trent's party.

Nausea swam in her stomach, then as it did now.

Pray.

She closed her eyes against the thought. What good would praying do? She wanted to believe her mother hadn't lied to her, believe that God did indeed care. But God hadn't healed her mother. Nor had he stopped her father's gambling or preserved her future. Rather, she'd been left with a loneliness that had grown deeper and darker with each passing hour. Only a few more hours and she'd be bound to Glover for the rest of her life.

She raised her eyes to the tall ceiling. "Lord, I..." she whispered. "I...please."

She said no more, just simply rocked her nephew and daydreamed of a life—a family—that might have been.

Trent glared through his bedroom window at the street below. He ran his fingers through his hair, released a ragged breath, then took to pacing once again. He had to find Rosalind. She hadn't come home yesterday. And with the party taking place within a few hours, she'd need to return to prepare, wouldn't she? What if she had decided not to attend? He must see her one final time, whether she wanted to see him or not.

His chest tightened. *There's nothing for you in Boston,* she'd said. How wrong she was.

He'd prayed into the night looking for direction, a dream, anything that would confirm he should stay in Boston. Yet God remained silent. Had God brought him here only to have him leave Rosalind once again? He shook his head. The idea made no sense. He couldn't believe after their recent kiss that she still planned to marry Glover.

A light knock sounded on his bedroom door. "Rosalind?" he called and opened it.

"It's me." His mother stood there with a bewildered look on her face. "Sydney is here to see you. She's in Rosalind's room gathering her things. She said Rosalind won't be returning until later in the week."

"That doesn't make sense. Rosalind told me yesterday she was marrying Glover today." He headed for Rosalind's bedroom.

"Wait." Mother placed a hand on his arm as he passed. "Are you sure you understood her correctly?"

He hadn't planned to share their conversation with his mother, but something in the way she asked concerned him. "We had a bit of an argument, and she blurted it out."

"An argument?"

He lowered his voice to match hers, hoping Sydney hadn't overheard them speaking. "I told her I'd stay in Boston for her, but she told me to go home." He rubbed the back of his neck, kneading his tensed muscles. "I'd give up everything for her, Mother."

She glanced toward Rosalind's room, then met his gaze. "Go speak to Sydney. Find out if Rosalind plans to attend your party. And don't mention what we've discussed."

Trent strode down the hall and stood at the entrance to Rosalind's room. Her scent filled the air, and he inhaled deeply, his need to see her even more severe. Sydney stood at Rosalind's dresser holding a carpet bag.

"Sydney."

She turned and grinned. "Trenton. It's good to see you. I'm just gathering a few things for Rosalind. Please, enter." She set the carpet bag on the bed and stuffed a hair bow inside.

It was as if he held his heart in his hands, willing to give it away for any news about Rosalind. "How is she?"

A slight frown tightened her lips. "Do you know why my sister is upset enough to want to stay with me?"

What could he tell her? They'd kissed and he basically asked her to marry him, but she refused him for Glover. "During our last conversation, I told her I'd stay in Boston for her."

Her gray eyes, remarkably like Rosalind's, widened. "You did? And what did she say?"

He shoved his hands in his pockets. "Go back to Texas."

"I see," she whispered, collecting a few more items from the dresser and placing them in her bag. "Please tell me you're not giving up so easily."

He wasn't, but until the Lord showed him what to do or which way to go, he had only one choice—wait and be still. "What do you suggest I do? She's marrying Glover."

She closed the dresser drawers and met his gaze. "I don't know what she sees in the man, but I know she has feelings for you. Strong feelings, and that's why I brought this." She pulled a folded handkerchief from her dress pocket and opened it. "Mother was alive when I married Joshua. She gave him her blessing. She's not here now, but I am. I give *you* my blessing."

His heart pounded in his ears as she placed the linen in his palm. The initial S was embroidered on the white cloth, and inside was a gold and diamond band.

"Glover can't make her happy. She doesn't love him. Don't give up, Trenton. Pursue her. Don't let her get away this time." She lifted her bag from the bed and smiled. "We'll see you tonight."

Trent blinked, taking in what she'd said, then realized Sydney was leaving. "Let me walk you out." He hurried to follow her.

She waved him off. "I can see myself out. Besides, you must ready yourself for the party. Who knows what tonight may hold." She grinned and descended the stairs.

"I'll send a carriage." Trent gripped the rail with one hand and squeezed the rings in the other. What had just happened? He looked down into the foyer and watched Sydney leave.

Be still, a familiar quiet voice said in his heart. *Wait.*

Glover leaned back in his desk chair and twiddled his pen. He smirked. No matter what, today he would marry Rosalind.

Roger knocked, and he enjoyed the sly grin sliding over his face as he made Roger wait. One, two, three seconds. Four. Roger knocked again.

"Come in, Roger."

Roger hurried to Glover's desk, speaking in hushed tones. "You summoned me from a meeting with investors?"

"It's good to see you pride yourself in something besides gambling. A man must take pride in his work." Glover chuckled.

"If you're playing games, whatever you have to say can wait." Roger turned to leave.

"I'm changing our arrangement. I'm getting married and

wanted you to be the first to hear of it. Well, the second if you count my lovely bride-to-be."

Roger turned back and pushed the door closed. "I know you're getting married."

Glover's smile stretched wider. "But *when*, dear Roger? That's the question. Are you not going to ask? Aren't you a bit curious to know when the happy couple will be united before witnesses and *God*?"

"You know nothing about God."

Glover placed his hands on his desk and rose. "And you do?" He laughed. "You're a gambler. Although it hurts Rosalind to see you this way, you care more about feeding your addiction than how your actions affect her. Let's not forget, you used me to pay off your debts. You're no better than I, Roger. We both have gotten what we wanted—well, I'll soon have what I want. If this is the God you know, then he and I would get along wonderfully."

Roger hung his head. "This isn't the God I knew."

"Then you must not have known God very well." Glover skirted his desk and sat on the edge. "The Eastons will have Rosalind all to themselves tonight at the party—a concession I gave out of the goodness of my heart. However, after the party, I'm claiming my bride."

"That wasn't our deal!" Roger hissed. "She's not yet nineteen."

"I've held up my end of the bargain long enough. The mourning period is over. Everyone knows we've been courting." He reached across his desk and lifted a white envelope. "Surprisingly, I've grown fond of you, Roger. Now that we're to be family, I have a wedding present for you."

Roger took it, opened it, then counted the contents. He glanced up. "I don't understand. Money?"

Glover leaned back and lifted his cigar. "You will leave town. I want you as far away from here, from Rosalind, as possible."

"I can't leave my daughters. I can't do that."

"Boston can be a dangerous place, Roger. Men die in alleys or go missing and are never seen again. You remember Scott Tomlinson?" He took a puff of his cigar.

"Yes, he went missing right after …"

Glover smiled at the fear in Roger's eyes. "If you want to live, move away. It's up to you, but I'd much rather you live for Rosalind's sake. Yet again …" He set his cigar down and rubbed his jaw. "My wife would need much comfort if she were grieving."

"You can't be serious. What would I say to Rosalind? Or the Eastons?"

He shrugged. "Tell them you plan to visit them."

"In Texas?"

"Yessssss. Texas." And what a perfect, perfect idea. "Rosalind will accept that. Then, you will simply stay there. Away from here. Away from Rosalind. You may leave now."

"You can't do this."

"Oh, yes, I can. And Roger, no need for you to attend the wedding. It will be a very private ceremony." He stared into Roger's cowardly face and leaned forward. "I want tonight to be the last time I see you."

Roger squeezed the envelope. "Glover, I beg you—"

He chuckled. "Get out of my office. Or, if you prefer, I have a couple associates that can help you out."

Roger scurried through the door like the whimpering fool he was.

Glover checked the time. At the party, he would admire Rosalind from afar. Soon, he'd admire her *much* more closely.

CHAPTER TWELVE

"Rosalind, are you listening?"

Rosalind met Sydney's gaze. Her sister held a mirror before her. "What did you say?"

"Hmm. I'm curious to whom your thoughts have wandered, but I can guess."

"Glover," Rosalind answered quickly.

Sydney smiled as if she didn't believe her.

Truthfully, she was thinking of Glover. How could she dance with Trenton tonight without angering Glover, even with his permission? He'd be watching her, watching them. She must be careful not to let her feelings show and fuel his temper.

Tonight would be the last time she and Trent would be together, the last time she'd see him. Although her heart ached at the knowledge, she swallowed, stuffing down the pain, and focused on her sister's instructions.

"Turn your head to the left." Sydney pointed. "See, I placed the bow above your ear. Do you like it?" Small ringlets hung from her temple, and Sydney had pinned up the rest of her hair, with small pearl beads pressed in sporadic fashion.

"It's so lovely, Sydney." She forced a chuckle. "I think you missed a calling."

"Thank you." Her sister gave a mock bow and smiled. "When Anna's older, her hair will be quite fashionable. No doubt I'll fret over every primp and tuck."

"You will obsess, I'm sure." How she loved Sydney and was so thankful she and Joshua had returned to Boston. Rosalind drew a breath.

"Now listen, little sister. Every man at the party will be eyeing you from the moment you walk in. Including Trenton."

Rosalind said nothing. She ran her fingers over the fabric crisscrossing her torso, then tapering to bows on both sides. The green gown was breathtaking. Mrs. Easton said the color accented her brown hair and gray eyes.

"You look very lovely yourself." She touched Sydney's sleeve. "Who would have thought of black lace along the front and sleeves? I just adore burgundy on you."

She sighed. "It's Joshua's favorite color."

"You miss him."

Sydney rested on the edge of her bed. "Yes, it's hard on me when he's away, but when he comes home it's like heaven on earth. He loves and cherishes me. I thank the Lord he will be stationed on the naval base close to home."

"I'm thankful too." A wave of sadness washed over Rosalind. What would it be like to be loved and cherished the way Joshua adored her sister? She'd seen the love in his eyes when he and Sydney were together and how he catered to her when he was home from his required months at sea.

Rosalind blinked and steeled her emotions. Her marriage to Glover wouldn't have love. She'd simply have to endure it one day at a time and find a way to tolerate his touch.

"Are you all right?"

She stood. "Perfectly fine. Are we ready to leave?"

Her sister eyed her for a moment longer, an expression which said, *I'm letting this go for now*. Then she rose from the bed and checked her reflection in her vanity mirror. "Yes, I'll meet you downstairs. I want to give Doris further instructions about the children." Sydney left the room.

Rosalind didn't need a final look in the mirror. She knew she'd never looked more elegant in her life. Her most beautiful, most horrible night. She followed Sydney out and descended the stairs.

"Oh, Miss Standford, you look wonderful." Doris held Anna over her shoulder and patted the baby's back. "Now, you both have a lovely time and don't worry about a thing."

"Thank you, Doris." Sydney kissed Anna's fingers, then opened the door.

Rosalind was struck breathless as she exited. The light from an open carriage that sat waiting for them would guide their way. "Who sent this?"

Her sister said nothing, taking the driver's hand as he helped her into the carriage. Then he offered the same assistance to Rosalind.

The driver pointed to a blanket on the seat beside them. "We've only a few blocks to travel. Please use the blanket if you become cold."

"Thank you." Sydney ran her hand along the bench. "Oh my. This red cloth is so soft." The carriage rolled forward.

"We must thank whoever provided this carriage."

"Dear sister." Sydney covered her lap with the blanket. "As if you didn't know it was Trenton. I think you must be blind not to see he cares for you."

Rosalind took a moment to continue to dream of a life with Trent, full of simple moments like these. It wasn't only the luxury, but the man who loved her with all his being, like Joshua loved Sydney.

"We're close." Sydney pointed. "The Eastons' old residence." Several carriages—although none as nice as the one they occupied—lined the front of the house.

Rosalind's pulse raced as they rode into the driveway. She'd seen the estate many times since the Eastons had left, but now as the lights shone from the windows and guests entered the home, time seemed to have stood still and memories wove Trent and her together.

As they slowed to a stop, Trent came from the house. He was dashing in his dark coat, and as he neared, the light from the carriage shone on his handsome face. He assisted Sydney to the ground, but his eyes sparkled as he held out his hand for her. "Hello, Rose." He grinned.

"Hello." A blush warmed her cheeks as she took his hand, and he gave hers a small squeeze. She stepped down onto the paved walk and looked up at him. The way he smiled at her now made her feel special in a way she'd never known and would never know again.

Breathe.

He tucked her arm through his and led her up the path. They waited in line to enter the house.

Taking another deep breath, she glanced around hoping to see her sister, hoping *not* to see Glover.

"Are you looking for someone?" He covered her hand with his.

How could his covering her hand make her feel so safe and treasured? "My sister."

His gaze fell to her lips as his hold tightened. "Sydney's farther in line. I believe she left us alone on purpose."

"I see." Sydney had been encouraging her toward Trent

since his arrival and, no matter how much Rosalind tried to hide her feelings, she believed her sister knew her heart. So help her, tonight there would be no distance between them, and she would bask in Trent's affections and be thankful for every blissful hour. She wouldn't worry she'd be punished by Glover for enjoying herself. Tonight, for one evening, she would live as she'd dreamed of living.

The line began to move. "Father and Mother will be happy to see you, especially Mother. She mentioned you bought a lovely gown."

Rosalind glanced ahead and noticed his parents standing at the entrance and greeting guests. "Oh, Trent." She covered her mouth with her gloved hand. "You should be with your parents."

"Don't worry."

Finally, they reached his parents, both of whom hugged her. Then Trent's mother held her at arm's length. "Don't you look lovely." Mariam's eyed filled with tears, darkening their green hue. "You look just like your mother." She embraced her again.

"Thank you," Rosalind whispered.

A man cleared his throat, and Rosalind's blood ran cold. Glover. How had she not seen him? How long had he been watching them? Perspiration dotted her brow.

Glover, who stood next in line, bowed and then straightened. "Hello, Rosalind, dear."

Mr. Easton held out his hand. "Glad you could make it."

Glover accepted his hand and smiled. "I wouldn't miss this for the world." He then turned to Trent. "Knowing how much your parents will miss you, I'm sorry to see you leave our lovely city. But a man must protect his property, his cattle, his sheep, or … whatever it is you have in Texas."

Rosalind's anger pricked. Trent was more of a man than Glover ever had been or ever would be. She avoided Glover's gaze and smiled sweetly toward the couple behind him, hoping to move the line along and him out of her sight.

Trent must have known her thoughts because he accepted Glover's false regret and turned to greet the couple behind him. From the corner of her eye, Rosalind saw Glover stroll away.

She let herself smile, a real smile, reveling in the joy of standing with the Eastons as they greeted their remaining guests. For the first time in years, she felt part of a family, accepted and loved for herself.

Tonight, after the party, when she was forced to marry, she would remember this moment. And in the future, she would dwell on the memory against the loneliness that was sure to come.

As they greeted three more couples, Trent couldn't keep his gaze from Rosalind. Not only was she breathtakingly beautiful, but something had changed between them. She stood closer, taller if that were possible, and her smile radiated when she looked at him.

The last couple entered and was greeted. Trent shoved his hand into his pocket, and his finger slid over the smooth band and diamonds.

His father slipped his arm around his mother's waist and kissed her cheek. "Shall we?"

"I thought you'd never ask." She smiled, taking his arm.

Trent bowed and stayed low. "And I shall have the honor of accompanying you, my sweet lady."

Rosalind chuckled and clasped her hands together. "Do you act like this in Texas?"

He gazed up into her gray eyes. "Oh no. You won't find me

bowing or dressed like this." He rose and straightened his coat.

"I can't imagine what Texas is like. Will you tell me more about it?" She slipped her hand into the crook of his arm.

"I'd be glad to. Would you like to go to the balcony?"

"That would be lovely."

Out on the balcony, the unusually cool June evening had Rosalind shivering against his arm. He wanted to hold her to keep her warm, but doing what he wanted and what was expected were two different things. "We can go back inside," he said. "I don't want you to catch a chill."

Her eyes questioned him, and a moment later her hand slipped from his arm, and she strolled to the rail. "I'd much rather stay out here for a time. Tell me about Texas."

He stood beside her, staring out at the darkness, his mind drifting to his land. To home. "I really don't know where to begin."

"Start anywhere. What do the skies look like?"

"They're beautiful. Wide-open spaces. The sky stretches as far as the eye can see. My favorite times are early mornings and late afternoons. You can almost pick your color—orange, red, gold, blue, or pink. They all show up, as if God paints the heavens with His finger."

"Tell me about your land."

Trent turned toward her, and she was staring at him. Even in the dim lighting, he'd seen the longing in her eyes. Was her desire to be in his company or to see Texas for herself? He knew his own gaze reflected the desires hidden in his heart.

"I planted sunflowers for you." *And built a house for us to live in, to start a family in.*

For a long moment, she looked at the balcony floor, then to the house.

He was so tempted to lift his fingers to her forehead and

smooth out the wrinkles. "I wish—"

She looked away. "We should go inside. I believe I am feeling a bit chilled."

Were those unshed tears in her eyes? He hated to think he'd put them there, but she had to know he'd thought of her constantly since moving to Texas. Or was he torturing them both with a love they couldn't reclaim? "Of course." He held out his arm and she accepted.

At Rosalind's direction, they headed toward the music. Trent spotted Glover standing with a group of men. Glover's eyes narrowed as they strolled by. A whirlwind of emotions consumed Trent, but it was fear for Rosalind's safety that rose up within him. He covered her hand with his own. God brought him here for Rosalind's sake.

He'd be willing to give up his life to protect her, but he didn't know how to convince her not to marry Glover. *God, give me strength. Show me how to protect Rosalind. Show me tonight before it's too late.* They entered the crowd to waltz. Couples were gathering on the floor.

"Rosalind," he whispered. "I'm not sure I remember how to do this. I was sure once I began, I'd remember…except for my feet."

The music began and Trent froze.

Rosalind chuckled. "You seem frightened. Come on, cowboy. I'll show you what to do. Slide your right foot forward one step, three measures. Do you remember?"

No. "I'll follow your lead."

She tapped his foot, a prompt to move.

They circled each other holding hands in the air. She curtsied and he bowed, but when she pulled him to herself, he'd gladly let her lead any day. As Rosalind danced around the room with the other couples, her grace magnified. She was as elegant as a swan, and he couldn't tear his eyes away from her, nor did he want to. *Please, Lord. Answer my prayer. Show me how to protect her.* She returned to him.

He stepped with the music and realized his shoe had not met the floor. "Oh, Rosalind. Your foot."

She smiled at him and giggled. They both stood in front of each other once again. "I think I can walk."

He took her hand to guide her from the floor. They weaved through several couples and passed the stairwell to the balcony. Rosalind glanced at him. "Why are we coming back out here?"

"This is the only place we can speak privately without drawing attention. Especially from Glover."

She released his hand and stood at the rail, staring down into the darkness as if she saw the gardens below.

"Rosalind. What is it?"

"Dancing. Being near you. I wanted to believe I could enjoy this evening with you, but I can't. It's too difficult, even being here on this balcony." She turned to him. "The last time I was here was the night before you left, when you asked permission to write to me. My whole life changed that night. By the time we reached home, my mother was deathly ill. We didn't know if she would live through the night. I thought it was the most difficult thing I had ever faced. Then I learned that same night my father promised me to Glover."

"Your father had already decided you were to marry Glover, even before we left Boston? Before my letters?" She stood only inches from him yet seemed so far away. His heart was breaking at the growing distance. "Why didn't you share these things with me when you wrote?"

"I had hoped Mother would survive, to speak to Father and stop the wedding from happening. I thought it was you she …" She covered her mouth with her hand.

"Before I came out to the balcony that night, she asked if I planned to write you. I told her I would if she approved."

Rosalind met his gaze, eyes searching. "What did she say?"

"She cupped my cheek and said, 'Yes, please write to my Rosalind.' She said knowing I would keep in touch with you did her heart good."

Tears slid down Rosalind's face. "She knew she was dying, but she didn't tell us. It was you she wanted me to marry."

Lord, help me to set her free.

CHAPTER THIRTEEN

*I*t *was you she wanted me to marry.*

Rosalind shivered against the cold gripping her body. She recalled how her mother spoke of Trent and how she loved him. Hadn't Rosalind seen it before now … even the night of the party, the dress she wore? Yes, her mother encouraged her toward Trent. Why hadn't she seen that clearly? If Mother had been well, she'd have stopped her father from agreeing to her betrothal to Glover. Father would have listened.

"Rosalind, are you all right? You're trembling." Trent's warm hand caressed her cheek.

Her eyes closed in the truth. *I would have been saved.*

"Rosalind, you've grown pale."

"I …" Hearing heavy footsteps, her eyes flung open. Glover stared as he strolled toward them. She wiped her tears with the back of her gloved hand. "Glover." Her voice quivered, and Trent's palm fell. "We were—"

"Talking about her mother," Trent said quickly. "She's turned pale, and I was going to suggest she ought to rest in one of the rooms upstairs. Rosalind, would you like me to escort you upstairs? Or do you think you can manage?"

Glover had yet to speak, and her words caught in her throat, choking her. "I … I can manage … Thank you," she whispered and faced Glover. A nod told her he'd given his consent, but what would come of it later? Had he seen Trent's hand on her cheek?

She swallowed hard and hated herself for the fear Glover ignited within her. To be controlled regardless of who she was or how she felt.

Rosalind left the balcony and climbed the stairs to the second floor, continuing down the hall. In the Eastons' library, books lined the walls from floor to ceiling. She stood at the window and looked out. Darkness joined her there, but a figure grew within the reflection of the window. Glover. He reached her and stroked her arm.

"I know my caress will be much more welcomed than that of another man." His soft caress sent chills up her spine. He'd seen them. Trent's hand. What would he do to her now?

He gripped her arms, turning her, then leaned in for a kiss. Bile rose in her mouth.

She turned her face away.

Glover flexed his hands on her arms a time or two and took a breath, inching even closer. "Don't turn away from me. I'm not like Trenton. I get or take what I want, and no one can stop me." His fingers grabbed her jaw and forced her to meet his eyes. "Not even you." His lips devoured hers, promising what was yet to come. Ragged breaths filled her lungs when he released her. "Dinner is about to begin. You may sit with me."

Her hand flew to her stomach. "Glover. Please. I can't go out there right now."

"I don't know what has happened between you and Trenton, but I am not him. You will come because I say you will." He grabbed her hand and yanked her forward, causing her to fall to her knees.

"Let go. You're hurting me." She cried out in pain, but Glover didn't relent.

Mr. Easton came through the doorway at that moment. "Mr. Richards. I've been looking for you. Oh, Rosalind, did you fall?"

Instantly, Glover bent and collected her against him as they rose. "Are you all right, dear?"

She nodded. "I need to sit," was all she could say as Mr. Easton collected Rosalind's hands from Glover possessively. She winced from the pain in her wrist but said nothing.

"Yes, of course, Rosalind. I'll take you to a more comfortable room. Glover, supper is being served. Will you be so kind as to ask Trent to say grace and let him know I will return momentarily?"

"I shall leave you then, Rosalind. Rest. I'll be by later." He kissed her cheek but didn't linger.

Rosalind's body quivered and she could barely breathe, much less stand. "I need to sit, Mr. Easton." She choked back tears as he guided her down the hall to the room farthest from the party and noise.

"You will stay here with us tonight. I made sure every room in the house has been prepared for company. Now we'll actually use it."

She couldn't stay with the Eastons. That would only add more fuel to Glover's anger, no matter that every instinct Rosalind possessed suggested she needed to hide from him. But where? Where could she go that Glover wouldn't find her?

In a bedroom, Mr. Easton led her to a burgundy chair.

She slumped onto it. "Thank you," she whispered, biting her lip to keep her tears at bay, eyes scanning the room, something for her gaze to land on.

Mr. Easton cleared his throat, and her gaze found his. "Rosalind, I have a question I must ask. It's quite personal, but I need to know."

What could he possibly want to know? Did he see Glover's anger? Should she tell him what he'd done, hurting her? How she was being forced … "I will try to answer."

"When is the wedding? Mariam told me Glover planned it for tonight, and I hoped she'd been mistaken."

What did it matter if he knew? He couldn't stop the wedding. No one could. Not even her prayers, for God never heard her cries. "After the party."

Mr. Easton squeezed his eyes shut. "With the Lord's help, we will keep you safe. You will not marry Glover tonight or ever."

What was he saying? A sinking sensation grew in the pit of her stomach, and fear jolted her to her feet. She grabbed his jacket, her wrist throbbing. "Leave Glover be, Mr. Easton, please. He will hurt you and your family. He has ways. I've heard of them. I can't allow you to be hurt because of me."

His focus remained on her, compassion in his eyes. Rosalind released him then. "It would be the death of me for any one of you to be hurt … or worse. I'd rather marry Glover." She slid back into the chair. "When Mother was alive, I had dreams of a life filled with happiness, love, and growing old with someone." She met his eyes, knowing he was a Godfearing person like her mother. "Why did God take my dreams away? Why did He abandon me in the process?"

"Oh, child, God hasn't taken your desires away. He wants to give you the desires of your heart. But Scripture also says the devil prowls around seeking to devour. Stand firm in your faith, Rosalind. God is with you, even now."

"I have no faith. All I feel is anguish and fear."

"Rosalind, I know this is hard to hear, but you need to know God is near. God will rescue you."

She wanted to have faith. Faith in the God her mother spoke of, and she once too believed in. But how could she now, when there was no peace, only loneliness? "God ignores my cries."

"The Lord hears, Rosalind."

Trent entered the room. He looked from his father to Rosalind, then to the wrist she cradled in her lap. He knelt at her feet. "I couldn't find you. What happened? Are you hurt?" He gently took her wrist, and she winced at the pain once again. He studied her hand, fingers, and wrist intently, then her face. "It doesn't seem to be broken. What happened?"

Mr. Easton closed the door before he spoke, his brows drawing together in a frown. "Glover."

Rosalind stood, and Trent rose with her. "Mr. Easton. Please." She wanted to deny it but remained silent as Trent's blue eyes peered into hers. Something passed over his features, and his lips thinned into a fine line.

"He's the one who caused you pain before—the bruise on your cheek, the marks on your arms—when Mother attended you. He was the cause of it all."

It wasn't a question. Trent knew regardless if she admitted to the abuse or not.

"I walked in and saw him hurting her," his father continued, "forcing her to the ground. "I need the train ticket you bought for tonight. Do you still have it? Rosalind is in danger. We need that ticket."

It took them both a moment to understand what his father was asking. Trent was the first to respond. "You're sending her to our home?"

"As long as Glover doesn't suspect she's there, I believe she'll be safe."

"I can't leave." Neither man looked her way but continued as if they hadn't heard her speak.

"Then I'm going with her to make sure she'll be safe."

"You can't. What happens when Glover comes in the morning and you're both gone? He will assume you are together and hunt you down, but if you remain here and Rosalind disappears, you will not be involved."

Rosalind was stunned into silence. She couldn't believe what she was hearing. Leaving for Texas? "I can't go! I won't go!"

Both men turned.

"You don't understand," she pleaded. "Glover threatened my life. My father's and Sydney's, too, if we don't agree to his terms. I will not put my family's lives at risk. I must marry him tomorrow."

Trent's brows rose. "But it's fine for your father to put your life in danger and sentence you to death. That's what might happen if you marry Glover, and I won't allow it, Rosalind."

"I'm glad to hear you say that, son, because she leaves tonight. Tomorrow, you'll leave on the train everyone knew you were taking. We will have her stay in Fort Worth and wait for you until you get there the next day."

"I don't want to let her go alone. It's not safe."

"God will protect her."

"How, when we're not together?"

"By giving her your name."

Trent stilled. A question held in his gaze.

A tightening clenched Rosalind's chest, and her pulse began to race. She couldn't believe what his father suggested. She shook her head. "I can't … I can't marry you. I… My family…"

"Mariam and I will stay to make sure Glover doesn't touch your family. I have my ways. You have my word. I won't leave them. I made that mistake before, especially with your father, and it won't happen again."

Trent came to her, and Rosalind's breath caught in her throat. "Be my bride. Allow me the honor of being your husband. To love, honor, and cherish you for the rest of our lives."

Heat stole into her cheeks. She couldn't answer, nor did she know how. This is what she dreamed, yet what about her father, Sydney, and the children? Mr. Easton gave his word, but could he protect her family and themselves? What would happen if Glover retaliated against the Eastons?

She said nothing.

Trent reached into his pocket and withdrew a white cloth, then unveiled a gold band with a set of diamonds shaped in a circle. She gasped. Her mother's wedding ring. "How did you…"

He knelt in front of her. "Marry me, Rose."

CHAPTER FOURTEEN

The only thing Rosalind could hear was the echoing of her heart pounding against her soul. Was this a dream? Was she even breathing? She laid her hand against her chest. She was awake. This was truly happening. Trent wanted to marry her.

Glover's face flashed through her thoughts, and she fought to push the angry image away but failed.

"I love you, Rosalind." Trent's blue eyes remained fixed on her, his voice raw with emotion.

He'd loved her all this time. Could God have loved her all this time as well? Could it be He'd never left her, as her mother said? Or, as Mr. Easton said only moments ago, that He would rescue her? Was God rescuing her now by sending her to Texas, to leave her loved ones in danger?

Faith, my child.

Trent rose to his feet. "God will protect you. He will protect your family."

His voice left little doubt he believed his words to be true, yet tears filled her eyes, and one by one, they rolled down her cheek. "I want to believe you. I want to know God loves me and will protect me and my family—to have faith."

He wiped her tears with the tip of his finger. "I dreamed about you."

"Me?"

"On the way here. On the train. I dreamed you were in the middle of a field, within a sheepfold."

"What was I doing there?"

"You were one of the sheep, but as I continued to dream, wolves snuck in and all the other sheep vanished, but it was you who remained."

"I don't understand."

"The dream never finished, but I realize now I'm the one God called to rescue you … from Glover. You believe I love you, yet you're struggling to know God's love, and He's the one who sent me." He slid her mother's ring into one palm and dabbed her cheek with her mother's handkerchief with his other hand. "The way to have faith is to step out, forgetting about your fears and doubts, and to trust God that whatever happens, He will be there."

A movement caught her eye, and Trent turned to where her gaze traveled. Mr. Easton had walked to the door. "There's not much time," he said, causing Trent to pull his hand away.

She felt lost without the comfort of his touch. Loneliness settled around her shoulders like a heavy quilt.

"We need to head back to the party or Glover will be suspicious." Trent met his father at the door.

No! Don't leave! Her chest tightened as she took a step toward them. She wanted to believe, to have faith, to trust. *Forget your fears and doubts … trust God … step out … faith.*

She could barely breathe. "Yes."

Both men turned back to her, and Trent's gaze intensified. "What did you say?"

"Yes. I'll marry you. Tonight."

Trent scooped her up and kissed her soundly. She couldn't explain it, but joy and peace lit the dark shadows of her heart. Faith, foreign only moments ago, took root, clenching her soul. How could this have happened? A dream? No, this was definitely not a dream, for Trent's embrace held a promise and a future.

Mr. Easton cleared his throat. "We need a plan since the marriage will take place during the party. We will need to keep everyone in the dark of what's going on, especially Glover. Dr. Clark will be sitting at my left during dinner. I will ask him to see to you, Rosalind, though we know the outcome of his visit. Nevertheless, it's for Glover's benefit. After he leaves, I'm certain Glover will come to see you." He slid his timepiece from his pocket and flipped the latch. "Two hours until the train departs from the station. We need to hurry."

Trent intertwined their fingers and gave hers a gentle squeeze. "I'll speak with Pastor John."

Rosalind inhaled a deep breath, and a fluttering took flight within her stomach. Within the hour, she'd be Mrs. Trenton Easton.

Yes. Rosalind's word still echoed in Trent's ears and radiated within his heart, even now as he took the back stairs to the kitchen. Mother was with Rosalind in his old bedroom, and his father was filling his mother in on what transpired only moments ago. He still couldn't believe they were to be married.

By the time they entered the dining hall, their guests were halfway through the meal. Trent sat in his chair while his father went to his place at the head of the table. Still standing, he smiled to their guests. "I'm terribly sorry we are late. One of our guests has become ill, and Mariam is attending to her now. As some of you are aware, Trent will be heading back to Texas tomorrow morning and we will miss him greatly." His father raised his glass. "To my son, whom I love. It gives me great pleasure seeing the man you've become and the man you will continue to be, trusting God every step of the way."

Trent nodded and smiled at his father as he claimed his chair. Voices rose and filled the dining hall once again. Trent glanced at Dr. Clark, who sat closest to his father. Their plan had to work precisely.

Yet it was God who led him to Boston for Rosalind. Even if the plan didn't work as they hoped, God was in control, and He alone would be their protection, their fortress.

"Mr. Easton." Glover got Mr. Easton's attention the moment he walked away from a group of men that included the mayor and governor. Although the man no longer lived in Boston, his influence couldn't be denied, and it angered Glover that much more. For the first time since he'd seen Rosalind visit her father at the bank several years earlier, he sensed himself losing control of his plan to make Rosalind his wife. Their hold over Rosalind couldn't be allowed, but with Trent leaving, and their marriage tomorrow, the ties were about to be cut. For good. But for now he needed to find Rosalind.

Glover held out his hand, and Mr. Easton returned the gesture with a firm shake. "Wonderful party."

"I'm glad you're enjoying yourself, Mr. Richards."

"I was wondering if you've seen Rosalind? I haven't been able to locate her. She isn't with your son or your wife."

"Oh, yes. I told my wife to escort Dr. Clark to where Rosalind is resting. He's checking on Rosalind's wrist. It seemed to be bothering her, and since the doctor was already in the house …" He chuckled. "Less on the bill, you know." He began walking, and Glover followed.

"I guess you are right. Did she say how she hurt her wrist?"

"No." He directed him away from the guests. "I told her not to be concerned about missing the party. Trent will understand."

"So, she's resting. Good." Good girl. She knew the cost if she spoke a word of what happened. Maybe he would reward her with a new gown. Chocolate. A reminder to stay on his good side. "Do you know if she's eaten? I'd like to take her a tray. If she's feeling ill, she'll need to keep up her strength."

"Nonsense. I'll order a tray to be taken to the room. I shall be but a moment, then we may go together to see how Rosalind is faring."

Glover quickly sidestepped to allow a woman with blonde hair, hands full with dishes, to enter the kitchen. Mr. Easton was on her heels.

Within minutes, the man exited, and Glover followed right behind him, up the stairs to another hallway. The doctor came through the doorway as they were about to enter.

"How is she, Dr. Clark?" Mr. Easton blocked Glover from entering the room, yet he could see Rosalind. She sat in a burgundy chair, her shoulders slumped, eyes closed. A sense of pride rose up within him as he watched her. She was an exquisite creature like no other woman before her, and his desire for her tormented him. He had waited much too long to take her as his wife. Even now, he couldn't touch her if he so wished, and it angered him.

The doctor announced her wrist wasn't broken but would be tender.

He knew she was fine. If he'd broken anything, he would

have felt the pop in his hands. A feeling he was familiar with. He inhaled several breaths, reining in his pulse.

"Thank you." Mr. Easton shook the doctor's hand. "We appreciate you taking a look."

"Not a problem. Glad I could be of service. If you'd excuse me, my wife and I have a waltz to dance." He smiled as he left.

Finally able to enter, Glover eyed her, willing her to hold her tongue. "How are you feeling, Rosalind?"

"Still a bit tired."

Mariam laid her palm on his arm. "I told Rosalind she is staying with us tonight and that *no* is not an acceptable answer. When I leave, I will speak with Sydney about getting her things for the night."

Mr. Easton nodded. "I will send the driver to collect them."

Glover opened his mouth to protest, just as the woman with blonde hair from the kitchen strolled in, placed a tray on a table near the corner of the room by the window, then left.

Mariam bent down and kissed Rosalind's forehead. "I will be back after I speak with your sister. Thomas, may I speak with you in the hall?"

Glover waited until they were out of earshot, although he could clearly see them outside the door. He forced his irritation under control before whispering, "How did you manage an invitation?"

She stiffened.

"No matter. I will be back for you tomorrow shortly after breakfast. Be ready." He dragged a finger along her jaw, eyes filling with the view. When Rosalind's face grew pale, satisfaction lifted his lips. She'd finally be his. "Yes, be ready."

Only moments ago, Glover's gaze had burned Rosalind as his eyes raked over her body. The promise of tomorrow caused fear to plummet deep within her soul, sickening her stomach. Now, hidden within a bedroom on the second floor as the party continued downstairs, Pastor John stood and opened a small Bible he withdrew from his pocket. Trent gently collected her trembling hands, his calloused palms reminding her of the new life awaiting her in Texas.

Mr. and Mrs. Easton came quickly to stand next to them.

"Let us begin," Pastor John said.

Did the pastor always carry a Bible for occasions such as this? Did that mean there were others in the same situation? She had a feeling the answer was no. Her mind rambled in any effort to block out the fear knotting within her heart. Glover could walk in on them. Was she placing her entire family at risk for another rash moment? She glanced at the closed door and inhaled a deep breath, fighting the tremors in her hands, as the queasiness rose even more within her stomach.

"Dearly beloved, we are gathered here today to witness the joining, in holy matrimony, of Trenton Parker Easton and Rosalind Lynn Standford ..."

Rosalind glanced at Trent. Fear led her to this moment. But selfishness took over at wanting to be free of Glover's abuse. How could she put her loved ones in danger like this?

As if Trent could read her thoughts, he said, "Have faith, Rose."

Fear slowly ebbed away at the gentleness of his words and the strength she felt as he held her hands. No longer was he the boy she once knew. Trent stood tall. A man. Strong in body but even stronger in his faith. Faith she was afraid to call her own. But as Trent's thumb gently rubbed over her knuckles, she so desperately wanted to believe. Believe that God did indeed hear her cries in heaven and that He had brought the Eastons to Boston. For Trent to marry her. Rescue her.

"Do you have a ring?" Pastor John asked.

Trent released her hand, reached into his pocket, and pulled her mother's ring out. Tears filled her eyes. Her mother had given her approval of Trent long ago. If only she were here. She wondered if she were watching from heaven. Never had she missed her mother more than now.

"Trenton, place the ring on her finger and both of you repeat after me."

The pastor began the vows.

"Rosalind," Trent whispered. His blue eyes drew her and held as powerful as a magnet, like the love they'd shared. Slipping the ring on her finger, he repeated the pastor's words.

Rosalind's tears hung heavy from her lashes before falling down her face. By the end of Trent's vows, when he finally said, "I do," both her cheeks were wet with tears. Trent brought his hand up and dried both with his handkerchief.

Barely able to think or breathe, she repeated every word Trent had just said, and when the last "I do" passed her lips, the minister addressed them.

"In the eyes of Boston and in the eyes of God, you are now man and wife. You may kiss the bride."

Trent cocked his head and ran a finger along her cheek, wiping away any remnant of tears. When he opened his mouth to speak, his father came up behind them.

"I need to return to the party, and you need to go, son. You don't have much time. Rosalind, when we all return to Texas, we'll celebrate, but for now, know how much we love you." He hugged her.

"Thomas, move." Mariam gave her husband a playful nudge and moved to face Rosalind, clasping her in a hug. "You were always my daughter. It's official now. Be safe. We'll be pray-ing."

"Thank you, Mrs. Easton."

"No, dear, that's your name. Call me Mariam."

Rosalind gave her another hug.

"Follow me," Mr. Easton said, grabbing the overnight bag Sydney collected at Mrs. Easton's request.

She hated to leave her sister, the children, or her father with not so much as a goodbye. But what choice did she have? Sadness filled her as she and Trent rushed down the hall.

"Take the back stairs. Hurry." His father continued to lead, but when they reached the stairs, he glanced back to them and nodded before turning in the opposite direction down the hallway.

As they descended, someone came from the shadows and any hope of escape evaporated. She gasped. "Father!" Something passed over his eyes, but Trent took her hand and rushed them outside toward a covered carriage. Once inside, the door closed behind Trent, and her heart pounded along with the horse's hooves on the ground.

Rosalind shut her eyes. She inhaled, exhaled, fighting the tightness in her chest. Did her father sense her leaving or that she had married the man she loved against his wishes? Would he tell Glover her secret to save his own life?

"Not much longer and you'll be safe." Trent's warm hands took her cold ones and caressed her palm and wrist. "Does it still hurt?"

Emotions Rosalind couldn't begin to explain welled up in her throat. "A … a bit, but it will be all right."

"He'll never hurt you again." Trent released her hands. "You'll go to Chicago. Get off. Then buy your ticket to Fort Worth, Texas. The day after you pull in, wait for me at the station. My train leaves tomorrow morning so I'll be right behind you." He pulled money from his pocket. "This should be enough."

She'd never seen so much money. She shook her head, pushing it away. "I can't take this."

"You must, Rosalind." He placed the money in her hand. "You need to get home."

"I have no place to keep it safe."

"Your bag. You can hide the money within your things."

When they arrived at the train station, Trent hurried out, grabbed her bag, and stuffed the money between her clothes. He took her elbow and quickly led her to the station platform. Though it was dark, steam from the train filled the air and hung heavy like her heart. She was leaving everything and everyone she'd known behind, even her husband. She found it hard to look away from him.

The train's whistle screeched. Her pulse sounded in her ears. She swallowed.

"I'll be right behind you," he whispered, taking her in his arms and brushing his lips gently across hers. Before she could respond, he released her. "I'll be praying for you."

Her heart hammered as she tried to steady her nerves and walk toward the train, but her feet wouldn't corporate. How could they when all she wanted was to cling to him, beg him to leave with her?

"Please, Rosalind, you must hurry."

The strain in his voice snapped her to her senses. She wouldn't be safe until she climbed aboard and the train barreled down the tracks, away from him, away from Boston. She nodded and, without another thought, did as he asked and boarded the train. Several heads turned in her direction. One woman whispered something to the other woman sitting with her and pointed. Rosalind's gaze fell to what the ladies saw. She was overdressed. The reality of what transpired in the last hour hit her full force. Her ball gown had become her wedding dress.

Rosalind was married.

She glanced at her mother's ring, and tears filled her eyes once again. *We're married, Mother. I finally married Trenton.*

The train's whistle shrilled, and, with a jerk, the train pulled away.

Chapter Fifteen

Shadows danced against the light of his house as Trent ordered the driver to stop and let him out several yards away. Stepping out of the carriage into the crisp air, Trent scurried up against the stone home and entered the way he and Rosalind had left. Music sifted through the stairwell, and he closed his eyes for a moment. *Rosalind. Lord, please protect her.*

The music ended, and he hurried into action to blend in with the guests. Several couples took the stairs as he descended and rounded the corner. One, he believed, was the mayor. "Mr. and Mrs. Hart, I hope you're having a wonderful time."

Mr. Hart's gray beard shook as he turned. "Why, Mr. Easton. Lovely party. I would like you to meet my wife, Elizabeth."

Trent bowed. "Wonderful to meet you."

Mrs. Hart gave a smile, then nodded. "Likewise, Mr. Easton. We were about to dance. Would you care to join us?" She raised a reddish eyebrow.

It seemed odd, but was she daring him to turn down her offer? "Thank you, but I have no partner."

"Nonsense." Mrs. Hart looked past him and waved her hand. "Rita, dear," her voice boomed. "Where is that daughter of yours? Mr. Easton needs a partner."

No. I need no partner, he was about to say when a short, stocky woman pushed through the crowd and sauntered to Mrs. Hart's side.

The woman—Rita, he assumed—twisted toward his guests. "The last I saw Mary, she was dancing with a gentleman."

Mrs. Hart spun back to him. "We'll find her. Come, Mr. Easton. You will make a fine pair." She took the mayor's arm.

Mr. Hart laughed, slanting a look at him. "Watch out. My wife is a matchmaker."

Mrs. Hart patted her husband's arm. "Don't listen to him, Mr. Easton. Come, Rita. We must find her."

What had just happened? Trent didn't know, but before he could think on it, Rita chuckled and slipped her arm around Trent's elbow. He shook his head to himself. This wasn't what he intended. As they neared the couples gathering on the floor to dance, Trent hoped Rita's daughter was committed to someone else for the next waltz.

Rita squeezed his arm and pointed. "There she is, in the golden-colored gown."

A young woman with dark hair came toward them. Two men followed on both sides.

Rita released his arm. "Mary, dear, I want you to meet Mr. Easton, our host. Mr. Easton, my daughter, Miss Mary Ondervan."

Mary curtsied, her violet eyes holding his.

"Mr. Easton needs a dance partner and I thought—"

"Of course, Mother." She batted her long lashes at Trent.

He, on the other hand, forced back a sigh and nodded. She was beautiful, but he wasn't interested. *Rosalind.* The thought warmed him. *She* was the one who held his heart captive from the first moment they met. He was nothing without her. He couldn't dance with Mary, but as he was about to explain his heart was taken, Glover appeared in the corner of his eye.

Trent needed to convince Glover his interests weren't with Rosalind. If he could put doubt in the man's mind about his affections for her, it might be easier to leave once the word spread of her disappearance. Trent held out his hand to Mary and smiled. "Shall we?"

Mary took his arm like her mother had done moments ago, dismissing the men. Without a word, they left her side and moved through the crowd of guests.

Once they joined the other couples on the floor, the music began. Trent caught a glimpse of Glover watching them from a distance, and he struggled to recall what Rosalind told him. *Slide your right foot forward one step, three measures.*

Right or not, that's what he did. He led Mary through the dance, but the way she moved and the frequency of her touches on his arm, his hand, were more than he bargained for. She was a flirt.

Five dances later, Trent not only had Glover's attention, but everyone else's as well, especially his parents. Nothing he did was improper, but he didn't stop Mary from her advances.

"Miss Ondervan, would you like some punch?" He extended his elbow. She looped her arm through his.

"I'm having such a wonderful time, Mr. Easton." She shook her head back and forth, her hair swooshing across her shoulders.

His mother strolled up to them. "Hello. I don't think we've met."

Mary's eyes flitted between Trent and his mother. "You must be Mrs. Easton. I'm Mary Ondervan. My parents are close friends with Thomas and Elizabeth Hart."

"Yes, of course. Would you care to join us?"

Mary smiled. "I'd be delighted."

Weaving their way through chairs and tables, Trent's father stood. "I don't think I've had the pleasure." He bowed.

Trent released his hold. "May I present Miss Mary Ondervan? Miss Ondervan, my father, Thomas Easton."

Trent quickly scanned the room. Glover and Roger sat together at a table, both of them looking on. His heart pounded. *Lord, please have Roger hold his tongue. Don't let him tell Glover what he witnessed tonight. Or had he already?* He took in steady breaths.

A warm touch caressed his hand, bringing his attention to the woman next to him. Mary was staring. "Will you walk with me to my mother?"

"Of course." Trent held out his arm and glanced at his father, praying his look conveyed his need for help.

"Your train leaves tomorrow, Trent," his father said, retaking his seat.

With a smile, he gave his father a nod and then strolled in the direction Mary led.

"You're leaving tomorrow?" Mary's soft voice came through the noise around them. Her exotic eyes peered at him.

"I am. My home is in Texas." And it would forever be. A life he'd waited years to claim.

She slowed her steps. "She's a lucky woman."

He glanced at her. "Is it that obvious?"

She took his hand and drew him aside as people strolled by. "I've never met a man who doesn't reciprocate my flirtations, unless his heart is taken. It's a shame I've not had the pleasure until now, Mr. Easton." She curtsied. Her smile lit her face. "Until next time."

There would be no next time. "It was wonderful spending

the evening with you, Miss Ondervan." He bowed.

Rosalind stood in the aisle, looking around the train. A family jostled her as they passed. The whistle blew. The conductor yelled the final boarding call.

"Who can I possibly ask for help?" she mumbled.

A woman and child strolled in her direction, the little girl's auburn pigtails bouncing as she skipped.

"Excuse me," Rosalind asked, still feeling off-balance from the sway of the train she had just disembarked. "Which way is the dining car?"

"We're going there." She gestured to the next car. "You're more than welcome to follow us."

"Thank you."

The mother took her child's arm. "Come, Lilly."

Rosalind followed, holding her bag close. Where was that ticket she just bought? Heavens, she could be thrown off the train…or worse.

They entered the dining car through a tiny doorway. She'd never dreamed a train could be so splendid. The last one paled in comparison. Tables—covered in white cloths and decorated with china and glassware—lined each side of the aisle. The brown pull-down window shades held back the darkness as light from crystal chandeliers lit the dining car.

Rosalind slowed to a halt. The young woman she'd met moments ago waved her over. Firmly clasping her bag, Rosalind crossed the room. "Hello again."

"The other tables appear full, but we have plenty of room. Would you care to join us?"

The tension in her shoulders eased. "Are you sure you don't

mind?"

"Not at all. Please. My name is Catherine Hadley, and this is my daughter, Lilly."

Lilly's freckled cheeks stretched to a wide grin.

She sat by the window. "My name is Rosalind St—" She glanced down at her mother's ring—her wedding ring. She touched the smooth band with the tip of her finger. "Rosalind Easton."

The name rolled. The name she'd always wanted. Rosalind touched the swaying curtains and caught sight of the dark sky. By now, everyone would know she was gone. Glover's face flashed through her mind. His dark, hard eyes, the little smirk of pleasure he always showed just before he hurt her. A shiver shot up her spine. If Glover learned how the Eastons had helped her escape …

"Rosalind. Are you all right?"

Rosalind swallowed hard and focused on Catherine's kind face. The overhead lights brightened the auburn wisps framing her face below her hat. "I was married just prior to boarding the train. I'm riding alone." *And I'm lonely, worried for my husband and his family.*

"Oh, I'm sorry. I know it's difficult. When my husband and I first married, he often took short trips for the railroad. But after Lilly's birth, when the travel times lengthened, he started to carry us with him. He told me Jesus once said of marriage, 'What God has joined together, let no man put asunder.'" She leaned forward and chuckled. "And that includes the railroad."

After dinner, Catherine and Lilly stood. Rosalind was about to stand as well but recalled her ticket. She had to find it, or she'd have no place to go.

"Will you be staying a bit longer?" Catherine took her daughter's hand. Lilly placed her napkin on the table, but it fell on the floor.

Rosalind bent and snatched it up, placing it next to her plate. "I think I will."

Catherine smiled. "We hope to see you tomorrow then. Say good night, Lilly."

Lilly, the spitting image of her mother, curtsied and then grinned. She looked up at her mother. "I did it without falling this time."

Catherine laughed. "You did, sweetie." Her gaze returned to Rosalind. "Good night, Mrs. Easton."

Rosalind nodded. "Tomorrow." If she hadn't been taken off the train before then because of her ticket.

An hour later, after searching through everything she owned, looking for her ticket, she glanced around the dining car. She was the only person left and still had no idea what to do. One thing for sure, her eyes weren't cooperating. Her eyelids slowly shut. She was so tired. She shuffled in her seat and forced a blink.

A man strolled up to her, wiping his hands on his apron. "Is there anything else I may help you with? We are closing for the evening. Breakfast will be served at seven o'clock."

"I need nothing else. Thank you." She grabbed her bag and reticule. She had no choice but to leave. Yet he held her gaze as if searching her eyes. Did he somehow know her predicament? But how could he? She stood and turned.

He cleared his throat. "Ma'am."

She took a few steps away.

"Ma'am? You don't have a ticket, do you?"

She slowed her pace and turned, glancing down at her bag and reticule. "I do, but I can't find it. I have friends I met. I'm sure they'll allow me stay with them."

"They must."

Was it the rocking motion from the train that made her

stomach queasy or the emphasis he added to his words?

He gave her a small smile, as if to reassure her. "Your secret is safe with me, but if others find out, they'll not be so concerned for your well-being."

"Thank you."

"If you need further assistance, just ask for me by name. Oliver." Oliver cleared off her dishes. She hurried to look for her friends where she assumed they'd gone. Standing in front of two compartments, to the right and left, she knocked on the left. The door opened. An elderly man leaned on a cane. "May I help you?"

"I'm sorry, sir. I believe I have the wrong room."

The elderly man coughed, his thin frame shaking. As she was about to offer her assistance, he moved and closed the door. She took a deep breath and knocked on the next compartment. There was no answer. She knocked again but a little harder.

A gentleman answered, running his thick fingers through his thinning hair. "Yes?"

Rosalind glanced down the hallway. She was no more able to locate them than she was to find her ticket.

"Now you look here." His eyes narrowed and pointed a thick finger in her face. "Young lady, do you not know the hour?"

Rosalind felt a hand on her shoulder. She jumped, and her breath caught. She'd not heard Oliver's approach. His hand fell.

"Forgive us, sir. I believe we've forgotten our cabin." Oliver stood inches from the man as if to protect her, with a smile she'd guess could turn even a foe into a friend.

The man gave a hard nod, then slammed the door without a word.

"Didn't mean to frighten you, but…it's not good for you to be alone."

Rosalind took a few steps back and grabbed her wrist against her stomach. Glover's hard eyes flashed before her. What would happen to her if Oliver were like Glover, or worse? Could she trust a total stranger? But what choice did she have? Today was to be her wedding to Glover, and he could never find her. A chill ran up her spine. She had to get to Forth Worth.

"I will help you. Follow me." He turned and led the way to an area meant only for train personnel. He entered a room, but she waited in the hall. He came out with a handful of papers. His keys jingling as he placed them in his pocket. "Let's go back to the dining car so I can take a better look at these." He motioned for her to walk ahead of him.

They re-entered the dining car, and Oliver slid into the first chair. She sat across from him. He laid the papers out and ran his hand over them, then pointed to several lines. "There are two empty compartments. The passengers didn't show up."

Who was this man who seemed to be a waiter one moment, then spoke with authority and wisdom on train business the next? "Why are you helping me?"

He held his finger on the paper and glanced up. "You have a look about you, a look I had once when I needed help. Someone helped me then, and I promised God if I ever got that feeling from someone, I'd help them." Oliver rose from his chair. "You can use the first compartment to your right outside the dining car. You'll be safe there."

"Thank you," she said as exhaustion weighed down her limbs. "Truly, I thank you." She accepted the key and headed to her room. When she reached the dining car exit, Rosalind looked back. Oliver smiled, his deep brown eyes full of such kindness it brought tears to her own.

CHAPTER SIXTEEN

Rosalind rose from the bed with a sigh and crossed the small area to the window. Colors blurred past her.

Trent.

A day. That was the difference between them once she arrived in Fort Worth.

She'd never left Boston before, never wanted to, except when reading Trent's letters. *Land spread as far as the sea… Skies as blue as a robin's egg… Clouds like cotton…* She couldn't imagine it, just as she couldn't imagine being married to Trent. Until now. How things had changed.

Rosalind propped her arm against the window frame and fingered the shimmering diamonds of her mother's ring. Her mother's ring was proof enough they were married, yet her mind still couldn't wrap itself around the fact. And where had he gotten the ring?

The smell of bacon seeped into the room and caused her stomach to rumble. Rosalind stepped into the hall. A stream of people pushed past her, leaving the dining car, while others pushed against those to get in. With little effort, Rosalind moved through the hall behind a short, round man, entered the dining car, and found a table unoccupied.

Slipping into the bench, she glanced at the burning gas lights. Everything was brighter this morning, even the sun poking through the trees into the dining car. But thoughts of Trent weighed heavily along with those of Glover. If Glover found out about their wedding, she was certain he would retaliate. But if he never found out, would she actually be free? Free from his touch and the pain he caused her?

She glanced down at her hands, remembering Glover's cruelty, then how afterward, on the way to the train, Trent caressed her palm and wrist. His gentleness warmed her then as it did now. Her heart lifted and she smiled. Today was the start of a new life and future. One that included Trent.

Rosalind heard something to her left and glanced up. "Well, don't you look lovely."

"Catherine. I was lost in thought. Where is Lilly?"

"My husband is getting her ready." She clasped her stomach and her face paled. "You don't mind if I sit?"

"Of course not. Please. Have a seat. You must eat breakfast with me." Rosalind stood and placed her hand under Catherine's elbow for support. Catherine sunk into the chair. "Is there anything I can do?"

"It's been like this for months." She leaned forward. "I'm with child and the mornings are the hardest. I'm sorry. That was most improper." Her whisper faded as she sunk further into her seat, taking the napkin from the table and blotting her neck.

Rosalind shifted a bit closer. "No need to worry." She smiled at her new friend, wanting to bring comfort, although she had no understanding of the sickness expectant mothers often endured during pregnancy. If given the chance, she'd gladly endure any sickness to have a child with Trent. A child, one as cute and adorable as Lilly. She looked down the aisle, then back again. "You said Lilly and your husband are joining you, yes?"

Catherine dotted her forehead with a napkin and inhaled a long breath. "He is the most wonderful and caring husband. He tends to Lilly every morning while I nibble on something to settle my stomach."

Rosalind nodded as if to say she understood such adoration, but in fact she hadn't a clue, being wed only for such a short time. Come to think of it, never had she seen her father take on such a role. Rosalind pushed the thought of her father away when the waiter hurried to their table.

After Rosalind and Catherine placed their orders, a thin man in a dark conductor's coat entered, waving train tickets in the air. "Tickets, please! Tickets!" he bellowed across the dining car, drawing everyone's attention. No one had asked for tickets since she'd been aboard, but she'd known the conductor would come eventually. She had devised a plan of escape, but she couldn't simply walk out without drawing attention now. But did she have a choice?

The conductor paused at the table before Rosalind's. Her heart pounded in her ears.

"Rosalind? Are you all right?" Catherine chuckled. "You look a little like how I feel."

"I … um …" Her body trembled. She rose quickly, sending her chair into a girl walking past balancing two glasses on a round serving tray. One of the glasses wobbled on the small tray and the other tipped over, sloshing milk on the server's dress.

"Oh, my." Rosalind bit her lip, then swiped her napkin from the floor where it had fallen. White splats dotted the poor girl's face. "I'm terribly sorry." She extended her napkin.

The girl set the tray down, then shook out her arms. Liquid slung from her sleeves. Catherine appeared at the girl's side with more napkins, patting her arms.

The conductor stared in her direction.

She glanced toward her friend, scrambling to think of a reasonable response for leaving so abruptly. "Catherine, I must go."

Catherine pushed her auburn hair from her face. Worry creased her brow.

Lifting her skirt, Rosalind rushed out of the dining car.

Rosalind was desperate. With nowhere to go and no one to turn to, she hid in her room until evening when hunger drove her out. Would the conductor be searching her out even now? The dining car was empty, but the aroma of roast chicken caused her mouth to water.

"Would you happen to be the brunette I heard about today?"

Rosalind jumped and bit her lower lip as she turned. "I didn't see you there."

Oliver sat in a corner near the kitchen hunched over a stack of papers, his eyes gazing up at her. He dropped his writing instrument and sat up. "No answer. Are you hungry?" He stood and entered the kitchen area and came back with a plate. "I figured you'd come." Gently setting the plate down on a table, he nudged it toward her and returned to his paper. "If anything were to happen to you, my wife would be quite upset. You should have seen her when Lilly and I came to breakfast. She barely ate, and I can't have her not eating." He shot her a poignant look, then smiled.

Rosalind gaped. "You're Catherine's husband?"

"That I am." The corner of his eyes wrinkled, and his face beamed. "And to say I'm blessed to be so is an understatement.

She is a loyal companion and has taken a liking to you right off."

"Did you know who I was yesterday?"

"You matched the description Catherine gave." He lifted his pencil and pointed to the food. "Now, please eat so I may take you to Catherine. She'll be thrilled to see you." He leaned his elbows on the table and began to scribble something.

She turned her focus to the chicken and potatoes. Feeling the need to pray and thank God for her food, she stalled in response. She willed the words to come, yet nothing came to mind, except for the sweet smell from the glaze on her chicken. Rosalind licked her lips.

As she ate, her thoughts turned to Mr. Easton, who had once implied God sent his family to Boston to rescue her from Glover's clutches. That God was with her and working for her through everything. But did sending her to Texas also apply? Or the food Oliver waited for her to eat? Was God truly with her no matter what she faced? If so, why didn't God answer her prayers? Yet a hunger deep within her soul yearned to know God cared and loved her still.

Emotion tightened her throat. *Thank You for providing food for me ... and, Lord, I pray, as your Word says, that You do know my voice. Amen.*

She wiped the tears on her lashes and glanced at Oliver studying the papers before him. He scribbled something, then flipped the page over and repeated the motion on the next sheet.

After eating, she smiled at Oliver. Butter lingered in her mouth. "Thank you. Supper was wonderful."

"Good. Let me roll these drawings up and we'll be on our way." Oliver directed her to follow him, then glanced back at her. "Were you looking for Catherine last night?"

"Yes, but I had no idea which room she and Lilly were in."

"You came very close to finding them. I was on my way to

them when I saw you. Come." Stopping at a door down the hall from where she stood the night before, Oliver entered first, hiding her behind him. "Catherine."

Catherine pulled the book down from her face and spotted her instantly. "Oh, Rosalind!" She leapt from her seat and wrapped her arms around Rosalind's neck as though they were long-lost friends. "I was so concerned about you. Why did you leave so abruptly this morning? Is everything okay?" She took Rosalind's hand, guiding her to sit. "Lilly is sleeping, so we'll have some time to ourselves."

"I guess that means I should go." Oliver chuckled, switching his papers to his other arm.

"Oliver, how did you find her?"

"I'm sure you two will have time to discuss it. But for now, maybe we can be properly introduced. I'm Mr. Oliver Hadley." He bowed to Rosalind and winked at his wife.

Rosalind started to rise, but Catherine chuckled and held her hand to keep her seated. "You will find my husband to be quite playful when business isn't his focus."

"I'm Mrs. Rosalind Easton." She nodded. "Nice to meet you."

A puzzled expression crossed his face. "Are you related to a Thomas Easton from Texas?"

"Yes … I've just married their son, Trenton Easton. I'm heading to Graham now."

His eyes lit, and his playful expression returned. "I met Thomas and his son the first time they drove their cattle to Fort Worth. The Eastons are contracted with the train line. They give an exceptional rate for beef on the hoof. It's always a pleasure to work with them. We've kept in touch on other matters since."

Catherine smiled. "Yes, we met with Mr. and Mrs. Easton on our last time through Fort Worth. Oliver, perhaps we can make another visit soon." She squeezed Rosalind's hand.

"A wonderful idea." He bent and kissed the top of his wife's head. "Now, if you ladies will excuse me, I have a few more details to go over before I retire for the evening." He pulled the door closed as he left.

"I'm intrigued. Tell me, Rosalind, how did you meet your husband? With our families already connected, I feel we are destined to be good friends."

Rosalind began. She told Catherine everything since the day she met Trent, the death of her mother, to why she sat next to her on the train. She had never once taken someone in her confidence as she did with Catherine, and it wasn't pity she witnessed on her friend's face but admiration.

Trent stared down at the cobblestone driveway from his bedroom window, waiting for his carriage to pull to the front of the house to take him to the train station. With an exasperated breath, he spun on his heels, marched a few steps, and gripped the frame of his bed.

Everything was different now. So different from his last trip to Texas. More so than he ever thought possible. This time, the journey to Texas brought him hope like he'd never known. God brought him back to Boston to rescue a lamb. His wife. He still couldn't believe they were married.

It came to him last night as he wrestled with his thoughts, lying in bed—the thought that maybe God had sent him ahead years earlier to Texas for this very purpose, to protect Rosalind, to protect their future together. Trent was to care for her. Love her in a way she'd never known, showing her God's love. And his own.

He swallowed against the knot in his throat. God had been giving him the desires of his heart all along, only in *His* way and in *His* timing.

A knock sounded at the door. "Son." Trent heard his father's voice through the thick wood of the door. His father entered and sat on the edge of the bed. "Your mother and I told Rosalind we would stay for Roger. In my opinion, people give up much too easily on others. I won't abandon my friend again. While we're here, I will try to throw Glover off your trail. I don't know if I can. He's not a fool. But I must try."

"Do you think that's a wise decision? Maybe if you went to the authorities, they could help."

"I have no proof except for Rosalind and what I saw. It's not enough."

"How about Roger's testimony? Doesn't he care about his daughter's life?" Trent wanted to punch something. Instead, he took to pacing yet again. A man owed it to his family to love and protect them. If he got his hands on Rosalind's father, he might have to take him out to the barn, as his cowpokes would say, and teach him a thing or two.

Trent clasped his shoulder, then pulled him into a hug. "I'm proud you're my father. I don't know if I ever told you that, but it's true. No matter the reasons we left Boston, I know now you were protecting us from harm. *No greater love than that a man lay down his life for those he loves.* I only wish Rosalind's father was more like you."

"No, son." He smiled as he pulled away. "Like Christ."

His mother's voice chimed in from the doorway. "Yes, like Christ."

Trent glanced at his mother and her face shone. She walked over to him and gave him a hug of her own. "I will miss you, Trent. And when you get home, you take care of that daughter of mine."

He moved her to arm's length and chuckled. "I see how it is."

It didn't take long for them to arrive at the train station. But as Trent began to take the white stone steps up to the platform, he heard his father behind him.

"Son, I'm going to head back. I think it might be best in case Glover comes looking for Rosalind with Mariam alone at the house. Please be careful. My prayers will be with you and Rosalind."

After they said their goodbyes one final time, Trent stood and watched his father climb into the carriage. As the carriage rolled into the cobblestone street, his heart grew heavy. He began to pray for his parents' safety, Rosalind's family, and for his wife.

Trent turned back and climbed one cold stair at a time toward the train station entrance. He pulled his jacket tighter around him as it began to rain.

A familiar sound of horse hooves pounded the ground, and as the rapid sound grew louder, he stopped. He turned to see three riders race toward him from the opposite direction his father had taken.

CHAPTER SEVENTEEN

"Easton!" Glover's voice rumbled like thunder.

Trent turned back to the station, noted the time on the large clock on the front of the railroad depot, and entered. The posted train schedule was directly ahead, and it wasn't much longer until the train would board. He scanned the exits. Pulling at a door handle to leave, Trent's pulse raced. Glover's loud voice carried as he left the building. There was no one outside. He'd face Glover and the others alone. "God, whatever happens, protect Rosalind."

The three men pursued him out to the platform beside the tracks.

"Trenton! Where is my wife?" Glover's voice cut through the air like a knife. His companions, both wearing pommel coats, passed in front of Glover and approached him, standing only inches away. Glover strolled toward him, his pace slow and sure as he removed one glove, then the other.

Trent's fingers tightened around his bags. He bit the inside of his cheek from speaking what he truly felt toward the man who caused his wife so much pain. His first concern was to put

Glover off his trail. Second, to fight. "How kind of you to see me off." The man on his left, somewhat shorter than the other man, clenched his fists. Trent recognized them as the men he saw Glover speaking to from time to time.

Glover chuckled, stuffing his gloves into his riding coat. "I wouldn't call us friends…business associates, maybe. And when a business associate wrongs me, there is always a price to pay."

"Not sure I'm following." Trent's muscles tensed. He wasn't a man of violence and never strapped on his gun as his cowhands did, but right now he'd give anything to have his pistol within reach.

"Where is she?"

"I assume you mean Miss Standford?"

Glover nodded, and the men grabbed Trent's arms. He struggled, dropped his bags, and punched one of the men across the jaw, causing him to fall to the ground. Trent held up his fists as one man came toward him and the other jumped up from the ground. *Give me strength, Lord.*

Lay down your life.

Trent blinked twice at the words that rang so clear as if someone whispered them in his ear. His arms fell to his sides. The two men grabbed him again, but this time Trent didn't fight.

"Not so strong are you, *boy*?" Glover's hot breath reached his face. "Now, tell me where she is, and I'll let you go. Otherwise, you'll pay the price." His dark eyes narrowed. "And let me warn you before you answer. My price is steep."

Trent wrestled with telling him they were married and that Glover would never have her. But just as he was about to speak, Glover punched him in the ribs and knocked the words from his mouth. The pressure around his arms grew as both men held him tighter, whether to keep him standing or for another punch, Trent wasn't sure, but he forced himself not to struggle.

Glover spoke through clenched teeth. "Tell me or you'll never reach Texas."

"I haven't seen Miss Standford since the party last night. I'm on my way home now, to my life. My land."

One of Glover's brows rose, and his jaw twitched. He took a step back.

"Do you want us to let him go, boss?" the man on the right said.

Glover nodded.

Python-like hands released him, even as a fist landed squarely on his skull. Trent fell to the ground, and his head hit hard, then his body came to a stop. He tried but couldn't fully open his eyes. Warmth oozed down the side of his head.

"He's still alive."

"Of course he is. If I wanted him dead, he'd be dead."

Trent forced his eyes open. A shadow hovered over him. Rain poured harder as he lay there, trying to focus.

"He's awake."

Glover leaned in. "Since you're a praying man, you better start praying I find her. If I don't—"

"Boss. Someone's coming."

Trent focused on Glover's face. Something flashed across his features, but what, he didn't know. Then the three men left.

Trent rose up on his elbows, watching Glover and his companions disappear around the brick wall of the train station. Another man hurried to Trent from the direction of the depot. "Are you all right, young man? You're bleeding."

Trent nodded and immediately regretted the action. Dizziness washed over him. He touched the back of his head. His hand came away bloody. "I'm fine. Really. Just hit my head is all."

"I'll be back." The man stood and headed inside the depot.

Glover had threatened him, though he never had a chance to finish. From now on, Trent would wear his gun and protect what was his with his life.

He needed to get on that train. Nothing would stop him. Not even Glover.

Glover fisted his hands and kept his eyes focused on the Eastons' home from his parked carriage. He had his men watching the house, but today his anger boiled and demanded that something be done. But what? Roger never left. He couldn't very well force himself inside a second time and demand answers, no matter how much he wanted to. Rosalind had been missing for nearly a week, and no one would admit to seeing her.

Not her father. Not Mr. Easton nor Mrs. Easton. No one had seen her since the night of the party. Yet Glover knew the Eastons were involved, or else a missing person's report would have been ordered and, with wealth dripping from the ex-bank-president-turned-rancher, his money would move society to find her. Of that, Glover was certain.

When Glover had barged into the Easton home on Tuesday, demanding answers to her disappearance, he discovered Roger hadn't left town after all. How much he had revealed to the Eastons, Glover wasn't sure. But he had already destroyed any proof of their agreement. Nevertheless, Glover's word could be taken to the bank. He would soon prove to Roger that promises to him were always paid in full.

Until then, Glover would wait. Someone would eventually make a move, and when they did, they'd lead him right to Rosalind.

Chapter Eighteen

"Lilly, how many servers can you count?" Once again, Rosalind tried to occupy the child with questions. She ran a finger along her water glass as moisture formed a ring on the tablecloth beneath.

The little girl rotated in her seat, then pointed at each in succession. "Five."

"Very good. And how many tables are there?"

"Can I get up and count them?"

"Maybe we should wait until we've finished our desserts before trying that one."

Lilly nodded, her pigtails bouncing, then her face sobered. "Is Mama okay?"

Rosalind's stomach lurched. She hoped Catherine would indeed be fine, but what could she say to ease little Lilly's mind? Catherine hadn't felt well enough to leave her cabin in over a week. Oliver was pulled between his duties on the train, tending to his wife, and simply kneeling at her bedside. At Oliver's request, Lilly had stayed with Rosalind in her cabin.

"Your mother doesn't feel well, but your papa is taking good care of her. And of you, by having us spend lots of time together. Besides, your papa knows how much you like desserts. He insisted we come and have ice cream, remember?"

"My favorite."

"It's one of my favorites too. Ice cream and chocolate bars."

The server brought them their ice cream. Lilly picked up her spoon, dug a big scoop from her bowl, and shoved it into her mouth.

"Be careful or your head will hurt from such a big, cold bite." Rosalind took a small amount from her own bowl just as the conductor approached their table.

"Ma'am, I don't believe I've seen your ticket." He gave her a scowl, impatience ringing in his tone.

Rosalind blinked, lowered her spoon, and looked at Lilly. Heat flamed her cheeks, for she didn't know what to do. Tell the man she lost it? She had already told Catherine and Oliver about the ticket, but they said for her not to worry. They would help her now, she was sure. Oliver was associated with the railroad somehow, but she'd never used people and didn't want to start now. Catherine was her friend, and they had done so much for her already. Not only that, but with Catherine having problems with the baby … Rosalind couldn't worry her for any reason.

She regrouped and leaned close to the conductor. "I've lost my ticket, sir. I've looked and I can't find it anywhere."

"I thought so when you left so quickly several days ago. You can't get away with stealing, and you will be prosecuted for theft." The conductor had raised his voice, and other diners looked toward them. "The two of you need to come with me."

Arguing with everyone watching was pointless. She had no proof she'd paid legitimately and lost her ticket. Still, Lilly shouldn't be witness to this. Rosalind would explain to the conductor after Lilly was taken back to Oliver.

"Sir, this little girl needs to be returned to her parents. She isn't mine. She's simply in my care. Will you allow me to take her to her family?"

The conductor's forehead wrinkled. "I will have someone take her to her mother and father."

Lilly glanced at the man as she ate her ice cream. "Papa said I have to stay with Mrs. Easton."

Rosalind bit her lip. Oliver had indeed admonished the child to stay with her.

"Unless you'd have me make a scene." The conductor moved aside to let Rosalind out of her seat.

"Not necessary." She slid out of the bench and looked to Lilly. "I'm sorry, sweet pea, but I have to take you back now. You can have ice cream later."

Lilly nodded, disappointment registering in her slouched posture as she slid out and grabbed Rosalind's hand.

Rosalind sensed eyes boring into her back as they walked out of the dining car, the conductor close behind.

Lilly's small fingers tightened around Rosalind's. "I don't want you to go. Don't you like playing with me?"

Rosalind stopped and knelt in the aisle. If she were forced from the train at the next stop, would she ever see the Hadleys again? In a matter of days, they had come to mean a great deal to her.

"Oh, Lilly, this has nothing to do with liking you. I like you very much. I wish I didn't have to go." Lilly hugged her, and a yearning seared Rosalind's heart. Perhaps she would tell the Hadleys what was happening so they could help her.

The conductor cleared his throat.

Rosalind met his gaze. "Her room is down this hallway. You can see the rooms from here."

"I'll wait." He eyed Lilly. "She looks familiar. Who are

your—"

"Time to go to your mother and father." Rosalind stood and pushed her lightly through the cabins. Lilly ran ahead of her and into her family's room, leaving the door open behind her.

Oliver met Rosalind at the door. Tears were in his eyes, and she decided then not to tell them about her predicament. Catherine must have worsened. Stealing herself for what was to come, Rosalind took a breath. "How is she?"

When he gave a slight shake of his head, her heart fell.

"The doctor has already left." He bent, lifted Lilly, and held her close. "Thank you, Rosalind. You've helped us more than you know."

"I'm thankful I could help." She tried to give him a reassuring smile but failed. Instead, she placed a hand on his arm, then turned and walked away. There was nothing more she could say. Nothing more she could do.

The conductor waited at the end of the hall. "Follow me, Mrs. Easton."

With a heavy breath, she obeyed, yet everything within her wanted to baulk.

"In a few minutes we will be stopping. You'll be escorted off at that time." He took her to a small office compartment where another gentleman was busy cleaning the space. The conductor pulled out a chair from the wooden desk and motioned for her to sit opposite him. He opened a cabinet and withdrew a white sheet of paper. "Now tell me your name, where you boarded, and your destination."

Rosalind glanced at the other man, who now leaned on his broom and stared. "My name is Rosalind Easton, I boarded in Chicago, and I'm heading to Fort Worth."

"Mrs. Easton, you've broken the law riding without a ticket. You will be held accountable. If you couldn't pay for the train fair, you shouldn't have gotten on the train."

"I purchased a ticket, but somehow I lost it. If you'd allow me to go back to my room, I can prove I have the money for the ticket. I have spoken with Mr.—"

"How do you have a cabin without a ticket?" He eyed her, a frown forming on his lips.

She studied her hands and remained silent. Should she involve the Hadleys and cause Oliver to lose his job?

The train jerked and the whistle blew. They were slowing. She faced him again. "Please. If you'd—"

The conductor held up his hand, stealing her words. He tapped his fingers on the desk, then rose, narrowing his gaze. "You stay put." He whispered something to the other man who had been cleaning, and they both left the room.

He didn't believe her. Rosalind was sure of it. She needed her things from her cabin if she'd ever prove her innocence. She peeked out into the hallway. All clear. Lifting her skirt, she hurried back the way she'd come, passing through several cars. One more and she'd be back into the dining car.

As she approached the last door, it opened suddenly. There in the doorway stood the conductor, blocking her way.

Rosalind glanced around. She was caught, trapped. Her heart raced within her throat, and she tried to swallow against the knot it made. The conductor came toward her.

She backed away. "I was going to my room to grab my things."

"You never answered me. How do you have a room without a ticket? Did you break in as well?"

Before Rosalind could answer, she watched Oliver come through the doorway holding Lilly in his arms. "I gave it to her," he said.

The conductor spun to face Oliver. "Mr. Hadley. D-do you

know this woman?"

"Mrs. Easton is a friend, and our families have known each other for years. And right now, my wife is in distress. My daughter has informed us you will be taking Mrs. Easton by force from the train. Is this true?"

"She … she cannot prove she purchased a ticket. It is the law."

Oliver set Lilly down, his gaze softening. "Take Mrs. Easton to see Mama. Mama will want to see her before we leave the train."

Lilly ran to her, grabbed her hand, and tugged. Rosalind met Oliver's gaze as she squeezed past him. Oliver and Catherine were getting off the train? Was that fear she witnessed in his eyes? Catherine must be more ill than Rosalind thought.

She gave Lilly's hand a light squeeze. "Hurry, sweet pea."

When they reached the room, Rosalind knocked before they entered. A trunk and two other bags sat by the door. Lilly's hand tightened around hers, drawing her gaze to Catherine lying in bed, shivering. Sweat dotted her forehead. Rosalind needed to distract the child for a brief moment in hopes of speaking with Catherine alone.

"Lilly, do you know where your rabbit, Mr. Sanders, is?" Rosalind asked.

Lilly nodded and began to search her luggage for the stuffed rabbit.

Rosalind hurried to the side of the bed and knelt. Catherine's once-rosy cheeks were deathly pale, her hair matted with sweat against her forehead. "Catherine. What can I do?" She slipped a handkerchief from her pocket and dabbed her sweat-soaked hair and face.

"You're safe." Her lips lifted slightly, but tears ran from her eyes and down her cheek.

Oliver entered at that moment and knelt beside his wife, next to Rosalind, pulling a handkerchief from his pocket. He took over wiping Catherine's face.

"I lost my baby, Rosalind." Catherine's breath became labored. "I might not live."

"Don't say that." Rosalind shook her head. Her mind flashed back to the night her mother died. *I might not live*—the same words spoken mere hours before her death. "You won't die." Yet Rosalind had uttered those same words to her mother.

With her rabbit in hand, Lilly ran to the bed and climbed in beside Catherine. Her little eyes filled with moisture. Oliver rose and motioned for Rosalind to follow him outside the cabin.

Tears formed in his eyes. "I need you to do something, Rosalind. It's important."

"I don't know if I can." She looked toward the doorway, unable to meet his eyes. "The conductor … I'm going to jail."

"No, Rosalind. I oversee this train and the others. You will not be prosecuted. Everything has been taken care of as I promised you, and I spoke to the conductor about a few other things."

"What other things?"

"I need your help. I need you to take Lilly with you to Texas. She will need you." He looked away. "What Catherine said is true."

Rosalind cringed, unable to speak. What was Oliver asking? Was this really happening? *Please, God. Not another death.*

His jaw clenched. "I can't let her watch Catherine die."

"You can't separate Lilly from her mother. She'll be devastated."

"I'm trying to do what is right, Rosalind." His voice lowered as he met her gaze. "Catherine is so worried about Lilly seeing her this way … and the blood. Please, I'm asking you to be her guardian. Would you rather Lilly watch her mother die?"

Rosalind listened to Oliver's plea as years-old pain and fear swept over her again. How could she take Lilly from her mother? But the alternative … watching her mother die as Rosalind had done … she'd never wish that on anyone, especially a small child. And she'd never want Lilly to feel hopeless and alone.

"Please, Rosalind. We have no family that can take her."

Rosalind swallowed against tears. "Does Catherine know what you're asking?"

He shook his head ever so slightly, yet Rosalind expected she knew the answer. "She will accept my wishes. It will tear her apart, sending Lilly away, but she will understand this is for the best." Oliver cleared his throat. "Please."

Closing her eyes, Rosalind fought back the memories of how she watched her own mother gasp for air, taking her last breath. If only she would have had someone to help her through… "Yes. I'll care for Lilly." The train slowed and the clickety-clack echoed in her ears, then slowly stopped.

Oliver pushed through the door and Rosalind followed. "Lilly, Mama and Papa have to go somewhere, but you're going to stay with Mrs. Easton for a little while."

Catherine struggled to sit up. Fresh tears rolled down her jaw. Rosalind watched as she reached over and gently touched her little girl's face.

"Mama, I want to go with you. Why can't I go with you?"

"Because, my sweet girl, I don't feel well. I need to go to the doctor, and I don't know how long I will be there. Rosalind will take good care of you until Papa comes for you." A flicker of emotion skipped between them, causing Rosalind to jerk her eyes from the unspeakable pain she witnessed.

"We will be leaving in a few minutes." Oliver collected their things and left the room.

Rosalind glanced at Catherine. Had she given up hope she'd live by not including herself when Oliver came for Lilly? She slowly looked away from her friend, suppressing a sob, and collected Lilly's hand. "That's right, Lilly." She swallowed hard, fighting to make her words clear and hopeful for all their sakes. "We'll go on an adventure together. How does that sound? We'll stay at a ranch where they have horses. Do you like horses?"

Lilly nodded, gripping her rabbit against her chest with her other hand.

Oliver returned and helped his wife stand. "A carriage will be waiting for us outside. Do you need me to carry you?"

Catherine looked down at her daughter. "I'll walk."

Oliver took his wife's elbow and wrapped his arm around her waist, helping her rise. Blood marred her dress and the bedding where she'd lain. Rosalind turned Lilly so she wouldn't see the stains.

Once off the train, Oliver supported his wife into the carriage, then took Lilly into his arms. "I love you, my dear girl, with all my heart. I promise I will come for you very soon. And you listen and obey Mrs. Easton … always."

"Yes, Papa. I will." She hugged him tightly.

A tear slid down Oliver's cheek. "Now give your mama kisses while I speak with Mrs. Easton." He put her in the carriage and returned to Rosalind. "Where did you say you'll be staying? At the Easton ranch?"

"Yes, in Graham, Texas."

Oliver glanced to the carriage, then back at her. "You both will stay in the room I provided—it's my personal quarters—but do not go back until it's cleaned. Take Lilly to get ice cream while you wait. And for the duration of your trip, everything will be provided for you both. I give you my word." Oliver wiped his tears with the back of his hand. "Pray, Rosalind. Pray she lives."

He walked back to the carriage and hugged Lilly a final time.

Never had Rosalind seen a man love his family more than Oliver, and it crushed her to see their anguish. Knowing she'd never felt the love of her father the way she witnessed through Oliver and Lilly hurt her that much more.

Rosalind bit her lip to keep from crying. Lilly came to her, and Rosalind lifted the child and they waved goodbye. With a deep breath, she turned back to the train.

Later that night, unable to sleep, Rosalind peered at Lilly's sweet face. She pulled the sheet under her chin and listened to her light breathing. Oliver had asked Rosalind to pray. But he didn't know that God had never answered her prayers when she cried out for Him to save her own mother. Why would He hear her prayer now? But the ache for Lilly to hold her mother once again sent Rosalind to kneel by the bed.

God, if you would hear just this one prayer…

CHAPTER NINETEEN

Rosalind glanced at their bags in the room, then bent to button Lilly's red-and-yellow silk sweater. She pulled on one of her pigtails. "Are you ready for an adventure?"

Lilly shook her head slowly.

Rosalind wasn't sure she was ready to go either. Their routine on the train had given them a sense of home and security, but they had to leave. Lilly grasped her hand tightly. Whatever they'd face, they had each other.

The conductor came to their door, avoiding her gaze. "Ma'am, may I take your bags? Your carriage is waiting."

"But I did not call for a carriage. I had planned to stay in Fort Worth until tomorrow." *How would Trent find her?*

He eyed her then. "Mr. Hadley ordered the carriage. We … the driver has strict orders to take you to Mr. Easton's ranch."

"Papa?" Lilly's emerald eyes—exactly like her mother's—peered up at Rosalind.

She allowed room for the conductor to enter and collect their bags, then knelt in front of the child. "Your papa is taking very good care of you. He arranged for us to be carried to my new home. He will meet us there after your mama gets well." She clasped Lilly's small hands within hers. "Can I tell you a secret? I'm a little nervous about being in a new place, and I'm thankful you're accompanying me. And now I'll have someone to help me pick flowers. Would you like to pick flowers?"

A smile lifted the corners of her mouth. "As many as I want?"

The light in Lilly's eyes brought a smile of her own. "Of course. But first we must ride in the carriage your papa sent."

Lilly squeezed her hand and pulled her out of the room. "I like to pick flowers. Mama always lets me carry the basket."

They stepped from the train, meeting the sun's blinding rays head on. Dry heat tightened Rosalind's throat. And the odor …

"Rose, what's that smell?" Lilly pinched her nose.

Rosalind was tempted to do the same. What *was* that terrible smell? This was Texas? The place Trent lived? The place he *loved*? She raised her hand and shielded her eyes, scanning the crowds, she realized, looking for Glover. Her heart tripped at the thought.

I'm safe here. I'm safe here. She fought against the wave of fear and nausea rising in the pit of her stomach and forced her mind back to the task at hand. Maybe it was better she left Fort Worth sooner than later. The conductor set their bags down on the platform, said goodbye, then returned to the train.

Rosalind stood on the toes of her shoes and continued to skim the area. Tall horned animals ruled the roads, and men on horseback outnumbered the wagons. Where was the carriage, and who was taking them to Graham?

An older gentleman with a blue shirt, jeans, and a cowboy hat came straight toward them. He tilted his hat, revealing gray brows that almost touched. "Ma'am, are ya Mrs. Easton?"

Her brow raised at the question, noticing the twang in his

voice. "Yes … I am."

"I'm to take ya home." He snatched their bags from the ground and proceeded in the opposite direction without them.

"Excuse me, sir." Rosalind grabbed Lilly's free hand, the one she wasn't using to hold her nose, and as properly as she could manage, closed the distance between them. "What is your name?"

The driver glanced back at her, and his smile lit his eyes. "*Sir?*" He chuckled. "Haven't heard that one before. Walter, ma'am. But everyone calls me Walt."

Rosalind was so focused on Walt throwing their bags into the wagon that her foot caught on a hole and she stumbled on the edge of her dress, almost taking Lilly down with her. Rosalind pulled at her hem sweeping across the dirt like a broom. Surely it would be rags by the time she arrived wherever she was going. With her dress ruined, she'd only have her gown from the party and one other. She needed to find a place to purchase a few things, but she certainly couldn't ask this man to take them to a general store for clothes and undergarments. Remembering the night she left made her thankful she escaped at all.

"Let me help you." Walt hoisted Lilly in the back of the wagon and set her on her feet. He spun to Rosalind next, but she held out her hand to stop him, eyes wide. She didn't know this man, and who knew if he was telling her the truth. She needed to protect herself and Lilly. Yet how else would he have known they needed a ride if not for Oliver? Granted, it wasn't a carriage as the conductor mentioned, but so far, Texas wasn't what she expected either.

"I think we'll both sit up front with you on the bench seat." Regardless of where she sat, this strange man would *not* be taking her at the waist and lifting her the way he had Lilly. Just the thought made her cheeks warm.

When Rosalind was finally in her seat with Lilly perched between her and the driver, she looked over the crowd of animals and cowboys. She'd never seen so many animals.

A cowboy trotted up to the wagon and tilted his hat. "Well, ain't you a sight, little lady."

Rosalind glanced at Lilly. A sight? Lilly's hair was brushed. Her sweater, appropriate—although she really should take it off now. Rosalind didn't want her to have a heat stroke, but her pale-pink dress looked lovely on her. "I think she's a beautiful little girl."

The cowboy gave a deep chuckle. "I was speakin' to you." His lopsided grin showed a missing tooth.

Walt pointed. "Best be on your way, mister. Your herd's scattin'."

The cowboy yelled something to a man yards away, then yanked the reins to turn his horse.

Rosalind removed Lilly's sweater and watched in fascination as the men managed to move the cattle. Was this the kind of work Trent did?

As they drove, the heavens became a canvas of colors. Yellows, oranges, and pinks streaked the sky exactly the way Trent had described, as if God himself had taken His finger and run it through the clouds. Rosalind pointed. "Look, Lilly. Isn't the sun breathtaking? And the clouds? God's masterpiece."

"Mama always said we are His masterpiece. Oh, look, Rose! The sun looks like it's sinking into the ground."

"It *does* seem to be." She pulled Lilly against her side and wrapped her arms around her waist. They sat in silence and watched as the orange ball inched slowly to the earth. It was beautiful, like nothing Rosalind had ever witnessed.

"We're here." Walt pointed down the hill. A white two-story home with a wraparound porch seemed to rise up from the ground. "The Easton Ranch is the only place 'round with a two-level home."

Trent's house. She leaned her chin on Lilly's head. She was moving into his home. *Her* home.

As they approached, a motion to the right caught her eye. A man was exiting the barn. "Well, hello, Walt," he said as they stopped. He had brown hair, his voice deep and a bit raspy.

"Be right back, ma'am." Walt hopped down and shook hands with the man.

"Rose, can we get down?"

Rosalind glanced at Lilly. "Not yet, sweetie." Her legs and backside hurt from sitting on the hard wooden seat, but she didn't know what was better. Stay in the wagon where Walt—a man she'd only known for a few short hours—had left them or take her chances and get down.

Walt went into the house, and the other man turned to peer up at her and Lilly. A thousand questions seemed to race across his features and in his blue eyes. His jaw tightened, emphasizing a jagged scar that ran across his cheek. Rosalind swallowed hard and squeezed Lilly to her side.

"Mrs. Easton. Mr. Oliver Hadley sent word of you and his daughter's arrival. May I help you both down?" He held out his hand.

Lilly looked up at her. Rosalind hesitated, glancing around for Walt. It was almost dark now, and he was nowhere in sight.

"You may help Lilly, but I can manage." She stifled a yawn and rose from the bench. Her body ached all over, and her clothes were matted with dirt. But her thoughts were never far from Lilly and Catherine, and if she'd made the right decision to travel without Trent. Heaviness pressed on her shoulders, but she couldn't allow the fear she felt earlier to dictate her actions. She needed to remember that in the future. Once her feet touched the ground, she let out a long breath.

"My name's Blake McKenny. Hope your trip out here was fine." He retrieved their bags from the wagon.

Walt came out of the house with a wide grin. He was eating something. "That cook a yers is somethin' else." He licked his fingers. "I bes' be gettin' home. Thank ya, Blake." He climbed into the wagon, took the reins, and secured a package on the bench next to him.

"Anytime. Don't be a stranger. Preacher's comin' on Sunday. Hope to see you then."

Walt was leaving her alone with a man she didn't know? She looked to Blake and the scar on his face and turned back to Walt. She had the urge to ask Walt to stay until Trent returned, but held her tongue. What did she tell herself moments ago? Fear wouldn't dictate her actions.

When Walt began to slowly pull away, she waved. "Bye, Walt. Thank you for your help."

"Yes, ma'am." He tipped his hat and yanked the reins, leaving them.

"Let's get you both inside before night falls. Watch your step." Blake took the two porch steps in one stride.

Rosalind glanced back just as Walt disappeared over the hill. She took a deep breath, collected Lilly's hand, then followed Blake up onto the porch and inside. A stone fireplace nestled on the left wall, flanked by couches. To her right, next to the stairwell, stood a grandfather clock beside a desk. Though the furnishings seemed sparse for such a large area, the overall result was lovely. And familiar.

Rosalind bit her lip to keep her emotions at bay. The resemblance of this room reminded her of a house she drew so long ago, when she dreamed of her future. Had Trent built this home based on those awful drawings?

"Are you all right, ma'am?" Blake eyed her as he set their bags down. When he straightened, a sheriff's badge peeked out from underneath his vest.

She breathed a sigh of relief. She and Lilly were safe. "I'm fine. Thank you. I'm sorry I didn't introduce myself earlier, please forgive me. I'm Rosalind Easton, and this is Lilly Hadley, my charge."

Blake's eyes lightened as he stared at her for the briefest of moments, then he focused his attention to Lilly. He knelt before her. "Do you like horses?"

Lilly's eyes gleamed at the question. "Yes, sir. Rose asked me the same thing when we left the train."

Blake smiled up at Rosalind and then turned his attention back to Lilly. "Well, tomorrow I'll take you out to see the horses. Would you like that?"

The corners of Lilly's mouth lifted at his suggestion. She glanced at her. "May I, Rose?"

It was strange to see a grown man down on a child's level, but what surprised Rosalind more was the kindness radiating from him. She had little experience being around men, but not everyone would treat a person like Glover. Trent wasn't like him, and she sensed this man wasn't either. Swallowing any lasting doubts, she agreed. "Of course. As long as I can join you." She met Blake's gaze.

He nodded.

"Thank you, Mr. McKenny. Then we will enjoy seeing the horses."

"Please, call me Blake." He rose to his feet.

Rosalind nodded. "Blake. I know you mentioned receiving a telegram from Mr. Hadley, but did you receive word from Trent or his father?"

"No, ma'am. I have to be honest, when I received the

telegram from Mr. Hadley saying Mrs. Easton was on her way, you weren't who I pictured."

"Oh, I guess not." Rosalind didn't know what else to say or how much to reveal of her circumstances. They both stood in uncomfortable silence. Blake's gaze settled on her for a moment too long. Rosalind could only imagine what he must be thinking. Was she really who she claimed to be? If so, why wasn't Trent with her? She almost couldn't blame him if he was as unsure of her as she was of him a moment ago.

She decided to clear the air before they went any further. "I know this is a bit strange, us arriving here out of the blue, but I assure you I'm Trent's wife."

"We know who you are, ma'am. I have no doubt you're Trent's wife." Blake's expression struck her, as if something ignited behind his lit eyes. "If you don't mind, I'm not tellin' anyone who you are just yet, only that family has come to visit." He chuckled. "Matthew is Trent's right-hand man, and he's tendin' to the animals, but I hope to keep it from him a bit longer. I have some business to attend to in town. I'll return later this evening, but if you don't mind keepin' it a secret for a few hours, I'd like to see his reaction when he hears of the news."

Why didn't Blake want Trent's right-hand man to know who she was? Was she in danger from this Matthew fellow? Did she need Blake—the sheriff—to protect her? Rosalind's hands began to tremble. She clasped them together in front of her, and her thoughts leapt to the way Blake's eyes brightened when he spoke of Matthew. It wasn't a look of concern but…playfulness?

Lilly tugged on her skirt. "Do you think we can see the horses tonight?"

Blake ran his fingers over his scar and chin. "I'm not sure how long I'll be in town tonight, but I promise we'll see the horses right after breakfast. How does that sound?"

Lilly smiled again, but now Rosalind's wavering fear turned into panic and welled up in her chest. Breakfast? Was she to cook? Of course she was. She was Trent's wife now. "Can you direct me the kitchen?" she asked, glancing around.

He nodded to another room. "Through the entrance there."

As she made her way to investigate, Blake followed. The kitchen was a bit larger than what she was accustomed to. But once again, the design reminded her of her drawings. It ran lengthwise instead of being a square like hers or her sister's.

She inhaled a weary breath. How were Sydney and the twins? Was Joshua home now? She hoped so for everyone's sakes. Glover would think twice before taking his anger out on her sister or the children if Joshua was around.

Needing a distraction from her thoughts, Rosalind lifted Lilly in her arms and walked to one of the windows. Nightfall met the land as far as the eye could see. The evening gave way to a clear view of the stars winking at her from the heavens above. "How beautiful. So vast and wide."

As is My love for you.

Rosalind stood straight and listened for the voice she heard, yet none came. Had it been her imagination? No. The whispered words were clear as the stars above. She set Lilly down and stared out the window once again. The tension and fear she felt moments ago drifted away.

Lord? Is that You?

A man's voice wafted inside. "Just because you're sheriff now doesn't mean …" The screen door to the kitchen slammed behind the man carrying the voice. He gave her a cocky grin, then looked her up and down. "Blake, you've changed quite a bit since becoming sheriff."

Blake chuckled in the corner of the kitchen, where he was pouring a cup of coffee. "Don't mind him. That's only

Matthew."

So this fellow was Matthew? He reminded her of a redwood tree she read about in one of her books.

Matthew frowned. "What type of introduction is that? I'm not used to finding beautiful women in the kitchen. She's a lot better to look at than you and the other cowpokes. That's for sure."

"You better watch yourself. You don't know who this is."

Matthew tilted his hat above his eyes and lifted one of his brows. "Well now, ma'am, to say I'm intrigued is an understatement."

"Matthew, I'll let you introduce yourself, but behave." Blake turned to her. "Ma'am, I've got to go into town now, but no matter what he says, I am leaving you in capable hands."

Blake took a sip of coffee, then faced Matthew. His countenance fell. "Another longhorn is missin' from Boyd's ranch."

Matthew groaned and followed Blake into the living area. "Another one? How many does that make?"

The conversation turned, and so did Rosalind, taking Lilly and their bags upstairs undetected as the men's conversation became strained. A light guided them to the top of the stairs where it grew and flickered all around her as they stood in front of two rooms, one to the right, one to the left. Rosalind set the bags down and entered the doorway to the right. An oil lamp burned next to the bed along the wall. A dresser nestled in the corner, and a rocking chair sat across from the bed, curtains set behind it covering most of the window. The room was spacious enough for both her and Lilly.

She opened one of the dresser drawers. Empty. "This room doesn't look like its being used."

She exited the bedroom and was drawn to the light seeping

from under the door opposite hers. Rosalind gave in to her curiosity and stepped across the wide hall to peek inside the second room. Relief was her reward, as there was a chamber pot and a bathing tub. No running water, but perhaps Blake could help her carry the buckets upstairs. Maybe Texas wasn't as rugged as she thought.

She grabbed the bags she'd deposited outside the bedroom, then reentered. Lilly sat in the rocking chair with her rabbit.

"How about we right ourselves with a bath and dispose of our dusty clothes? How does that sound?" She opened their bags and unpacked, placing her things in one side of the dresser, Lilly's on the other.

"Come on, Mr. Sanders." Lilly slid from the rocker and sniffed her rabbit, scrunching her nose. "You need a bath."

Rosalind stifled a giggle, grateful for the joy the child gave and hoped she too was being a comfort to Lilly in return. Rosalind couldn't help but think of Catherine and wonder how she was. She wanted to let Oliver know she and Lilly arrived safely, but even more, she wished to know Catherine's health. Was she even alive?

Rosalind glanced at Lilly. The child had set the rabbit down and was untying her shoes. She wanted to ask how she was managing without her parents but thought better of it. She didn't want to cause the child pain. Maybe it was best not to mention her parents unless she brought them up first. They both had so much to adjust to, and they'd do it together. But what would Trent think once he returned home to find Lilly? And could she tell him that no matter how much she loved him and enjoyed the heated kiss they shared in Boston, she wasn't ready to share his bed?

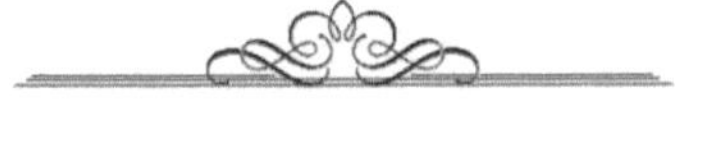

CHAPTER TWENTY

Rosalind blew hair from her eyes with a quick puff of her lips and continued to cut a row of circles into the dough. She hoped what she fixed would be enough. When she and Lilly finally ate supper last night, the house was dark except for the light she carried from her room. She and Lilly had set out everything she'd need for breakfast. Blake and Matthew never came back in, but she was sure she'd see them sometime this morning.

After placing the dough on a tray, Rosalind slid it into the oven. She found eggs in the icebox and set them to boil. As she put away the lard and salt, the screen door screeched open to admit a gray-haired man. He stopped cold and frowned.

She smiled regardless of the older man's perplexing stare as if she'd grown another head. *Boy, the cowhands come in early.* Tomorrow she'd make sure to have things ready. "Hi. The biscuits are cooking and the eggs are boiling, so it shouldn't take long now for everything to be finished." Rosalind glanced outside—it wasn't even light yet. "Would you care for some coffee?" She opened a few cabinets, having forgotten to find the coffee the night before.

"No. I'll get the coffee. You sit." He pulled out a chair.

That was nice of him, but she had too much to finish. Still, she didn't want to be rude. A few minutes should be fine. Rosalind sank into the chair, thankful she'd done most of the cooking for her and Father these last two years. All those meals had prepared her for today. Although it was her mother who taught her to cook—at least some. Biscuits and desserts were her specialty.

The gray-haired man set a pot of water on the stove to boil, then reached for a bowl labeled COFFEE. How had she missed it? Well, one less thing to find tonight at supper.

The clock in the kitchen ticked away the silence when the front door creaked. She stood and went to her boiling eggs. Small crackles began to appear across the shell. Done. She removed the pot and placed it in the sink.

Matthew entered the kitchen and tipped his hat in her direction. "Good morning." He grabbed a mug from a shelf.

"Good morning," she replied, peeling off eggshells.

"I see you met Martin." Matthew handed the gray-haired man the cup. "Ma'am, you disappeared upstairs yesterday, and I never found out your name. I think Blake is keeping you a secret for some reason."

Martin poured Matthew a steamy dark brew that resembled rich, dark chocolate, then cast a look at her.

Matthew leaned his hip against the counter. "So what's for breakfast, Miss …"

Rosalind inhaled. The last thing she wanted to do was start her visit off on the wrong foot. "I'm afraid I haven't been a good hostess. Let me introduce myself. I'm Rosalind Easton, Trent's wife."

Matthew choked, set his mug down, and sucked in a heavy

breath. His watered eyes found hers. He tried to speak but coughed out her name. "Ros … a … lind?"

Blake came into the kitchen with a wide grin, obviously having overheard their conversation. "Oh, did I forget to mention that?" He turned toward Martin and said, "I'll take a cup, Martin," before sending a wink Rosalind's way. "I would like to introduce you both to Mrs. Easton."

It grew so quiet and still, Rosalind's face heated under their gazes. She mumbled a hurried "Excuse me" and left from the room. She needed to check on Lilly anyway.

Matthew called to her, his boots sharp on the wood floor as he followed her to the stairs. "Rosalind. Wait. I mean … Mrs. Easton. I've waited a long time to meet you."

She stopped halfway up the staircase and craned her neck to see him. "Meet *me*?"

"Yes, ma'am. It wasn't so much Trent's words, though he spoke of you, but it was clear by his actions you were special. He only had eyes for you."

Her face warmed even hotter than before. Did all cowboys speak so plain with someone they'd only met? "Thank you." Her gaze fell to the wooden stairs. "Trent should be on the train today. I was to meet him in Fort Worth."

"Trent can find his way home." Matthew chuckled. "He'll never leave again." He sniffed the air. "Do you smell something burning?"

"Oh, no!" She ran past him. When she entered the kitchen, Martin was lifting a tray from the oven. She'd baked her mother's biscuits to perfection many times before, but now, when she needed it the most, "golden" wasn't in her repertoire. It had been replaced by dark-brown and—Rosalind was certain—rock hard. Her shoulders slumped.

Martin threw her biscuits in the trash. "I'll make more, Mrs.

Easton. Don't you worry yourself none."

First day as Trent's wife and a *man* had to offer to cook where she'd failed. Rosalind nodded in embarrassment and, once again, headed upstairs to check on Lilly.

After breakfast, Lilly sat next to Rosalind at the kitchen table and read her book to Mr. Sanders. To listen as she recalled the story Catherine must have read to her warmed her heart. How was she?

Blake came into the room, and she could see him clearly as he sunk onto the couch in the living room, several papers in hand. The front door banged hard against the frame, and Matthew pushed through the doorway, his expression strained. Rosalind leaned forward in her chair, thankful her view extended to include the living room. She captured Matthew's every hardened step.

He yanked off his Stetson and flung a sheet of paper on Blake's lap. "Read this."

Blake set his other papers aside and lifted Matthew's. "What is it?"

"A telegram from Mr. Easton. There might be trouble."

Rosalind's heart jolted. Trouble? She stood and quickly walked to the living room. Although tempted to snatch the telegram from Blake's hand, she refrained by clasping her hands together. "What does it say?"

Blake rubbed his scar and jaw as he met her gaze. "I don't mean to pry, ma'am, but why wasn't Trent with you on the train? Seems a bit peculiar he'd send his wife on ahead without 'im."

Rosalind opened her mouth to demand to read the telegram but then clamped her lips closed. She was in no position to demand anything. She was no one to them, but should she tell them that with her living here, their own lives might be in danger? She swallowed the lump in her throat. "To protect me."

Blake rose and handed her the telegram. "And Mr. Easton seems to want to protect you both."

Rosalind's hand trembled as she accepted the paper.

Matthew and Blake,

Trent and his wife will arrive in Fort Worth on separate trains but will meet, then return to Graham together. My greatest concern is for their safety, which caused the delay of this telegram. Mariam and I will follow at a later date when things are settled here in Boston.

T. E.

Chills dashed up her spine as Rosalind folded the paper. What had stopped Mr. Easton from sending word earlier? Had Glover … Sydney, the children … Father? She pressed a hand to her stomach. Surely they were safe.

"Ma'am, is there anything we should know?" Matthew ran his fingers along the brim of his hat.

Yes … No …

So much, Rosalind didn't know where or how to begin. Aware of their gazes, she averted her eyes. "I'll let Trent explain after he arrives."

"Yes, ma'am." Blake's gaze shifted as he clapped Matthew's shoulder with his hand and moved him toward the door. "Do you remember Mr. Oliver Hadley? We joined Mr. Easton and Mr. Hadley for lunch in Fort Worth after bringing the cattle to market a few times. Did you know he and his wife are acquaintances of Rosalind as well?"

Matthew looked over his shoulder at Rosalind, then Blake.

"What does this have to do with the telegram?"

"Nothing, but Lilly is his daughter, Rosalind's charge, and I promised her yesterday I'd take her to see the horses. Which means you—"

Matthew hesitated at the door, then shoved his hat onto his head. "And how is it you get the *fun* job while I get to muck out the stalls?"

"Just lucky, I guess."

Matthew slid on leather gloves, a teasing gleam in his eyes. "Oh, there will be payback." He thumped Blake's chest with the back of his hand, his expression turning serious. "One of the fences was down. In light of what's going on over at Boyd's ranch, I had two of the men fix it. Thought you ought to know." Matthew left.

Blake came and stood near her. He hesitated as if considering his next words carefully, then looked toward Lilly in the kitchen and lowered his voice. "Are you all right, ma'am?"

Rosalind couldn't wrench her eyes from the look of concern on Blake's face. "You sent him away for me?"

He nodded. "There's plenty of time to talk after Trent returns. No need right now. Just know we're here if you need anything." Blake entered the kitchen and held out his palm to Lilly. "Ready to see the horses, Miss Lilly? They need a good brushin', and I thought you'd like to help."

Lilly set her book down on the table, scooped up her stuffed rabbit, and slid her hand in Blake's. "I'm ready."

"We better be goin' before Matthew changes his mind and has me cleanin' the stalls." Blake chuckled, giving Rosalind a smile as he passed, as if knowing that what she might have said about the telegram would cost her.

And it would have—sharing the details of a cruel man she feared she'd never forget.

Trent stepped from the train and searched the platform for Rosalind as the whistle blew. He had to find her and make sure she was all right. Although he'd made certain he wasn't followed on the connection to Fort Worth, he couldn't help but be concerned.

A herd of cattle moved down the street, blocking all other traffic. In another two months, he'd be rounding up his own herd to take to market. But he'd have time to think about that later. Right now he needed his wife.

His wife. The thought lightened his heavy heart.

Where was she? His eyes roamed the streets, catching a glimpse of a group of women as they ambled down the boardwalk. She wasn't with them. She wasn't anywhere. Maybe she'd needed to use the privy.

"Trent!"

He jerked around. Pete*?* Trent's cowhand rode up through the cows. "Did you leave me while I was gone?"

Pete yanked his hat off and wiped his forehead with his sleeve. "This is my brother-in-law's herd. One of his men came down with somethin', so I'm helpin' today."

"Good to hear you're still with us."

"I'd never leave you, Boss. Besides, you have the finest herd." He quirked a questioning brow. "I didn't realize you were in town. Boston that bad?" He snickered. "Glad you're back. Listen, before I head out. I heard somethin' you and the guys should know about. Someone's rustling longhorns in Graham. This might explain what's happenin' with *our* horns."

"Have we lost more?"

"Seven head."

Trent chewed on the side of his lip. "Thanks for letting me

know."

"I'll be in town tonight to rest up, but I'll be back in the morn. My brother-in-law's cook is nothing like Martin."

"No one is as good as Martin."

"Even if the man never smiles." Pete steered his horse to the herd. "See you tomorrow."

When Trent sent a telegram to Matthew from Boston, he'd asked for his horse to be taken to the livery. Thankfully his horse was still there. After settling with the livery owner, he stripped down to his buttoned shirt, rolled up his sleeves, and climbed onto his horse. An hour later, he resigned himself to the fact no one had seen a woman matching Rosalind's description, or heard of her—and fear gnawed at him.

He didn't want to think what might have happened. He couldn't get home fast enough. Trent rode. Hard. "God, please let her be there." He wiped the sweat from his face with his forearm. His heart raced as he passed the tree marking the beginning of his property. Hot adrenaline pumped through his veins as the house came into view. "Let her be there, God, please."

Blake came out from the barn with a young child. Trent rode up to them and hopped off the horse.

"Blake, have you seen—"

"She's in the house."

His body was spent and rattled. The fear he'd harbored for his wife these last weeks gave way to emotions he couldn't control and had hoped to release before seeing her. His gut told him she was okay—Blake said she was inside—but the door to the house swung open, and he was robbed of the opportunity to relax first.

She spotted him, and he froze on the last step to the porch. Just the sight of her made him crazy. Her hair was down, shining in the sun like a beacon. Eyes so clear … so beautiful. She stole his breath. "Why didn't you wait for me? Hadn't we decided when I put you on the train?" His tone came out harsh, although it wasn't his intention. She had to know what she'd done to him. Even now his heart pounded.

Her smile faded. "I …" She looked away, then back at him, but said nothing.

"That's not an answer." He huffed.

She turned her back to him and went inside, leaving him on the step.

He took several breaths and followed, stomping up the porch. "Rosalind." She wasn't in the living room or the kitchen. He climbed the stairs to the second floor. A sound caught his ear as he came to one of the extra rooms. Her bags lay on the bed, and she shoved clothes into them.

What was she doing?

It took him a moment to understand the scene before him. "You're leaving?" The same fear that rode with him from town intensified. No longer was it the fear that Glover had found her. Now he feared he'd never see her again.

Rounding the bed, Trent grabbed her waist and pulled her to him. Rosalind's eyes slammed shut, and her body cowered in his arms.

She thought he'd strike her?

He released her immediately, and pain gripped his heart for what she had endured at Glover's hand. "Please, look at me," he said in a gentle tone. When she didn't move, he whispered her name, coaxing her to meet his gaze. "I promise, I will never raise a hand to you."

"But you were angry. I saw it in your eyes. I will never allow another man to hurt me."

"Yes, yes, I was angry. I was afraid. Afraid of losing you.

You weren't at the station, and I feared he had found you."

She cocked her head to the side, biting her bottom lip.

She had no idea how appealing she was to him right now. She was safe, in his home—their home—and he'd never been more relieved in all his life. "May I kiss my wife hello?" He held out his hand.

She took hold of his fingers, but when he didn't pull her toward him, she came freely. He wanted her to feel safe, in control. So he waited. Before long, her mouth found his. He praised God within the warmth of her soft lips teasing him, making him fully aware of God's blessing. His fingers found their way to her slender shoulders, sliding through her hair as he deepened the kiss. Within those moments he collected every taste and breath as his own, promising God and himself he'd be the husband she deserved.

She pulled in a gasp of air.

He released her neck, and his fingers cooled where they had touched her. He breathed deeply, and the fragrance of roses tickled his senses. He leaned his head against hers, holding her close as he whispered, "Thank you for being my wife." He bent to kiss her again when a knock sounded at the door. Trent exhaled as Rosalind slipped from his arms. "Come in."

Blake entered with the child he'd seen when he rode up. The little girl ran to Rosalind, who knelt and embraced her.

CHAPTER TWENTY-ONE

Rosalind's lips burned, and her heart pounded wildly as she tried to catch her breath. If not for Lilly, right now, she and Trent would be …

Heat crawled up her neck at the way his kisses claimed her. With difficulty, she focused her attention on Lilly.

Lilly squeezed her tightly, then collected her hand. "Can we go?"

Rosalind smiled at the anxious child, knowing exactly what she was after. She poked her chin. "Where would you like to go? You want me to see the horses?"

Auburn hair bobbled. "Mr. Blake is waiting to take us."

She glanced at Blake and caught a glimpse of his back as he retreated from the doorway. When she turned to Trent, his eyes pierced hers and his forehead wrinkled in confusion. "First, I want you to meet someone." Rosalind rose, inhaled a breath, and turned Lilly to face Trent. "Lilly, this is my husband, Mr. Easton. The one I told you about on the train. Trent, this is Lilly Hadley, my charge."

Trent glanced from her to Lilly. Questions raced across his

features. "Hello."

Lilly pulled her hand, but Rosalind held fast. "Trent, would you care to join us?"

"Let me wash up and I'll meet you." He glanced down at her bags, then at the bed. "Will you be sharing this room with Lilly?"

Heat rose to her cheeks. She had hoped they'd have time to discuss their room arrangements, just not with Lilly standing at arm's length. She needed to talk with him, needed him to understand the situation. Instead, she answered his questions with a nod.

Disappointment shadowed his eyes, and her stomach plummeted from his silence. She wanted to give herself freely, to share his life fully, but for so long the desire of others gave her no choice but to obey. How could she explain?

"Lilly, go find Blake and tell him I'll be down shortly." She waited until Lilly left, then turned back to her husband. "Trent."

He took a step closer and lightly rubbed his index finger over the bridge of her nose and forehead. She released a sigh and relished his touch and the way he eased her tension. He grinned in return. "Now, that's better." He raised her chin with his finger and caressed her lips with his own. "Then we shall wait. It won't be easy, but we will wait." He kissed her forehead, then strolled from the room.

Rosalind's heart pounded. She floated down the stairs to the barn and pushed the heavy door as it creaked in protest. She'd barely slid through when Blake yanked the door wide. "I appreciate you watching Lilly."

"I'm sorry for interruptin'."

She waved her hand, face warming at the thought of what he and Lilly had interrupted. "Oh, no need to apologize."

He pointed in Lilly's direction. "She seems like a well-behaved child. She told me her father takes her riding. I was sorry to hear about his wife." They walked through the barn to the gate where a horse grazed. Lilly stood peering between the rails of the fence a few steps away.

Rosalind lowered her voice. "If only I knew how to ride. I'd do anything to make things right for her. I wish her parents were here now." She could still see Catherine's face as they pulled away from the train station. The longing in her friend's green eyes stabbed Rosalind's heart.

She'd felt it too when her mother died, and she knew it was the last time she'd see her. The last breath she'd ever take. Rosalind reached the fence next to Lilly and closed her eyes for a moment to break her thoughts from the pain and hurt she'd tucked away so long ago.

Blake knelt alongside Lilly and rolled on the heel of his boots. "Little miss, how would you feel about going for a ride?"

Lilly's eyes widened at Rosalind. "May I, Rose?"

"If Mr. …"

"Blake will be fine." His mouth turned up at the corners, causing his scar to seem less noticeable. "My friends call me Blake."

She nodded. "All right. On both accounts."

Blake rose and chuckled under his breath. "Would you care to help saddle the horse, Miss Lilly?" He held out his hand, and she grasped his fingers, pulling him farther into the barn.

A moment later, the barn door squeaked open and Trent sauntered in, his hat shadowing him, yet she couldn't pull her focus as he moved toward her. His shirt protested against his build, defining broad shoulders and strength that had only been hinted at under his Boston attire. His blond hair curled at the collar of his shirt, and his eyes, although hidden, caused her heart to skip, remembering how dark his blue orbs had turned moments ago after their kiss. She was married to a cowboy, and to an exceptionally handsome one at that.

A horse whinnied, and Blake appeared, holding Lilly with one hand, reins in the other. When they passed, Lilly waved and Rosalind waved back. She turned to Trent. "Tell me." Her voice almost pleaded, recalling Glover's threats. "How is my father and sister? The twins? Are they all right?" She swallowed.

"They're fine, Rosalind. They're safe. I believe with Joshua home, with his work with the navy and his large stature, your sister and her children will be safe. Sydney is quite upset you left without saying goodbye, but when I told her we were married and I sent you to Texas ahead of me, she was very pleased. And as for your father, he is staying with my parents. God is protecting them."

She let out a long breath and turned her focus back in the direction Blake and Lilly had rode.

"Tell me about Lilly." He moved alongside her.

Where should she begin? "I met her and her parents, Oliver and Catherine, on the train coming west. They were very kind to me. When I needed shelter, they provided."

"What do you mean, shelter? I gave you enough money for a comfortable passage. I wouldn't have sent you alone any other way."

Rosalind cleared her throat. "I … I lost my ticket on the train and had no proof I'd purchased one. If it weren't for this family, I'd have been taken off the train and arrested."

"Arrested?" His voice held the same timbre as it did when they first met on the doorstep.

Rosalind wished to take his hat off to see him fully. His eyes were expressive of his feelings long before he reacted or spoke a word. Still, she'd misread his reaction earlier. She *knew* he was nothing like Glover, but for a moment, the fear Glover had instilled in her for the last two years rose, and she reacted. Trent only cared for and loved her.

He rested his forearm on the fence, boot on the bottom rail.

She reached over and cupped his hand. "I'm all right."

He nodded and looked at her. "What happened to Lilly's parents?"

Rosalind paused for a moment. "Her mother went into labor and the baby passed. Catherine became very ill, and they had to leave the train. Oliver asked if I'd take Lilly"—her voice broke—"into my care. When we arrived in Fort Worth…her father provided transportation to the ranch without delay."

"How are *you*?" Even though she couldn't see his concern, she heard it in his voice.

It had been so long since someone asked how she was, and the question took her by surprise. She glanced at the dirt and hay scattered at her feet. She finally whispered, "I don't know. I'm a bit overwhelmed with everything that has happened since your parents' party. I haven't had much time to think. I've simply reacted to the situations around me." Rosalind glanced down at their hands. "What happens if I can't take care of Lilly as she needs?"

Trent laced his fingers through hers. "Do you recall the time you found a baby bird that had fallen out of a nest, and how carefully you tended to its needs?"

"Yes. It was hurt. I couldn't let it die, knowing the mother wouldn't be able to care for it."

"You were so gentle. I was taken back by you, the way you tended to the bird. Never had I seen such sympathy for another creature. And now you've taken in another baby bird. Lilly. You understand what she is going through. I believe God brought her into your care for this very reason. You are what she needs."

Did God really bring Lilly into her path so she might help her? Did God truly care about Lilly … about her?

Behold the fowls of the air: for they sow not, neither do they reap, nor gather into barns; yet your heavenly Father feedeth them. Are ye not much better than they?

Was she valuable to the Lord? Did He bring Trent and his family to Boston to help her in her time of need, as she was helping Lilly in hers? "Your father told me once that God would rescue me from Glover. And now I'm here."

"I'm thankful He brought you to safety—to me."

"But am I safe?" She closed her eyes. "I'm scared, Trent."

Trent collected her within the warmth of his arms and held her. Rosalind knew she was loved, wanted, for the first time in years—but she was just as aware that her fear of Glover wasn't far behind.

It was almost dark, but Trent needed this ride. His muscles tightened as each hoof hit the ground. He grasped the leather reins, and his body moved as one with the horse. He didn't want to think another minute of how Rosalind lived through abuse at Glover's hand. So he rode harder until the wind blew against his ears, soothing his mind and nerves.

He slowed his stallion and took a deep breath of grass and manure mingling in the air, remembering what Pete mentioned at the station. Someone was rustling cattle. He'd get with Matthew and Blake for sure. But right now, he headed toward the two-acre pond.

As he got out of the saddle, Trent's boots crunched the bridle grass near the pond's edge. He rolled up his sleeves and plunged his hands into the warm water and grabbed a few rocks, then skimmed them across the surface. "Lord…" Trent looked toward heaven. Dark clouds had pushed into the area. "Although Glover isn't physically here, he's here with us, in fear, within both Rosalind and me. Please bring comfort to my wife and protect our lives together."

Thunder rumbled in the distance, and a light drizzle fell as he mounted his horse. He lifted his face one final time. "Thank you, Lord, for providing rain in our drought. But most importantly, for providing Rosalind with a safe journey to her new home. Now provide me with wisdom and understanding for the two women You've placed in my care."

It was dark by the time Trent halted his horse at the barn. Blake was inside, scribbling something on a tablet. He spoke without looking up at Trent. "Have a nice ride?" He tore the top sheet off the tablet and stuffed it in his shirt pocket.

Trent dismounted. "Can't complain."

Blake rose and eyed him for a moment, then took the reins from him and led the horse through the barn to one of the larger stalls.

Trent leaned against a post, taking off his gloves. "Something on your mind?"

"Yes and no." Blake yanked the saddle from the horse and hung it over a rail. "I received a wire from your father today."

"Rosalind told me."

"And Rosalind told me you were trying to protect her." Blake closed the stall door behind him. "What I find strange is how a man who has never shown an interest in women because his heart has been set on one comes home with fire in his eyes for that same woman, his bride … Why would he send her on the train without him? What happened in Boston?"

"Does this questioning have to do with the new hardware on your chest?" A clap of thunder crashed, and Trent glanced in the direction of the house. Had the thunder frightened Rosalind as it did as a child? He turned back to Blake.

"No. It has nothing to do with the badge, but my concern for you and your family."

"Where's Boyd? Did he decide to retire being sheriff early?" Trent asked.

"Shot dead."

Trent stood upright. "Shot? What happened?"

"Not sure really. His cowhands found him in one of the fields along with a few longhorns."

Trent couldn't believe it. Boyd was the first person he'd met when his family came to town, and the last he saw before he left for Boston. They'd spoken about the ranch and taking the herd to Fort Worth when he returned. Trent slumped back against the post. "Any clues?"

Blake shook his head. "I'm following up on a lead, but not much to go on."

The sky rumbled and echoed in the rafters of the barn. "I never took you as a lawman, with your love for horses."

Blake let out a deep sigh. "I thought Grace and I had a future, so I took the job when they offered it to me. Shortly after, she told me she didn't want to marry a lawman."

"Sorry to hear."

"I keep telling myself she wasn't the one."

"God has someone special for you. You'll find her." Trent knew all about God's timing. He'd waited much longer than he'd anticipated or cared to relive, but God brought him the desires of his heart in the woman he'd loved since they were children. "You plan to stay on?"

"I plan to stay if you don't mind. But I'll get me a place at the boardin' house and split my time. No job can keep me away from my horses." Blake smiled.

"As long as you know this is your home. You and your horses will always have a place. Where are you staying tonight?"

"I had planned to stay in town for a few weeks while you were gone, but Rosalind showed up." Lightning lit the dark sky, and the crack of thunder rolled from one end of the barn to the other. "The weather is getting worse."

A growing sense of anxiety grew as Trent glanced toward the house. "I should check on Rosalind and Lilly."

"Congratulations on your marriage. And for the record, I know you're avoiding my question about Boston. When you're ready to talk, I'm here."

Trent nodded and pressed his hat on his head before running for the house. The rain plopped hard against him. He entered the kitchen and found Rosalind arranging a jar of sunflowers. She froze at another clap of thunder, and her petite fingers spread across her stomach. He swiped the Stetson from his head and ran his fingers through his hair. "Hi."

She noticed him for the first time and greeted him with a worried smile. "Blake said you were riding your land. Everything okay?"

Had she been waiting up for him? "It will be with time…and rain."

"Too bad God had to invent thunder."

"Still unsettling?"

"At times."

They stood there in silence for a few moments, and he set his Stetson on the table. "Are you heading to bed?"

"I was waiting for you, to make sure you got in okay."

She had been waiting. He smiled and took her hand in his. "Let me walk you to your room."

At the bedroom door, he opened it and she entered. Light from a candle flickered softly against the walls as they both tiptoed to the bed and peered down at Lilly.

"Storms don't seem to affect her."

"I guess not," she whispered back, glancing at him. "Thank you for understanding about …"

Trent knew what she meant, and he meant what he said. It would be difficult to be without her to love and hold at night, but he would wait until she was ready. "You're welcome." He leaned in to kiss her, but thunder shook the house and Rosalind gasped, clinching his arms. Nails stabbed his flesh.

A tentative smile crossed her lips as she released her hold. "Sorry. A bit jumpy at times too."

He noted her eyes darting to the curtains and then back to him with every flash of lightning. "Once your head falls against the pillow, I'm sure you'll doze off quickly. You've had a long day and much to adjust to." He leaned in once again and this time kissed her cheek. Though he wanted to linger, he took a step back. "God will keep you safe … in every way."

"Thank you."

"See you in the morning." He closed the door behind him and entered his room, recalling the storms she feared as a child, taking shelter under tables, in closets, or his arms during the worst of storms. As he listened to the rain pound the roof and thunder roll across the sky for the next hour, he ached to hold his wife, hoping she needed him again. Wishing she'd come. Yet the door remained shut.

Chapter Twenty-Two

Trent's eyes opened in the darkened room. Within the hour, light would seep through the curtains. There was much to do on the ranch, and he was already behind. But one thing he intended to do was uncover what was happening to his longhorns. If someone had stolen them, they were also capable of killing a man, like his kind friend Boyd, in the process. Instantly, what Glover said at the train station turned in Trent's mind. *If I wanted him dead, he'd be dead.*

Yes, Glover was the type of man who'd kill anyone who crossed him, including Trent, but he wasn't in Graham. Trent realized then that no matter how much Glover continued to invade his thoughts, Rosalind quickly followed.

He prayed silently for his wife to have peace within her heart, mind, and soul, knowing that the One who rescued her from Boston would never leave nor forsake her. A Father who truly loved her and was willing to sacrifice His own life. Unlike her earthly father.

Oh, Rosalind ... my Rose.

How long had it been since he spoke the name that fit her so well? The rose scent of the bath water she bathed in, the pink tint of her cheeks, the softness of her skin. He smiled. The beauty of a rose … but had she wilted through last night's storm?

Trent doubted she had closed her eyes until the lightning passed in the wee hours, but surely she was resting now. The temptation to check on her and Lilly pushed him from the bed to dress.

He slid on his clothes and froze. He sniffed the air, then lunged from the room, instantly snatching his hat on the way out. Trent hurried down the steps and prayed the house wasn't on fire. Following the stench to the kitchen, he found Martin leaning over the stove with a tray. Brown shriveled rocks lay on the pan.

Trent took two steps farther into the kitchen. "Please don't tell me this is what you planned to serve. First I thought the house was on fire, but I don't know what would be better. The house or my stomach."

Someone cleared their throat to the left of where he stood. He glanced over to catch Matthew's signal that someone was behind him. He turned to find Rosalind biting the inside of her lip, eyes glaring. "I made those."

"Why would you?"

Again, Matthew cleared his throat. His friend shook his head, and his gaze dropped to the floor.

Rosalind hurried past him and Martin, snatching a towel from the table. "I'll take those." She grabbed the pan of biscuits from Martin and upended it on the table. She rushed into the other room, came back carrying a basket and swept the biscuits into it, then spun and marched out the door.

Trent watched her go, then turned his gaze on both men. "Can someone please explain what's going on?"

Matthew shrugged. "I tried to warn you to keep your mouth shut, but you wouldn't take the hint."

Martin gave a mock cough and laughed. White teeth shone across his face. Never had Martin laughed nor smiled since his employment began two years before. Trent glanced over at Matthew, whose eyes lit with laughter but stared openly at Martin.

Martin straightened his shoulders and his frown returned. He went to the icebox and came back with premade dough he was known to make for the next day. "I don't believe anyone's told her I'm the cook. I thought it was strange yesterday when she was cutting the dough in circles. But when Blake explained she thought she had to cook for everyone, and remembering how she burnt the biscuits for supper, I didn't have the heart to tell her."

Heart? Who *was* this man? Trent dragged his gaze from Martin and ran his fingers through his hair. "And no one had the *heart* to share this bit of information with me?"

Martin unwrapped the dough on the table, saying nothing.

"Well, at least the house is still here." Matthew coughed, then smiled.

Trent narrowed his eyes at his friend, settling his hat on his head. With determined steps, he ventured outside in hopes of apologizing to Rosalind for not explaining who Martin was yesterday—or any other thing she'd deem as important.

Light broke through the darkness with pink and yellow hues across the horizon.

A horse's easy canter sounded in the distance. Rosalind wouldn't try to ride in frustration, would she? She didn't know how to ride. Small giggles erupted as Blake carried Lilly on horseback from the barn. Trent smiled and waved. As he turned and caught sight of Rosalind at the side of the house, he was keenly aware of her beauty, and how his heart battled to have the intimacy that a husband and wife shared, but most importantly, how God had blessed him and his future.

He took a few steps forward. "Rosalind?"

She whirled and faced him, her fingers gripping something he couldn't see. She turned away and released the object. It landed with a hard thump on the ground. Her biscuits.

Trent could see the hurt in her eyes, the anger in the firm set of her lips. He recognized her symptoms of injured pride as certainly as he had his own when he thought Rosalind didn't want him. But he wouldn't let her push him away, as it seemed she was willing to do.

He took a few more steps, coming alongside her, and she reached into the basket by her feet and took hold of another. She was about to pitch it when he snatched the biscuit from her hand and took a bite. His teeth ripped into the rock-hard bread.

She gasped as her eyes widened. "What are you doing? They're terrible."

He continued to chew. "I'm a lucky man to have a wife who's willing to cook for me and my men when she doesn't have to."

She glanced down at the basket by her feet. "Martin is your cook? He cooks for everyone?"

"He does, but it's your choice. If you'd like to cook, you can. Just let me know and I'll tell Martin." He took another bite, then tried to swallow the first. He could have used some water. Nevertheless, he planted himself in front of her and chewed.

She stared into his eyes. "I'm sorry… The bread… I don't understand it." Her crystal gray eyes pleaded for him to say something.

And he would have offered to say something, if only he could speak. His mouth was so dry. But he wasn't sure if it was from the biscuit or his wife's presence that had dried it. Instead, he touched a strand of her hair that had come loose from her ribbon and rubbed it between his fingers. *Like silk.*

She watched him but gave no indication of how she felt, or if his nearness stirred her heart like hers did his. He wanted to know. *Had* to know. He suspected over the last two years she'd learned to keep her feelings and emotions tucked away from anyone. But not here. Not with him. He wanted her to know she was safe and free to be the woman God called her to be.

He tucked the strands behind her ear and grazed her jaw with his finger. A small sigh passed her pink lips, and his heart thumped against his chest. "You're free to live again, Rose, even if it means throwing rolls in the yard, at my head, climbing trees, or eating chocolate bars in the afternoon."

She cocked her head to the side and smiled. "Does that mean you're willing to give up your share of the chocolate?"

"Never." He chuckled, lifting the basket of bread from the ground, and held out his arm for her, as he had many times in Boston.

She slipped her hand through his arm. "Thank you."

Trent's chest tightened, as did his fingers, which now covered hers against his arm. "You're welcome, Rose."

Rosalind's heart swelled from the nearness of her husband as they walked across the field, arm in arm. She loved him to the very depths of her soul. She inhaled, enjoying the warmth from the sun on her skin, as they moved farther away from the house. "Where are we going?"

"I'd like to show you something, if that's all right."

She glanced over her shoulder. "Blake has taken Lilly for a ride. I'd hate to be far off if she needs me."

"We won't be gone long."

She nodded, and they continued toward the large tree at the beginning of the property.

When they neared, Trent set down the basket he'd been holding, then slid his hand to the small of her back. "My first instinct was to build us a home here, but Father suggested it would be better down the hill where the land is leveled." He shrugged. "After I laid out how I planned to build the ranch, I knew he was right."

Us? She struggled to focus. Thoughts of her poor drawings of the house she drew years before came to mind, as did how oddly similar Trent's living room seemed.

"This is our land, Rose."

Her gaze followed his callused finger, pointing to the bark of the tree. Carved within the wood was a heart. She fingered the shape, then the names nestled inside, Trent and Rose. Moisture filled her eyes. "*Our* land?"

"As far as you can see, from this tree and past the house."

She slowly turned to where he indicated. They stood on a hill, overlooking the house, two barns, and, in the distance, another long building. Longhorns scattered about the flat land to the right, some wading within a pond, and to the left was a field of sunflowers. The flowers' yellow petals sprung toward the feathery sky, brightening the dry land with a golden hue. It amazed her how this land, which she'd never seen before stepping from the train, called to her in its beauty and simplicity. "Sunflowers are my favorite." She was tempted to run down the hill and collect a basket full, but Lilly would enjoy helping, especially carrying the basket.

"I know."

Every word Trent had written to her in his letters was true. He had included her in his dreams, and ever since he had left Boston, she was the only one. He did this for her all along. For them, a new life, to share together. Rosalind avoided his gaze, for she knew one look and he'd see the tears clinging to her lashes. She didn't know if she was crying because her hopes and dreams of loving Trent had come true, or because she felt truly wanted and loved inside and out.

Trent wrapped his arms around her as if he understood. Her mother's words written within her Bible took hold. It was true. God directed her path and prepared a place for her ... for *them*.

"This is our Promised Land, the land I believe God intended for us all along. Our hopes and dreams were solely fulfilled by the work of the Lord's hand," he whispered close to her ear.

Rosalind tried to speak, but her voice squeaked. She couldn't deny the peace she felt at this moment, or describe it, as Trent held her in his arms. She cleared her throat. "I think you might be right."

Trent loosened his grip and turned her to face him, but his mouth closed as a tear escaped her eye. He wiped her cheek with his finger. "Would you like to go back?"

She nodded. "I think we should. Lilly might be waiting for us at the house."

Trent bent down and collected her basket, but she dumped the rest of the biscuits onto the ground. He glanced at her. "I would have eaten them."

"I know." She chuckled for a moment when her stomach rumbled, and she recalled that they hadn't eaten. "Oh, dear. You must be hungry."

He held out his arm and she looped hers through. "I'll eat later. Nothing is more important than spending time with you."

She smiled at him, fighting every ounce of strength not to yank that hat off his head and request a kiss from her cowboy. He reciprocated with his own smile and then stopped walking. Had he read her thoughts?

A loud crack broke the silence of the morning and echoed through her mind.

Trent grabbed her to his chest and glanced around.

"What was that noise?"

His focus continued to scan the area. "We need to get you to the house." He took her arm and quickened their pace. A single horse trotted toward them. Blake had one hand wrapped around Lilly, reins in the other. Lilly waved feverishly at them as she neared.

Trent shielded his face and glanced up at his friend. "Did it come from the west?"

"Yep," Blake said. His features were tight, his voice controlled. "The same place Pete had mentioned, I'm sure. I'll take Lilly to the house and get your horse ready."

"Tell Martin to fill however many canteens I have in the house. We're going to need them."

Blake's eye twitched and his lip tightened. But as he leaned toward Lilly, he teased. Still, the lightheartedness she'd seen in his eyes previously had vanished. "Ready, little miss?"

Small giggles lingered, trailing Blake and Lilly back to the house.

"Trent." Rosalind pulled back from his arm and stopped. "I'm not taking another step until you tell me what is going on. What was that noise?"

"Gunfire. Either that was a warning shot, or someone is dead."

CHAPTER TWENTY-THREE

It had been nearly three weeks since the gunshot ripped through the peace Rosalind and Trent had shared. She thought of nothing else than his declaration. Although he never said the words, his actions spoke of love in a way she'd never expected. And, oh, how she longed for his kiss. She recalled his lips were warm against hers and dreamed of a moment they could share another, but the days lingered. The nights were even longer.

Rosalind punched the dough with her knuckles, letting out her frustration. Until now, he'd come home far into the evening. His absence during the day was hard enough, but now she'd have to go without even the sight of him … for how long? Sixteen days so far.

Martin turned the stove on and slid in an apple crumb cake that was Rosalind's mother's recipe. It had always been her favorite growing up, and Trent had enjoyed it too. She only hoped it would remind him that he had a wife waiting for him.

"The venison stew is cooking. I need to get several jars from the cellar." Martin's voice brought her back to what she was doing. Or trying to do. She shook her head. Would she ever make these biscuits right? With a huff, she glanced at Lilly, who was sprinkling flour on the table.

"I know when you get older, you're going to make some of the best biscuits around, the kind that melts in your mouth like my mother used to make." Rosalind rolled out the dough.

Lilly came to stand beside her. "I don't want to cook when I get older. I just want to eat."

Rosalind bit back her chuckle. They both cut the dough into circles, then laid them on a pan.

"Rose?"

"Yes, sweet pea?"

"Can Martin make these so we don't have to?"

At this point, Rosalind couldn't give up. *Wouldn't* give up. All the work and time she'd put into this had to count for something. "Sometimes if you want something bad enough, you can't give up no matter how hard it is or how many times you might get disappointed. You keep trying."

"Is that why you stay up every night … to see Mr. Easton? Why don't you and Mr. Easton sleep together in the same bed? Like Mama and Papa do?"

Rosalind's cheeks burned. "Um … I … Why don't we finish this up and then go outside?"

Lilly clapped her hands together in excitement. A plume of white dust burst from her palms. "Who do you think will come today? Blake or Matthew? I guess Blake. I like Blake. Why does he have the scar on his face?"

Since Trent and his men had been out in the field putting up a fence around the property, either Matthew or Blake would come to the house and let Martin know they were ready for dinner. Rosalind had decided to make a game out of guessing which one it would be each day. "I'm not sure what happened to Blake's cheek, but it's not polite to ask."

"All right." Lilly's head fell, and her auburn hair swooped over her face.

Rosalind hadn't braided the child's hair this morning. Instead, they'd sat in the morning sun and brushed it more than a hundred stokes, then left it undone. Texas's way of life was much freer than Boston's, yet not free enough to ask such a personal question, no matter how much she wanted to know herself. "Matthew. I say Matthew will be the one to come."

"Actually…" Martin came through the back door, a jar of beans tucked under each arm and stuck in each hand. "Someone else is here to see you."

"Oh my." Rosalind looked at herself. She was a mess. But she was finally going to see Trent. She hurried to the sink and washed her hands. "Lilly, you stay here. I'll be right back."

When she opened the front door, her heart sank. "Can I help you?" she called to the stranger who stood off to the right of the porch. He had his back to her, but something about him seemed familiar, as did the wagon.

"Yes, ma'am. I've got these things for ya." He turned around with a few boxes in hand. His bushy gray brows rose, connecting into one.

She almost laughed. "Walt! How are you?" She smiled and joined him beside his wagon.

"Doin' just fine, ma'am. Ross from the general store in Fort Worth said to give ya and Mr. Easton his apologies since this has taken so long to get to ya, bein' a present and all."

Had Trent remembered her birthday? "What's inside the boxes?"

"I don't rightly know, ma'am. When I got to the store, these were waitin' for me, but they have yer name on 'em. Where would you like me to put 'em?"

"Oh, inside by the clock is a small table. You can put them

there." While Walt was inside, she glanced at the other boxes. What were these? Every one of them had either hers or Lilly's name on them. She headed inside, where Lilly jumped up and down by the door.

"I see my name! I see my name! Are those for me?"

"Let's ask Walter, all right? He'll know for sure."

Lilly ran to the kitchen. "Are the presents for me?" Before Rosalind reached the kitchen, Lilly flew back past her to the brown boxes and yanked the top off one of them.

"I didn't hear him answer, Lilly."

Walt and Martin both came into the living room. Walt nodded.

Lilly yanked a white-embroidered, fuchsia dress from the box and held it up against her small frame. "Pink is my favorite color!" She grabbed another box.

Walt went outside and returned with more packages. Each box had Rosalind's name written across the top. "This is the last of them. It was good to see ya again, Mrs. Easton. I best be goin'. Bye, Martin."

"See you." Martin nodded, then headed back into the kitchen.

Rosalind sat on the edge of the couch, fingering a blue-printed cotton dress Lilly would look lovely in. Trent must have bought these. No one else would have done something so kind and thoughtful. How did he know she needed these?

"Aren't you going to open yours?" Lilly bounced in front of her.

Lilly wrapped her arms around her and contentment nestled on each side of Rosalind, hemming her in. As they sat opening the rest of the presents marked for Lilly, Rosalind made a decision. If Trent didn't come home tonight in time to see her, she'd go to him. She had a lot to tell him, and for once, she was sure the words would come with what she felt flowing from her heart.

The aroma of baked cinnamon apples teased her senses. Martin must have taken the cake out of the oven. Her mouth watered. "Do you smell that?" She held Lilly at arm's length and opened her eyes wide. "What do you think it is?"

"Your cake! Let's have a party! I can get dressed in one of my new dresses."

"Lilly, that sounds wonderful. What do you think about going to see Trent and thanking him for our gifts? I'm sure he would love to have some of our cake and so would the other men."

"Can I wear the pink one?"

"Yes, you may." Rosalind kissed Lilly's nose, then handed her the fuchsia dress. "Run upstairs and get ready. I'll be up in a minute. I'll need to share our plan with Martin."

"Do you think he'll let us go?"

"Don't you worry about that. Now hurry."

Lilly giggled as she climbed the stairs. Rosalind thought to do the same. They *were* going to see Trent.

"Martin," she said as she entered the kitchen. He took a pan of biscuits out of the oven and set it on the counter. "I forgot all about them." She poked one with her finger. It sprang back from her touch. "Did you do anything to these?"

"Just put them in is all. They really do look good, Mrs. Easton."

"Look, they're actually soft." She laughed, putting her hand over her mouth. "Trent needs to see these."

"And your cake." He smiled, his eyes twinkled. "In one of those new dresses he bought for you."

"I haven't even opened all of mine yet." She stared at Martin. He knew about the boxes, so Trent must have told him.

She glanced around the kitchen, excitement filling her. Could she do this? Put herself out there for Trent's attention? She wanted him to notice her. She wanted to be beautiful for him and to bring her husband home.

"Will you take us to where Trent and the men are fixing the fence?"

"Of course. When one of the men comes to let me know they're ready for dinner, we'll all go together."

"Thank you, Martin. I'd better ready myself." She pecked his cheek quickly and giggled like a little girl as she went to the table by the clock and snatched up the unopened boxes with her name scrolled across the lids. Tonight, she'd wear a dress that her husband had picked out and take the cake she knew he'd love and biscuits finally good enough to eat. Tonight would be perfect.

Trent scanned the horizon. Martin should have been here long ago. They still had a lot of work to complete on the fence line and taking longer breaks than necessary wasn't going to send him home any sooner. Trent paced.

Maybe there was a problem. No, Matthew would have ridden back and told him.

He still felt the way his heart dropped when Pete's shot rang through the air almost three weeks ago. His cowhand's warning shot meant business. Trent had to find a way to protect his property. If fencing every inch of his land would stop someone from risking his life to steal cattle, it was worth the cost. He didn't believe in killing, but the other men would have shot the rustler without a second thought. But this raised another issue— keeping Rosalind and Lilly safe. Martin was with them most of the day, and Matthew filled in when Martin couldn't be there. That was the best Trent could offer until he was free to protect them himself.

Trent walked over to Pete, who lounged against a tree while whittling away at a piece of wood with his knife.

"I don't know what's keeping them, boss."

"I'm heading back out to work. Tell Martin when he gets here." He shook his head, took a handkerchief from his back pocket, and wiped the back of his neck. "Never mind."

Pete slid his knife into his belt sheath. "Where we headin'?"

Trent didn't want everyone to get back to work when they needed to eat, needed their strength to finish the job. "You stay here, Pete. I'll check in after a while."

Pete leaned back against the tree and looked over the horizon. "I want you to know I told him to stop. I'd warn anyone who's on the property, but if I ever see someone stealing or if someone puts one of ours in danger, I'll shoot."

"You're a good man, Pete. I trust your judgment as much as any of my men. I only hope this deters others from making a grave mistake." He turned and whistled for his horse.

Trent headed away from the men and toward the work the other cowhands had done earlier in the week. He wanted to make sure the extension of the barbwire and the added rails were located along the property line. In the past, there'd been some discrepancies, but as he made his way down the line, everything looked in place. If he kept going, he'd be home in no time. Home. It never meant more than it did now.

He turned his horse and headed in the opposite direction. As soon as he finished this fence line, he wouldn't need to stay away so much.

If Rosalind didn't calm down, she might swoon. Were those stars flying past her eyes? She fanned herself with her hand. How could she be this anxious? Even wearing the three-piece blue cotton dress Trent had bought her did little to quench the heat. She couldn't think straight. Maybe it was because she wasn't wearing a bustle for the first time in her life.

Lilly climbed into the wagon and slid next to her. The child had beamed since slipping into her fuchsia dress. All Rosalind could do was smile. She couldn't remember being this happy and excited about anything in such a long time.

She took a deep breath, trying to quiet her heart.

Matthew came out from the house and set the last platter of food in the bed of the wagon. "Everything smells wonderful. I know the boys will be very happy to see this spread. Especially the cake." Matthew called to Martin, who came out of the house. "Why don't you make cakes, Martin?"

"Never was taught." The older man climbed into the driver's seat and took the reins. His gun stuck out like a thumb.

Rosalind tried to ignore it but wasn't used to seeing him with his holster on. She moved Lilly to the other side of her, just in case something did happen. Lilly preferred the outside seat anyway.

"Ready?"

Rosalind nodded. "Is it far?"

Martin whipped the reins. "Nope. Not far at all."

They were finally on their way. Rosalind rested in the seat while Lilly sat straight up, back stiff as a plank, gazing over the land. Rosalind took in the view as well. The land was flat as far as an eye could see. This was the land Trent loved and toiled over, but she looked forward to eating together like a family.

Family. Rosalind's cheeks heated thinking about what Lilly asked her earlier. Was she ready to share his bed? Her thoughts cleared quickly when her hand grazed Martin's gun. "I've never seen you with a gun, Martin. Why are you wearing it now?"

Lilly leaned over her to look. Rosalind set her back against the seat, and once again Lilly sat straight up and peered out.

"Trent asked all of us to wear one for protection. To watch out for each other."

Rosalind thought about that for a moment. "When you're with us, does that include Lilly and me?"

Martin glanced at Matthew, whose horse trotted alongside the wagon, then focused on the horse pulling the wagon. Silence spread between them until Martin finally answered. "Matthew and I are to protect you from whomever comes onto the property."

"Oh, I see." Rosalind tugged at her dress sleeve, touched her bonnet and ribbons. Trent told her someone had been stealing longhorns throughout the county, but he never said anything about her or Lilly needing protection. And by the way Martin's shoulders now slumped, she guessed Trent didn't want her to know this bit of information.

"Look at all the horses!" Lilly's voice caught her off guard. "Can I help feed them?"

Martin laughed. "You've been spending too much time with those horses in the barn. But I'm sure the men would love for you to help them serve the cake." He steered the horses to a patch of shade where a few oak trees grew. A dozen or more men rose to their feet.

Rosalind glanced at each one, but Trent wasn't with them. Surely he wasn't far.

Matthew came to help Lilly down, then returned for her. "Ma'am, may I help you down?"

She took another quick look around.

Matthew's hand rose for her. "He's not here," he said. "His

horse is gone."

Rosalind met his gaze. "Where could Trent have gone? Doesn't he normally eat with the others?"

"Always, but we took a bit longer than normal. This land means a great deal to him, so if he had to go without food for a while to get the job done, he'd do without."

She accepted Matthew's help from the wagon, biting her lip as he took her by the waist. In the last few weeks, she'd dreamed of the promise of intimacy with her husband, not only sharing a room, but intimacy of heart and mind. Being truly one.

Her heart fell as her feet touched the hardened ground.

CHAPTER TWENTY-FOUR

Trent hurried home. His wife had come to see him. How often he'd imagined her coming to him and now, when the moment he'd dreamt of finally arrived, he hadn't been there. Maybe she'd still be awake, though the chances were likely nil since they'd left hours ago.

He'd heard about the cake she'd made. All the men said he was lucky, not only for her beauty but for how she cooked. Matthew had come up to him as he was about to mount and unraveled a napkin to reveal one of Rosalind's biscuits. When he took it, he didn't know what to expect, but as he broke off a piece and placed it on his tongue, it melted like butter. Martin mentioned she'd awakened every morning before he arrived to roll out the dough. Trent wished he could tell her how proud of her he was for never giving up—a trait of hers he'd always admired.

Trent dismounted and walked his horse into the barn. A shuffling caught his attention. "Who's here?"

"What time is it?" Blake's groggy voice sailed over a few stalls.

"Time for you to go into the house. I thought you were staying in town until tomorrow?"

Blake came around the stall and helped Trent tend to his horse. "I was, but I needed to warn you. I learned that before Boyd died, he told the doctor there were three men in the field moving his herd."

Trent stilled. "Three?"

"I deputized four men in town to try to find the ones responsible for his death, but the trail came up cold. I have a feeling the men that killed Boyd knew these parts." Blake ran a hand over his jaw. "You need to be careful, Trent. You have prize bulls that bring in the highest bidders. These men aren't doing it for the beef. They're doing it for money."

With his horse tended to, Trent walked from the stall and Blake followed, closing the gate behind them. Trent understood Blake's concern, but they were almost finished with the fencing. "We have a few more days until the fence on the west end will be finished, which will help."

Blake glanced down at his hands before meeting his gaze. "For a while maybe, or they might come in a different direction altogether. You need to protect yourself and your family."

"That's what I'm doing. You should know better than anyone that my men are family and I want to protect them. If adding a new fence line, closing the open range, will do that, regardless of what other ranchers want, then I'll add one. I'm not willing to lose any of my men."

"I understand what you're doing and why, but Rosalind and Lilly are your main concern. I've seen how hard you've worked—all the men have. We know how dedicated you are, but your family comes first." Blake took a deep breath and walked a few steps. "I was married once, and with a new wife came big dreams. But two months after we were married, we were robbed.

I wasn't going to let them take what little money we had, so I fought them in the dead of night in our bedroom. While I fought hand to hand with one, I couldn't see where the other man was. There was a gunshot and then another. I stopped fighting to make sure Abigail was all right. When I turned to look for her, a knife sliced my face and I was hit on the back of the head. I awoke the next morning with a shot in my chest and a dead wife."

Blake's sorrowful gaze bore deep within Trent's heart, silencing him. "Your men can take care of themselves, but your wife and that little girl in there depend on you. Don't let them end up like Abigail." He cleared his throat.

The pain in his friend's eyes, even now after all this time, left Trent lost for something to say. "I had no idea, Blake. I'm sorry."

"We were so young. Abigail was my Rosalind. We grew up together, and when she turned sixteen, we married. I think about her often. I'd hoped Grace could help ease the memories, but it wasn't meant to be. I guess it's for the best. We wouldn't have been together for the right reasons."

Trent placed a hand on Blake's shoulder and bowed his head. "Please God, be with Blake. Heal him and his heart."

Blake nodded and cleared his throat again. "I need to be out here a bit longer. Go see Rosalind. If she's asleep, wake her. Don't let another day go by without showing her that she's loved, because tomorrow might be too late."

"Will you be here in the morning?"

"I will."

Entering the house, Trent took his Stetson off and set it on the table. He pulled out a chair, sat, and prayed, pouring out his heart once again for Boyd's family, for the safety of his men, and for Blake. But when it came time for Rosalind and Lilly, he couldn't speak. A few moments passed, and he laid himself bare before the Lord. "Lord, have I failed my family by not being here for them? I want to provide for them and give them all that I have, but I'm struggling to know what to do. I need to protect what You've given me, but what happens if I fail? Lord, I don't want to fail my men or my family, but most importantly, I don't want to fail with what You have given me. What do I do, Lord? Guide and direct my path. Lead me to do Your will. And please protect my family. Amen."

Trent opened his eyes as the moon shone in through the window. He wished Rosalind was standing there. He'd try to explain his absence and how his heart was troubled with all that was going on. But more than all that, he'd tell her how much he loved her.

Should he do as Blake suggested and wake her?

After Trent washed up, he found himself standing at her bedroom door. Turning the brass handle, he entered, making his way to the bed. Rosalind slept closest to the door with Lilly on her other side. He didn't know how long he stood there watching them as the moon crested his wife's face, but after a while, Lilly stirred. Small whimpers caught him by surprise, and he went to the child and collected her in his arms.

"Papa." Her arms wrapped around his neck.

He swallowed hard and whispered, "No, Lilly, it's Trent." But she didn't let go. Instead, she began to cry. "Shhh." He carried her to the rocking chair in their room and set it in motion. "I'm here, and I won't let you go unless you want me to."

Rosalind stirred and reached across the bed to where Lilly had been. She sat up and looked around. When her gaze found his, she drew the covers to her chest. "How long has she been crying?"

"Not long, but I'll need to change my shirt." He chuckled.

Lilly raised her head. "Is it dirty?"

He smiled at her. "It's clean. I wouldn't hold you with a dirty shirt."

"I don't mind." She snuggled against him, and his heart melted right then and there. He imagined what it would be like to have a child of his own. A child with Rosalind.

Trent didn't remember when he stopped rocking but began the motion once again. He ran his hand down Lilly's hair and continued to rock. "I'm afraid I missed you both today when you came to dinner. If I had known you were coming, nothing could have dragged me away. And what did I hear about this cake of yours, Mrs. Easton? Best thing the men had ever eaten, so I've been told."

Rosalind propped her back against the wall and brought her knees to her chest, still clinging to the blanket. "My mother used to make it. It's called an apple crumb cake."

He couldn't recall it. "Will you make it again sometime?"

"If Lilly will help me. She added the sugar and flour, the best assistant I've ever had."

Lilly yawned and nodded her head.

"I think that means yes."

Rosalind slid her legs down and laid her head against the wall. "Did you finish with the section of fencing you were working on?"

"I did. There's one last section to be done before it's completed. Maybe two, three days at the most. I hope this will deter anyone from stealing. Every inch will be fenced." He inhaled deeply, thinking about Boyd. How was Boyd's wife handling his death? And their daughter? He closed his eyes, pushing back the hurt of losing his friend, and gave in to the rocking motion.

A sweet yawn came from the bed. Rosalind held her palm across her mouth. Maybe he should try to lie the child down so they could sleep. He rose to his feet and walked to the side of the bed, opposite from where his wife sat. After laying Lilly down, Trent tucked the covers and kissed her forehead. Rosalind slid down under her blanket. He strolled over to her and whispered, "I'll see you in the morning."

She looked up at him wide-eyed. "You'll be here? I thought you said two or three days before you'll be finished."

"Do you want me to stay?" He wanted her to say yes, but she only stared up at him. "Or would you rather I go?" Still nothing.

He knelt and took a strand of her hair, rubbing it between his fingers. Without thinking, he brought it to his nose. The smell of rain and sunshine intertwined. Trent held it there for a moment longer. He released it and watched as it fell against the blanket that covered her. He wanted to be the one next to her, feeling her within his arms. "Share your heart. Tell me what you want, Rose."

When she didn't answer, he continued. "Your biscuit melted when I plopped a piece in my mouth. If I stay, will you make them for me in the morning?"

Her brows wrinkled. "You ate one? But how? They were gone."

"Matthew. It was the best biscuit I've ever eaten." He ran a finger along her brow, smoothing it out.

She closed her eyes and mumbled, "If you're here when I awake, then I will."

"I'll be here." He leaned over and kissed her forehead. "Good night." With a deep breath and much determination, he rose and shut the door behind him.

As he headed back to the kitchen for a cup of water, Matthew came in. Blake was close behind, hand resting on the butt of his gun, eyes focused. Matthew moved to the window and peered out from the curtain toward the barn.

Trent studied them intently. "What's happened?"

"We found someone outside the house," Matthew said and gestured toward Blake. "He has him tied up."

Trent's stomach tightened. "Do you know who it is?"

Blake's eyes narrowed. "Never seen him before, but he claims he knows you. Says he's from Boston."

Chapter Twenty-Five

Trent's pulse pounded in his ears as he hurried upstairs and grabbed his holster from his dresser before meeting Matthew and Blake in the kitchen.

Blake stepped in front of the door, blocking his exit. "What happened in Boston?"

Trent narrowed his eyes. "Nothing that concerns you." If he had to push through his friend, he would.

Matthew stood a bit taller and, as if he read Trent's thoughts, moved to stand alongside Blake. "What happened in Boston?"

"Why is that so important right now?" Trent's eyes burned into Matthew.

Matthew tilted his hat up above his brows and studied him a moment. "Before you got home, we received a letter from your father telling us to protect you and Rosalind. We know you're in danger. The question is why?"

Trent didn't care what happened to him. All he cared about was his wife upstairs. He'd do whatever he had to do to keep her safe. He felt for his pistol.

Blake's gaze followed his hand. "Lay your gun down,

Trent." His voice turned stern.

For a second Trent thought about telling them what had taken place while he was away. But they were wasting precious time when he could finally put an end to all this. Abuse would never touch his wife again. He gripped the butt of his gun and met Blake's stare. "What would you do to the man who killed your wife?"

Blake's eyes hardened. "As sheriff, I can't stop you until after you killed the man, but as your friend, I'll stop you from ruining your life and the life of your family."

Trent looked to Matthew, whose eyes flicked back and forth between the two men. He continued to block Trent's way. Both men's gazes moved to something over his shoulder, and Trent turned.

Rosalind slowly descended the stairs and pulled her long robe tight around her. "I know it's late ..." She stopped before the bottom step and tucked her hair behind her ears, a blush tinting her cheeks. "Lilly is asking for you. I can't get her to go back to sleep, and I was hoping..."

She was hoping he'd come. Trent let out a long, calming breath. Blake was right, his family needed him. "Tell her I'm coming, but it will be in a few minutes."

A small smile raised the corners of her mouth. "Thank you for being there for her." She spun and climbed up the stairs.

Trent inhaled another deep breath and turned back to Blake, meeting his gaze. "I'll give you my word. I won't use my gun unless it's needed."

Blake gave a slow nod, and Matthew's stance seemed to relax. Without another word, they left the house and entered the barn, single file, Trent behind the other two. He gasped at the sight of Mr. Standford tied up in a chair against one of the stalls.

"Trenton." Panic registered on his face. "Tell these men who

I am. Tell them I'm Rosalind's father."

Trent could sense Blake's and Matthew's gazes on him, but he didn't take his eyes from Mr. Standford. He didn't trust him. Any man who would allow a woman—his own daughter—to be beaten wasn't worthy of trust. "And because you're a relative, you think I should free you? I'm sorry, Mr. Standford, but you're sadly mistaken."

"Please, Trenton, I've come to make amends with my daughter. What I did was wrong."

"Wrong?" Hot anger trickled into Trent's veins, and he could feel it burning as his next words came. "How could you care so little? How could you let a man abuse her into submission just so he could have his way?" Trent took a few steps back, taking control of his emotions, and ran his fingers through his hair. "How could a father do that to his own *daughter*?"

"I … I had no proof he had been hurting her. She never said a word."

"She stayed with Glover to protect your life. Yours, Sydney's, and the children's."

Roger's gaze fell to the floor. "I should have been the one doing the protecting. When I finally realized who Glover was, it was too late. I tried to set Rosalind free from my promise of marriage, but Glover wouldn't have it." Roger looked up at him. "I was distraught over Sarah's illness, and that's when Glover told me he loved Rosalind and wanted to marry her. That's when I gave my approval. If I had known the type of man he was, I would never have said yes. That's why I had to come. I had to apologize. But now I know I have a lot more to apologize for."

"Where are my father and mother? Weren't you staying with them?"

"I don't know where they are now, but your father is one of the reasons I came. He told me you both would be here at the ranch. I brought you something to prove what I'm saying is true." Rosalind's father leaned to the side and twisted slightly in the chair.

"What is it?" Trent didn't really care to know. Tomorrow morning he'd make sure Blake took him straight to Fort Worth. Straight back to Boston where he belonged.

"It's in my pocket, but as you can see, I'm unable to reach it."

Trent nodded for Matthew to release him. When he was set free, Mr. Standford rubbed his wrists, reached into his pocket, and pulled out from his jacket a white envelope. "I've come to make amends, not only with Rosalind, but with you." With an outstretched hand, Roger gave Trent a letter.

Trent's grasp tightened around it. The letter in which he proposed to Rosalind. "We loved each other. Why wasn't I good enough?"

"Money, greed … I also knew Glover was wealthy and, with your father leaving from the position as bank president to become a rancher, I didn't see how he'd make it. I wanted Rosalind to be cared for. But I also had a gambling problem and needed money to pay off my debts. I thought Glover could provide both. I know it was wrong, and I'm sorry for what I've done. I can't change the past, but I can ask for forgiveness."

"I'm not sure how freely she will forgive, but you'll need to earn mine, and that starts with how you treat Rosalind from this point on. Matthew, get some money, enough for him to stay in Graham. He's not staying here." Matthew nodded and left the barn.

Trent pocketed the letter. "Roger, where's the last letter I sent Rosalind?"

"I have it, but I want to give it to her myself."

Blake held out his hand to help Roger up. "I'll take you to

town and get you settled in, but so you know, I'm the sheriff. I'm also real partial to the Eastons."

"I think we understand ourselves," Roger stated dryly, then glanced at Trent. "May I come back tomorrow?"

"You may visit only in the daytime while you're in town. Don't come at night, or I'll not be responsible for what happens. Now if you'll excuse me, my wife is waiting." Trent stalked out into the yard, wanting to hit something. Instead, he hurried as he entered the house to take off his holster and climb the stairs to their bedroom. Lilly was cuddled within Rosalind's arms, both sound asleep. He knelt by the bed and prayed for his wife, because tomorrow she'd have to face her past head on.

Rosalind stretched her legs. Little knees bumped hers under the covers as Lilly rolled over to face the wall. Streams of light filled the room. Rosalind sat up, rubbed her eyes, and blinked twice. Trent slept in the rocking chair across from the bed, arms crossed against his chest. His head hung to the left. Her fingers itched to run through his tousled hair and straighten each strand.

She let out a sigh. Yesterday hadn't turned out the way she'd expected, but last night, the way Trent cared for Lilly, and seeing him there now …

Rosalind pulled back the covers and tiptoed to the rocker. "Trent," she whispered, taken by her love for him.

"Hmm."

"It's morning."

His head turned to the sound of her voice, eyes still closed. She remembered the time he became sick as a child and there was a possibility he wouldn't live. She'd snuck into his bedroom while she and her mother visited, and seeing sweat on his brow, had taken the washcloth lying there and wiped his face.

Rosalind had stood over Trent while he slept then, but now she did so as his wife. Her heart raced as she touched his hairline. Her fingers inched through his blond hair, remembering its softness passing over her hand that day long before. His head moved, allowing her to wander. Her fingers found their way across his stubble, pricking her fingers. The roughness exhilarated her, as did the man she loved.

He looked up at her, his eyes dark with desire. She'd seen that look before in another man, but it no longer scared her. This time, she welcomed it.

Trent rose from the rocker and drew her to him, lifting her chin. "I'll protect you with my life. Know this. And know how much I love you." His words confused her, but as their lips met and his fingers moved along her neck, she nearly drowned in pleasure.

Tell him. You're safe. Tell him you love him.

Rosalind moaned.

He kissed her chin and then her cheek before pulling her against his chest. "I need to show you something. Will you come with me to my room? Lilly will be all right."

She nodded. From the edge of the bed, he took the robe he'd bought and slipped it on her, then escorted her to his room. Closing the door behind them, he withdrew an envelope from his pocket.

"I received this last night."

She looked at the letter, taking it in her hand. Her breath caught. "Where did you …? I threw it away, but when I went back for it, the letter had disappeared." She scanned the other side and met his gaze. "I don't understand."

He looked away, walked toward his window, and stared out.

She moved to stand beside him and followed his gaze to the

barn.

"Your father. He's here."

Her legs gave way, and Trent caught her elbow and sought the bed for her to sit. Trent knelt in front of her, set the letter aside, and took her hands. "He came here last night looking for you. He wants to apologize. I made it clear he was only to come in the daytime, and I expect he'll be here soon if he isn't already. Blake took him to town."

Trent tried to reassure her, but one question remained unanswered in her mind. Her body began to shake. "Is Glover here too?"

Trent's hand tightened around hers. "Your father came alone."

Tears sprang to her eyes. She pulled her hand away and stood, trying not to think of Glover. But how could she not think of him with her father here? She fought the nausea bubbling in her throat and pressed a palm to her stomach.

Trent stood and settled his arms around her waist, his mouth against her hair. "I'll protect you."

"I want to believe you could, but if Glover came and—"

"I *will* protect you."

Rosalind glanced at the door. Lilly's small voice penetrated her ears. "Lilly's calling me." She left the safety of his presence and opened the door to find Lilly descending the stairs, holding her rabbit by the ear. She went to call to her when she noticed her robe. As if Trent understood, he pointed to her room and headed down the stairs.

Rosalind entered and closed the door. What was she to do? Leave in case Glover found her? Would Glover be waiting in the shadows until the right moment to take her? He told her no one would have her but him. Would he truly come all this way to find her?

She fought against her thoughts, hurrying to right herself before they came back, but as she slipped into one of her new dresses, Lilly came in and slammed the door behind her.

"I couldn't find you." She clung to her waist.

"I was in Trent's room down the hall. Besides,"—Rosalind pushed Lilly's auburn hair from her face—"I'd never leave without telling you first." She knelt, hugging her in return. "I promise."

Lilly smiled and kissed her cheek, then went to the bed and tucked Mr. Sanders under the covers. "I want to wear a new dress." She went to the drawer and yanked out a light-blue cotton dress, holding it in the air. "I don't have buttons on this one."

"Then maybe you can help me with mine."

Lilly slipped hers over her head while Rosalind dressed. She struggled to fix the buttons on the back of her dress but couldn't slip the circular disks through the hole.

A knock sounded at the bedroom door, and Lilly ran to it.

"Lilly!" Rosalind tried to stop her from opening the door, but it was too late.

Trent entered the room, his gaze catching hers.

Rosalind tried to smile but frowned, holding her dress tightly within her hand. What a predicament she was in, unable to dress herself. Yes, they were married, but she stood there like a schoolgirl, heat rising to her cheeks.

"My papa does things for Mama," Lilly said, tugging on Trent's hand, pulling him to where she stood.

His eyes narrowed in on her. "What's the problem?"

Rosalind kept her back turned away from him. "I'm fine. Really. It just takes me a while to get these buttons closed."

Lilly spun, her blue dress swirling at the bottom. "See, I don't have them on this one."

"I *do* see." He shot Rosalind a glance. "I assume Mrs. Easton needs my help?"

She looked down at the floor, desperately wanting to send him away. "Trent, this really isn't—"

"On the contrary, Mrs. Easton, it is." He strolled behind her and tapped her tightened hand, playfully moving it out of the way.

With a deep breath, she released her hold. She bit her lip when his fingers grazed her skin. One, two, three soft tugs and the buttons were closed, but she stood frozen in place as she felt the warmth of his body behind her. He touched the ends of her hair and whispered over her shoulder. "You're a very beautiful woman." When he finished, Trent strolled past her and took Lilly's hand. "Martin has breakfast ready. We'll wait for you at the table."

Lilly skipped out of the room with him.

Rosalind walked to the vanity, taking long breaths in hopes of settling her racing heart. She rested her fingers along her flushed cheeks. He thought she was beautiful and, not only that, he had stayed behind as he said he would while the men fixed the fence. He did it for her.

Rosalind grinned. Her heart was light as she made her way down the stairs. But her joy quickly faded when, on the last step, her gaze collided with her father's.

Chapter Twenty-Six

From the look on Roger's face, Trent knew Rosalind had come down the stairs. Her father straightened his shoulders and took a step forward, nervously twisting his hat every which way. Rosalind's smile faded into a fine line, then her gaze fell on Trent and Lilly in his arms, avoiding her father's altogether. She seemed immune to his very presence. But Trent knew better. He sought to shelter her from this meeting, but there was little he could do now. Maybe he shouldn't have let Roger return. Trent reached for Rosalind and she accepted his hand, entwining her arm with his.

Roger exhaled. "Hello, Rosalind."

She frowned. "Trent told me you were here."

"Is this your papa?" Lilly asked, twirling a strand of hair with her fingers.

Rosalind glanced at her father for a moment. "It is. Lilly, why don't you go see Martin about fixing you a plate."

Trent placed the little girl on her feet. Lilly ran to the kitchen's entrance, stopped and looked back curiously, then continued in.

Rosalind reclaimed Trent's arm, and her nails bit into his skin. "Why did you come?"

Roger studied his hands for a moment. Exhaling, he looked at his daughter. "I came to see you. To apologize."

"Did Glover come with you?"

Her father's eyes widened. "No. Never. I was wrong. I'm so sorry for what I've done."

Trent watched the exchange and sensed what Roger said was true. In a way, Trent felt compassion for the man standing there, begging for forgiveness he didn't deserve. But wasn't that what the Lord had done for him, for Rosalind—given them undeserved grace and mercy? "Roger, we're about to have breakfast. Would you care to join us?"

Rosalind's arm tightened against his, nails biting ever deeper. Trent gritted his teeth.

"Thank you, Trenton. I would."

Rosalind released her hold and turned toward the kitchen. She walked tall, shoulders back, chin slightly elevated. She presented herself as a strong woman, and she was. Stronger than she realized.

All during breakfast, her father kept staring at her as if seeing her for the first time. Rosalind couldn't eat fast enough. She truly loved her father and under different circumstances would have wanted him to be part of her life. But she couldn't get past how he'd hurt her or the fear that Glover might have followed him. So she said little during breakfast and hoped he'd leave when they were finished.

Instead, he asked to stay several weeks. "I know I don't have the right to ask, but I would like to stay." His eyes pleaded with her.

Rosalind glanced away, biting her lip before the pain he caused her came out in words she'd regret.

"Roger, give us time to discuss it," Trent said. "You're more than welcome to come back in the morning about the same time if you wish to find out Rosalind's decision."

Her father nodded in agreement.

Rosalind rose quickly from the table and held out her hand to Lilly. "I could use some fresh air. Why don't you and I go out to the barn while the men continue their conversation?"

Lilly grabbed her hand, and Rosalind's shoulders relaxed as the two of them made their way down the porch steps. She took a deep breath and filled her lungs with warm air, appreciative of the barn smells for the first time.

"Well, lookie who we have here. I do believe it's Miss Lilly." Matthew pulled a red-and-white candy stick from his pocket and held it out, a grin pulling at the corners of his mouth.

"Is that for me?" Lilly's voice raised a notch.

Rosalind smiled and shook her head as Matthew bent down on one knee as if he were about to propose. "Of course it's for you," he said, smiling.

Lilly glanced up at Rosalind. "May I eat it now?"

"You may after we go for a walk. We can look at the horses in the pasture and maybe find some flowers to pick. What do you say?"

"Candy, please." Lilly threw her hand out.

Matthew plopped it in her small palm and chuckled. "Miss Lilly, if we're not careful, you'll have each one of us cowpokes wrapped around that pinky of yours." He tapped her on the nose and winked at Rosalind when he stood.

"Thank you," Rosalind mouthed, glancing down at Lilly, who smelled the stick between her pinched fingers. "Now where can we find a basket to put our flowers in?"

Trent strolled in with a basket held up in the air. "Are you looking for one of these?"

She wanted to ask Trent if her father had left, but with Lilly and Matthew near, she planted her hands on her hips instead and gave a mock frown. "Were you listening at the door? Isn't there anywhere one can find privacy here, where the land stretches as far as the eye can see, without a neighbor in sight?"

"Nope." Matthew chuckled as he climbed the ladder to the hayloft. He reached the top and placed a hand on a bale of hay.

Rosalind felt Trent's hand come around her waist, drawing her back. Trent walked her and Lilly to the side as Matthew tossed bales of hay, one by one, to the ground. Sunlight shone through dust that billowed up from the floor. "Why is he getting so much?"

"We need it for the horses. We refill the bins in the barn so we don't need to climb back up for a few days. Do you want to help me fill them, Lilly?"

The little girl's eyes widened, then watched Matthew descending the stairs. She shook her head. "I don't think I can."

Trent walked over to one of the hay bales. "Do what I do." He reached down and pulled chunks of hay apart from each other, then walked to a metal bin against the wall near the outer door and dropped it in. "That's it. What do you think?"

"We can do that. Can't we, Lilly?" Rosalind nodded and headed to where Trent pulled more hay apart, and as they did the same, hay clung to their clothes. After placing the hay in the bins and in several places in the field, Lilly and Trent took over filling a water trough. For a special treat, he went back to the barn and brought her a red apple. "I know the prettiest place to pick wild-flowers. Would you like to ride out and see them?" He reached into his pocket and pulled out a small knife and began slicing the fruit.

Lilly beamed, trying to wipe the hay off her new dress. She turned to Rosalind. "Please, Rose. Oh, please."

"It seems to me we need some working clothes." And maybe picking flowers was just what she needed to get her mind off her father. "Sounds wonderful. Let's go."

Trent closed his knife and slid it back into his pocket. "You can feed my horse while I get him ready." He handed Lilly the apple slices, then strolled to the stable door and swung it open.

His horse came out, straight toward them. Lilly giggled as the horse took one of the slices of apple from her hand.

Rosalind tilted her head. "We aren't taking the wagon?"

"I thought since Lilly likes to ride, we could all go together."

She looked at his horse. "And how will we fit?"

"I'll show you." He grabbed a pad off a hanging board and placed it on the horse. "Mother stopped using a side-saddle a year ago. You have no other choice. Ready?"

"I really don't know how I'm going to ride with this dress on." Rosalind tugged on her beige dress, touching the navy blue lines.

Trent patted the horse's back as if waiting for her to come to him, but she stood like a stone. How could she possibly ride? He pointed a firm finger at her and crooked it for her to come. He lifted his Stetson from his raised brow, showing a smirk on the side of his mouth, a dimple pressing in. She didn't know what he had in mind, but that look he gave made her heart gallop.

"Now, Mrs. Easton, would you care for me to lift you, or would you like to try to get on the horse yourself?"

She swallowed hard. "I … ah … I've never been on a horse." Trent already knew this. Still, she felt the need to warn him.

"There's nothing to be scared of. I'll never let you go."

She couldn't help being drawn to him, loving him, even now

as one look from those blue eyes pierced her. She never wanted him to let her go. Yet her father's arrival had stirred up old fears of abandonment, deceit, and lies, no matter how much Trent's words resounded within her heart.

Trent lifted her up and slid her on top of the horse. "Now one leg goes on this side and one on the other." He laughed. "You should see your face. Mouth wide open. Cheeks as flushed as that apple."

"My ankles … my legs … it's not proper."

Lilly wiped her hands on her dress, then reached for Trent. He scooped her in his arms and kissed her cheek. "I'm not sure we are going to be able to ride. Rose doesn't seem to know how to sit with a dress on."

Lilly's smile faded, and her head rested against Trent's chin. Rosalind swallowed her pride. She could do this. Gliding one of her thighs to the other side of the horse, her dress tightened, and her leg wouldn't budge any farther. She looked toward Trent as he came and placed Lilly against her chest, hiking her dress up even more. The warm air in the barn not only kissed her ankles but her legs. Trent's hand grazed her bare skin before he climbed onto the horse behind her. He yanked and pulled on her dress, tucking it in different directions.

Trent whispered close to her ear, "When we ride, hold on to Lilly, and I'll hold on to you. Now relax and let your body fall against my chest." His arm came around her stomach. "Relax." He moved them toward the end of the barn.

The rhythm of the horse soothed her, and her body released the pent-up tension. She felt secure. She never wanted to leave, except when the horse turned out of the gate.

Trent heard Rosalind's gasp as his horse trotted toward the open field. Did she think he was moving too fast? But he didn't mind in the slightest. Rosalind fit perfectly into the curve of his chest, his arm around her waist.

He leaned around Rosalind. "Lilly, are you having fun?"

"Yes, sir!"

Trent laughed, thinking about the first time he saw Lilly clinging to Rosalind. He recalled how concerned he was that she would complicate things with his new wife, but regardless of his initial thoughts, Lilly had nestled within his heart after only a few days. Trent prayed that her mother and father would return to her, but if for some reason God saw fit for him and Rosalind to stand in their place, he'd be honored. Gratitude for what God had given him surged through his heart. He'd love his family with his last breath.

Trent looked across the cloudless sky. They weren't far from the house, but a good distance for Rosalind to get used to being on a horse. He pointed to the east. "Look, Lilly. There they are. Sunflowers."

Lilly clapped her hands. "Those are the flowers on the table."

"They are." Trent rode a short distance away, stopped the horse, slid off, then helped Lilly and Rosalind down. Lilly ran to the patches of tall flowers while Rosalind followed close behind.

Trent strode to them, remembering the basket still sat on the ground in the barn. "Lilly, I forgot the basket. Do you think you could carry a few with your hands?"

"Yes, sir." She grabbed a stem and pulled. Yellow pollen from the flower dusted her hands. She glanced down and raised them in the air, lips puckered. "I got yellow on me. I can't pull them out."

"Point to the ones you want, and I'll cut them for you."

Lilly showed him several, and he cut at the bottom of the stems. Rosalind tried to brush the pollen off Lilly's hands, but only managed to collect the powder on her own. "Would you like my help?" He set the flowers on the ground, took Lilly's hands, and wiped them on his pants leg, leaving a yellow streak behind. Bending, he collected the flowers and handed them back to Lilly. Her face brightened as she touched the green leaves.

Trent turned to Rosalind and held out his hand. "Your turn."

"But you'll be a mess. Just look at your pants."

He took her hand within his and brought it to his chest, wiping the yellow dusting from her fingers and palms. But he didn't let go when he'd finished. "There was another reason I wanted to bring you here. I thought we could talk about your father while Lilly keeps busy with the flowers."

Rosalind pulled her hand slowly away. "I guess you're right, although I'd rather avoid the conversation altogether."

"I know."

Rosalind knelt next to Lilly, who sat on the ground admiring her flowers. "Trent and I are going to walk over there and back." She pointed to another patch of sunflowers that were a shade lighter.

Lilly met her gaze and smiled, then started counting the petals.

Rosalind rose and they strolled alongside each other. "How long do you think my father will stay?"

"I'm not sure, but he did say a few weeks … only if you want him to, of course."

"I don't know." Rosalind met Trent's gaze, pain casting shadows in her eyes. "He kept us apart."

"We're together now." He tried to reassure her, but her brows only deepened on her forehead. He was tempted to massage the tension away with his fingers but decided against it when she stopped walking.

"Not as we might have been. He put us through so much."

Trent couldn't begin to understand the pain she had endured and the memories she still faced, brought back with her father's presence. But her heavenly Father did. Trent prayed silently for wisdom. "We might not be together the way we hoped for in the past. We've both been through different types of hardships and pain, no fault of our own, but that didn't stop God's plan for our lives. He brought us together, Rosalind. This is God's plan. But God's plan also includes forgiveness."

Her gaze held fast, keeping him motionless. What was she thinking?

Rosalind turned away and walked back toward Lilly, who waved a sunflower in the air. Trent followed.

Rosalind bent, collected the flowers off the ground, and stood. "Ready to head back?"

Lilly smiled at them and got up, reaching for Trent. He lifted the child onto the horse, but before he could help Rosalind mount, she touched his arm. The flowers she held in her other hand were trembling.

"My father can stay."

"Fort Worth Station!" the conductor bellowed upon entering the car, then exited to the next.

A few minutes later, the pungent air of animal flesh and manure seized Glover's breath as he stepped from the train. A smirk lifted his lips. *I knew you would come through for me, Roger. It was only a matter of time.*

CHAPTER TWENTY-SEVEN

"How many more days until the fence lines are finished?" Trent asked Matthew as he milked, his head resting against their family cow. Trent hadn't realized how bad he had it for Rosalind when he named this cow Rose. Hopefully Rosalind would never find out. He smiled just thinking about her and the way her hair had shone in the moonlight the night before. He stood and poured his pail of milk into a large bucket.

"A day or two. I'll help finish one of the sections while Blake takes the other to make sure it's done right." Matthew raised his head from the cow, and the ring of milk against metal was quelled. Horse hooves scuffled against the ground, then came to a stop. "Do you think that's her father coming up?"

"I don't think so. It's too early. It's probably Walt. He has an order for me that hasn't come in yet. Besides, Rosalind and Lilly won't be up for a while. They slept restlessly all night."

"How have you managed, sleeping in that rockin' chair?"

Trent shot him a look. There were some things you didn't discuss, and he and his wife's sleeping arrangements was one of them. But everyone knew. "I'll do whatever I have to."

"Didn't mean to pry."

Trent nodded.

Matthew rose and poured his milk into the larger bucket. "I'm heading inside, but before I do, I haven't had a chance to tell you how happy I am for you and Rosalind." He grabbed his hat from the nail.

"I appreciate it, Matthew. Oh, make sure you leave me some coffee."

Matthew chuckled as he left for the house.

Trent finished milking the last cow and breathed deeply the smell of hay and manure. It wasn't that he minded milking. Still, he'd take Blake's place mending fences any day. But Trent needed to be close to home.

Rosalind's strained voice carried to him as he reached the front porch steps. He hurried into the house. Tears streamed down his wife's face and she waved a piece of paper in her hand. Her father stood on the other side of the living room by the stone fireplace, looking rather sorrowful. Matthew looked on from the corner of the kitchen.

Rosalind's voice broke as she read.

Dear Rose,

I hope you don't mind me calling you Rose. It's just, when I think of you, I think of roses. The softness of your skin, your beauty, and the way you ...

I hope you are well. I'm as well as I can be with such a distance between us. I'm looking out across my land and hope you will be able to see it for yourself soon. Would you be happy here? I pray you will.

I'm writing this letter while I wait for a few men to help me build the barn. We plan to build two, one for horses and the other for milking cows. I've never built a barn, but I love working with my hands. It has given me a sense of worth like I've never had before.

It's been two months since your last correspondence. I hope I wasn't too bold, asking for your hand in marriage in a letter. But I needed you to know my intentions and my plans for us. Please write soon.

Yours affectionately,
Trenton

"Answer me. How could you?" Rosalind hollered. "How could you keep this letter from me? Didn't you understand how much I loved Trent? Couldn't you see that? Yet you gave *me*—your *daughter*—away for money." Rosalind wiped her face with the back of her hand. "You tried to take everything away from me, but God wouldn't let you."

Roger stood ghostly white and still as a statue. "I'm so sorry, Rosalind. I can never take back what I've done. I can only apologize." He finally took several steps toward her, wiping away his own tears.

Rosalind held up her hand, letter gripped in her palm. "Don't." She spun toward the door, avoiding Trent's gaze as she rushed past him.

Trent looked at Roger, who stared at the ground. "I think it would be best if you left. Give her a few days. I need to go to her. You know your way out." He followed his wife into the yard. She stopped at the fence by the barn, where the horses fed on the hay Matthew had scattered earlier. Trent collected her in his arms.

"I'm tired of being strong … holding myself together. I can't do it anymore. I'm so weak." She cried. "I just can't. I'm tired of trying to survive."

"You don't need to survive any longer. You need to rest in the knowledge God will be the strength you need. Lean on Him, Rosalind. *Trust* Him."

After Rosalind's breathing settled and she wiped her tears for a final time, she turned her head against Trent's chest. "It's so beautiful here."

He wondered what she'd seen. The gray sky held a haze. Was this really beautiful to her? There were no flowers or trees, but what he planted. Only wide-open spaces and fenced-in cows and horses. Animal smells lingered in the air, and the chores never ended. "I meant what I said in my letter. I hope you will love it here. But I know—"

"I already do."

She said it so matter-of-factly, he couldn't question her words. She meant them. Trent kissed the top of her head.

Rosalind lifted her face and pointed. "Why is the brown horse pushing the black horse with its nose?"

"The brown horse is the leader. He decides who will eat with him, if anyone. I guess you can say there is an order of dominance with each pack of horses. After the brown horse eats, then the others will follow suit in that order."

"Seems a bit mean, doesn't it? Pushing others around to get what you want." She moved from his arms.

"I told your father to return in a few of days."

"Why do you keep insisting he return?" Rosalind folded her arms across her chest. "He belongs in Boston."

Trent recaptured the steps she took and tucked a few strands of hair behind her ear. He felt her body relax. "All right. If that's what you truly want, then I'll send word to him at the boarding-house."

Horse hooves sounded in the distance. It seemed Pete was riding in and their conversation was to be shortened.

Rosalind turned and shielded her eyes.

Trent hurt for his wife and the pain she continued to endure at her father's hand, and no matter how much he didn't want to forgive her father, he knew his heavenly Father asked it of him and Rosalind as well.

Pete halted his horse and crossed his arms on the horn of the saddle. "Hello, Mrs. Easton."

She gave him a genuine smile. "Hello, Pete. It's good to see you again."

"Thank you, ma'am." He nodded then turned to Trent. "The fence is almost completed. We need ya to tell us the size of the gate you wanna put in."

Trent placed his hand on Rosalind's lower back. "Care to go for a ride?"

"What about Lilly? Should we leave her?"

"She's still sleeping. Matthew can stay until we get back."

"I'll ask him while you get the horse saddled." Rosalind skirted the fence and headed toward the house.

Trent watched her leave. He couldn't pull his attention back to Pete, who waited on him. She was hurting. Was he only making it worse?

Trent finally turned his gaze to Pete and found him smiling. "What?"

Pete cleared his throat. "Oh, nothing, boss."

"Go tell Blake I'm on my way."

His cowhand's smile widened. "Yes, sir!" He hurried off.

Trent entered the barn and yanked the stall door open, calling his horse. After putting the bridle in place, he hoisted the pad and saddle on just as Rosalind appeared at the barn entrance, tying her bonnet under her chin. He walked the horse out, stopping before her.

"Lilly's still asleep."

"Good." He helped her place her foot in the stirrup, then up. Trent climbed behind her and slid an arm around her waist, grasping the reins in the other hand. "I'll take us along the fence line while I'm at it, if you don't mind."

Rosalind looked back at him at an angle, her soft cheek against his lips. "Not at all. Please tend to whatever it is you need to do."

His lips pressed along her cheek. She leaned back into him completely, holding her face to his. Could he love this woman any more?

They rode some distance before the start of the fence line. Rosalind pointed to an area of hardwoods where a few longhorns rested in the shade while others bathed in a small pond. The water had obviously receded even more, but there was still enough for them to wade in. "I hope it rains soon. We can really use the water."

Her back stiffened. "Will it storm like before?"

He remembered how she paced until late into the night the last time it stormed. "Chances are higher in the spring and fall, but you're safe in the house." He pulled her back to him, sensing her body relax yet again at his touch.

"You and your men did some fine work on the fence."

His heart quickened at his wife's praise. "Thank you." He studied the work as he rode, making sure the distances between the wood planks were spread evenly, nailed to the inside, and two strands of barbwire were attached. This was a costly endeavor, but well worth it.

They neared a clearing, just past a hedge of trees, where Blake waited, arms across his chest, feet spread apart.

"Sheriff." Trent tipped his hat.

Blake shot him a smirk, then flashed Rosalind a smile. "Good morning."

"How are you, Blake? Is the fence completed?"

"Doin' fine, ma'am. But we need Trent for one final detail before we're finished."

Pete strolled over to them. "Boss, do you think you could set the lines for how wide you want that gate?"

Trent hopped down from his horse and grabbed Rosalind's waist, setting her down on her feet. He met her gray eyes and momentarily found himself lost.

"The men are waiting," she whispered, peering over his shoulder.

"So they are." He lifted her palm and kissed the back of her hand. "I won't be long."

From under the shade of a tree, Rosalind watched in fascination as six men measured, stuck posts together, and dug holes for the gate. They worked together like a well-oiled machine, their shirts soaked through with sweat. Her dress hadn't fared much better with the heat of the afternoon bearing down. Sweat trickled along her spine, and she wiped the moisture from her brow, then untied her bonnet and fanned herself.

Rosalind wondered how Lilly was managing since they'd been gone most of the morning and afternoon while Trent completed the fence. She hadn't meant to stay so long, but she had no idea Trent planned to work. She had the feeling he'd forgotten she was there, until he turned and shot her a grin. She returned his smile, and her cheeks warmed even more. Could a man be any more handsome?

Blake and Pete walked toward Trent. Pete's hands motioned as he spoke, then Blake nodded and the three men turned. Trent pointed to the west and, after a round of brow wiping, Blake and

Pete headed to the other men, who were stacking supplies onto the back of a wagon.

Trent tugged at his shirt as he approached her. "The men are heading back to the house. I prefer you to go with them. I need to finish riding down the fence line."

"Oh." She wanted to go with him and didn't care how sweat clung to him. She felt safe in his presence and had almost forgotten her argument earlier with her father or the thoughts of Glover. Almost. She scurried to her feet but said nothing. "I'll go with them."

Later, as the evening settled through the curtains in her room, Rosalind rocked in her chair, fighting the fears racing through her mind and heart. She tried to keep them at bay, but they seeped in. And when she closed her eyes, Glover was there, forcing her into submission. Hurting her. She couldn't escape him.

A creak sounded in the hallway, and she stared at the door. Fear pricked her skin and pressed against her chest. *Glover? No!* She shook her head and bit her lip. It was Trent, she was sure of it. A door closed down the hall.

He wasn't coming to her tonight? She closed her eyes, knowing she needed to be strong. Yes, strong. It was the only way to survive. But Trent's words replayed through her mind. *You need to rest in the knowledge God will be the strength you need.*

"Rosalind."

She opened her eyes to see Trent's form in the doorway of the darkened room, a border of light traced around him. "You came."

"Why wouldn't I?" he said. She rose slowly from the rocking chair, tucking her hair behind her ear. "I thought you'd be asleep. Come, I'll help you in bed."

She didn't move. Couldn't move when all she wanted was him. "Hold me." Her words came as weak as she felt. "Never let me go."

He wrapped his arms around her and gently kissed her forehead. "Never."

Rosalind breathed in the scent of bar soap mixed with the scent of musk. The combination was all man, all her husband. "Trent," she whispered.

He kissed her temple and ran his fingers through the strands of her hair. "Is everything all right?"

She bit back her moan. How could she answer? Instead, she led him by the hand into his room. *Their* room. She stopped at the bed. "I … I need you. To hold me. To love me."

Trent cupped her cheek and kissed her so softly, so completely, she trembled. He pulled back the cover and helped her ready for bed, then slid in after her. The warmth from his body engulfed her, and tears filled her eyes. For the first time in her life, she felt truly safe. Safe within his arms, claimed by his touch, and made complete by her husband's love.

Chapter Twenty-Eight

Trent rode into Graham with one thing in mind—his wife and how he needed to speak with Blake about Rosalind's father. Several wagons were hitched in front of the general store as Mrs. Vines swept the front of the doorway. Trent tipped his hat to her as he passed on the way to the sheriff's office. "Good day, Mrs. Vines."

"Good day, Trent." She waved.

He entered the sheriff's office, surprised to find Roger speaking with Blake. Roger's gaze flicked to him, then back at Blake.

Trent stood by the door, arms crossed. "Why are you here?" He wasn't going anywhere without answers.

"I … um … I wanted to know if Blake thought I should go back to see Rosalind today. Or if I should wait a bit longer." Something mingled within the older man's features. Fear, hurt, whatever it was caused Trent to relax his stance.

Blake stood from his office chair. "I think you should. Rosalind needs to know you're a man of your word."

Though Trent didn't want Rosalind to be hurt by her father

again, forgiveness was the only way both of them would heal. "I agree. But if you plan to hurt her in any way, I suggest you leave on the next train."

Roger secured his hat on his head with two hands. "I don't. Never again. I will make it up to her, to you." He started for the door.

"Mr. Standford," Blake called to him. "God will work it out."

The older man nodded, then left, closing the door behind him.

"I guess you can expect him today." Blake rounded the desk. "So what brings you here?"

"I wanted to know if Roger was still in town. I guess I have my answer."

Blake snatched a note from the top of the desk. "They sent this telegram for you. I haven't read it. It's from your father. I was about to head to the ranch."

Trent's pulse quickened. He unfolded the telegram and began to read.

Richards Williams Jones are missing Stop Be careful Stop T.E.

Trent strolled to the window and stared out absentmindedly. His father was warning him. The first name on the telegram was Glover Richards, but who were the others? His father said they were missing.

In his gut, he knew the answer.

The telegram Trent hid in his back pocket burned a hole in his heart. No matter how hard he tried, he was unsuccessful at pushing back thoughts of Glover and the questions plaguing him. Had Glover already arrived? How would he tell Rosalind what he knew?

And what *did* he know, he asked himself, as he lifted an old quilt from a trunk next to his bed and took it outside for Rosalind and Lilly's picnic. He spread it on the ground, wanting to make their first picnic special. Martin came out with chicken stew and cornbread. Lilly followed with bowls and spoons, while Rosalind carried a pitcher of water and mugs. "I think we're all set."

Lilly plopped down on the red-and-white fabric and folded her legs beneath her blue cotton pinafore dress.

Rosalind touched his arm. "Sit so I can serve you."

Trent pressed a kiss to her cheek. "No. I'll serve." He led her next to Lilly and observed how Rosalind smiled as she sank to the old quilt. He decided then that there was no reason to concern her until he found out more about his father's telegram. With the decision made, he took the bowls Martin had scooped stew into and passed them out. When everyone had been served, he sat next to his wife.

Lilly took a bite of the cornbread Martin handed her and rewarded him with a grin. He patted her head like a grandfather would do, surprising Trent again by the changes he was witnessing in his cook. "Can we ride today?" she asked, her mouth full.

Trent chuckled at how excited the little girl was to ride. Maybe this was the distraction he needed. "I don't see why not, but maybe we should say grace first."

Lilly placed her bread in her bowl, lowered her head, and folded her small fingers together.

Trent collected Rosalind's hand and prayed. "God, thank

You for this food and our family. Help us to grow closer to You every day. Amen." He opened his eyes, wondering what Lilly thought about him including her in his prayer as part of their family. Did she even notice? He'd take her for that horse ride and talk with her about it. "Lilly, would you like to go for that ride after we eat?"

She smiled, bread showing between her teeth. Picking up her bowl, she swallowed her bread and shoveled stew into her mouth.

Rosalind touched her hand. "Slow down. You'll get a stomachache eating too fast."

"Yes, ma'am."

Trent set his bowl and spoon down. "I wanted to talk to you both about something."

Rosalind's gaze met his.

"I'll be taking the longhorns to market soon, and I wondered if you both would like to go with me. I know it will be a bit of hard traveling, but we could stay in town for a few days before returning home. I'm taking the herd a little later this year, but we'll get them there with plenty of time. What do you think?" He had already been thinking of asking if they wanted to travel with him, but now, with the telegram, he couldn't leave them. "I don't want to leave my girls behind."

Rosalind gave him a warm smile and then turned her gaze. "Lilly, what do you think? Want to go on another adventure?"

"I like adventures as long as Mr. Sanders can come with me."

Trent smiled. She sure loved that stuffed rabbit. "Mr. Sanders is always welcome."

"Then it looks like we're going." Rosalind patted her mouth with her napkin.

The breeze tossed a few strands of hair across her chin. He

gently pushed them behind her ear. "I don't know if I told you, but you're a beautiful sight." She blushed, and he had a mind to carry her back upstairs—until Lilly popped up from the quilt, breaking into his thoughts.

"I'll put my bowl in the kitchen." Lilly ran into the house.

"She's excited, to say the least." Rosalind leaned over and collected her bowl, setting his on top. "You're amazing with her."

"She's a wonderful child. And one day you will be an incredible mother." He picked up the tray of cornbread and leftover stew and followed his wife into the kitchen.

Lilly took a piece of candy from Martin and stuffed it in her mouth.

"I saw that." Trent chuckled, placing the food on the counter. "Lilly, are you ready?"

"Wes, swer." Her candy peeked from the corner of her mouth.

"Well, come on then. We've got a horse to ride." Lilly skipped through the house, and he gave a mock bow at the front door. "After you."

"You silly." She laughed, hopping down the steps.

Rosalind came and stood beside him at the door. "I've wondered how her parents are. It still worries me they haven't sent word."

"Remember, letters get lost out here. It took us a year to receive the letter about your mother." He turned. "You're more than welcome to ride with us."

"I think I'll stay here. I haven't made those biscuits I promised you the other day. I plan to fulfill my vow, and every other one I make to you in the future." She winked.

"I look forward to those biscuits even more." He lifted her chin with his finger. "Miss me while I'm gone."

"It would be hard not to."

Trent slowly caressed her lips with his, taking in her breath. "We won't be long."

"Take as long as you need. I'm not going anywhere."

"Promise me."

"I promise."

He took a step back and closed his eyes, inhaling a deep breath. She meant everything to him. *God, keep her safe.*

"Are you all right?" Rosalind was inches from his face.

What was he to say? *I love you more than life itself, and you might be in danger?* "I'm fine." He kissed her lips once again, then jumped from the porch to the ground.

Trent walked to the barn. "Lilly? Where are you, sweetie?" Trent glanced into a few stalls. "Lilly?"

"Here I am." She hopped out from the corner of one of the doors that led to where the horses grazed.

"What were you doing?"

"Feeding the horses."

Trent glanced in the direction she came from. "What do you mean, feeding the horses?"

"I found this big bag with food two days ago. They're hungry, but your horse isn't sharing. He pushed the others away, and he's been eating it all by himself."

Trent hurried outside where his horse seemed to be eating. He opened the gate and moved him out of the way to check the ground. He found manure and scattered pellets of food within the dirt and grass. Surely his horse hadn't eaten that much. To make certain the horse didn't eat any more, Trent brought him out toward the barn and saddled him, explaining to Lilly the dangers of overfeeding a horse.

Riding out a ways from the house, he looked down at her. Her back was straight, and she bounced with each trot of the horse. "What do you think, Lilly? Having fun?"

"I love horses. I wish, when I was on the train, Papa could have brought his so we could ride. Mr. Sanders doesn't like it when I leave him behind, so Papa's horse must feel the same way when Papa's gone."

"Do you feel the same way with your mama and papa away?"

Her head rose and fell several times. "I miss Mama and Papa. Do you know when they're coming back?"

Trent slowed the horse to a stop and got down, holding the reins. She gazed down at him. "Lilly, I don't know when your parents will be back." *God give me the words.* "But I want to ask you something. Is it okay if Rose and I love and take care of you until they do? As part of our family."

Her brow furrowed. "Can I still be part of Mama and Papa's family too?"

"Yes. You will always be their little girl."

Her face shone then. "You want to love me too?"

Trent smiled. "Yes, because I already do." He reached for her, and she came into his arms. He'd already lost his heart to her weeks ago. "Come on. Let's walk the rest of the way to the flower patch and pick flowers for Rose. I'll let you hold the reins. What do you say?"

Her small hand held out Mr. Sanders for Trent in exchange for the reins. "Rose loves flowers just like me."

Rosalind tossed the biscuit ingredients together and began mixing them with her hands. She wanted these to be perfect for her husband.

Trent. When they said goodbye at the door, he seemed

troubled. Should she ask him why or wait for him to come to her? Everything about their marriage was new, but a desire to pray rose within her. Had God even heard her prayers for Lilly's parents? Would He hear her prayers on other things that mattered to her?

A battle raged within her mind, but she closed her eyes against her thoughts and prayed. "Lord, help me to believe You hear my prayers. Give me faith to know You'll answer them. Help Trent with whatever is on his mind. Protect us. Please give us peace."

"Hello." Her father's voice floated to her ears.

Her eyes flung open as he entered the kitchen, hat in hand, and halted just inside the doorway.

"No one answered. I hope you don't mind."

She struck the dough with her fist. "I'm surprised you came back. I thought you would have returned to Boston."

"I couldn't leave, Rosalind. I thought about it, but I'm tired of hurting you."

"Tired? You have no idea what tired is." She slapped the dough on a pan and began rolling it out. The mixture stuck on the roller. She went to the cabinet, took some flour, and tossed it on the surface, some falling at her feet. She inhaled a long breath to calm herself.

"What would you do, Rosalind, if you were left with a child and no money to feed her?"

Immediately, Lilly came to mind. "I wouldn't sell or use her, if that's what you're asking me."

"No, you wouldn't, and neither would I … until it happened. I didn't mean for it to happen. I owed too much and I was afraid. I made a deal with the devil and lost. I sold my soul and lost you in the process. I was so wrapped up … I couldn't get out."

"Are you out now?"

"Yes. With Thomas's help, I'm free financially *and* spiritually. I've sinned against you, Rosalind, and I'm sorry. I hope one day you'll forgive me."

Rosalind looked at the roller enclosed within her palms. When had she stopped working and begun listening? Her father wanted her forgiveness and, deep down, she wanted the same. But there was just too much pain. Too much to forgive.

"Rosalind," he whispered.

"Yes, Papa." She swallowed hard. She couldn't remember the last time she called him by that name of endearment. Her heart sank as she met his gaze. "I never stopped being your daughter, and I never will." She went back to rolling the dough, then cut out circles.

Her father moved beside her and placed each round dough circle onto the tray, then slid the tray into the stove.

She stared after him.

Trent entered the back door to the kitchen, carrying Lilly against his chest. Tears streamed down her reddened cheeks. In between sniffles, Lilly cried out to Rosalind, "I killed him!"

CHAPTER TWENTY-NINE

Rosalind hugged Lilly tightly, then wiped the tears from her cheek. "Whatever it is… it can't be as bad as you say?" She mouthed to Trent, "Killed who?"

Trent moved Lilly's hair from her face so he could see her clearly. *Please, Lord, let the words I say be true.* "My horse will be fine. He has a stomachache. No need to worry."

"But Papa said horses can't have stomachaches or they'd die. I don't want him to die." She hiccupped. "I miss my mama." Lilly buried her face in Rosalind's shoulder.

Rosalind rubbed invisible circles along her small back. "I know you do, sweetheart. I know you do." Now Rosalind's eyes filled with unshed tears.

Roger slipped out the back door, and Lilly sniffled. "I want to go home."

Rosalind looked toward him, worry crossing her beautiful face. How Trent wished Lilly could go home to her mother and father, but it was impossible. He held out a chair and motioned for them to sit. When they did, Trent knelt and covered Rosalind's hand on Lilly's back. "We love you, Lilly."

A tear finally trailed down Rosalind's cheek. "I could never take your mama's place, but we love you, and we hope you'll think of this as your home too."

Lilly hiccupped again, lifting her face. "You mean it? Even if I killed your horse?" Her voice quivered.

Trent wanted to hold the child and reassure her. How quickly he'd begun to think of the three of them as a family. "Yes, Lilly. There is nothing you can do to take away our love."

"I like it here and so does Mr. Sanders."

"Good." Trent smiled and wiped a fallen tear. "How about if Rose takes you to your room, and you fix it however you'd like. It will be your very own room. If you wish to move any furniture around, ask Matthew to help. He'll be back soon." Trent exchanged a look with Rosalind and felt her approval. "You know, we leave for Fort Worth in two weeks, and after we sell our cattle, we'll buy something special for your room. What do you say?"

She cocked her head as if in thought and played with a wisp of Rosalind's hair that hung loose from her ribbon. "Rose, where will you sleep?"

"She's staying with me." Trent answered a little too quickly, but now that his wife shared his bed, he wasn't willing to let her go. "Like your mama and papa sleep together."

Lilly nodded, took Rosalind by the hand, and got down from her lap. Sending him a backward smile, Lilly led the charge up the stairs.

Trent removed his hat and plunged his fingers through his hair. The child was better, but he couldn't say the same for his best stallion. *Colic.* He'd do whatever it took to keep his horse alive, for his and Lilly's sake. He headed outside and rounded the corner to find Roger sitting on a bucket in front of the barn.

"I see how much you care for that child in there." He nodded toward the house. "You know, she reminds me of Rosalind at that age."

Trent had never thought about it before, but Roger was right. It wasn't that Lilly and Rosalind looked alike, but there *was* something similar between them. Maybe it was the way Rosalind loved with her entire heart or how she cared for others before herself. She trusted him to make things right, and so did Lilly. He'd do all he could not to let them down. "I can't let anything happen to my horse."

"How may I help?" Roger stood.

"Stay on for a few days. You're more than welcome to stay in the house, but we'll be up late tonight."

A wagon rolled into the yard, carrying Matthew and Martin. They laughed as it came to a halt. Matthew hopped down and fixed his Stetson. "Trent, you should've seen Pete. He ..." His eyes narrowed.

From the wagon, Martin looked at him, then glanced at the house. "The girls. They all right?"

Trent had never been more thankful for Martin than at this moment. Since the girls came to live at the ranch, Martin had been a different man. Caring, Trent would say, even protective. "They are. Matthew, would you mind checking on them in a bit to see if they need anything, like a piece of furniture moved?"

Matthew quirked a questioning brow and pointed to Roger. "Everything fine out here?"

"Well, not sure. Lilly overfed Midnight. She said she's done this for a couple of days now. While we were riding, he stomped his hooves a few times, but on the way back, he seemed agitated."

"Colic?"

"I think so, and Lilly is quite upset."

Martin shook his head. "I'll fix somethin' special for Miss

Lilly.”

Matthew patted Martin on the back, smiling. “You're fixin' dessert? I think I like this softer side.”

“Get your hand off me.” Martin barked. His face suddenly went ruddy. “You bes' check on those ladies to see if they need help. I've got work to do.” He marched off.

Trent chuckled, but when he and Roger entered the barn, a knot grew in the pit of his stomach.

Just after dawn the next day, Rosalind drew the curtains back and watched Trent pull the horse's reins, forcing the stallion to walk beside him, hoping the stomach condition would pass. It had been hours. Hours of praying the horse would live. Hours in her father's presence. At first, she wasn't happy that Trent invited him to stay, but she'd seen the reasoning behind his decision. Blake hadn't returned since he'd left for town, and with Matthew and the other cowhands getting ready to take the herd to market, Trent needed another man. And she needed her father.

Rosalind slipped into a dress and headed downstairs, where the smell of fried ham wafted in the air. She followed it into the kitchen. “Good morning, Martin. How long has Trent been out there?”

He turned from the stove as she approached, his face grim. “Good mornin', ma'am. Your father just left to relieve him.” He tossed two biscuits on a plate. “They've been workin' 'round the clock watchin' the horse, walking 'im every hour, giving mineral oil treatments, and constantly checking his heart and breathing rates. Even gums.”

Martin seemed to avoid making eye contact, his lips pressed into a fine line. She glanced around the kitchen. Did her father say something to hurt or offend him? She'd only known Martin for a short time, but somehow the thought didn't seem possible. Martin was made of a harder quality— steel perhaps—but behind that exterior, he had a caring and loving heart she believed not many had known.

She reached out and touched his arm. "Is something bothering you, Martin? You appear to be … I don't know."

He met her gaze then. "It's not my place, ma'am."

What wasn't his place? Her hand fell. "Please, share whatever it is you have to say." She clasped her hands together, readying herself.

"It's your pa—"

"My father?" Her heart raced. Hadn't she been up most of the night due to her thoughts of her father and God's prompting her to forgive him? "What has he done?"

"He told me about Boston. The pain he caused you."

"Oh, I see." She glanced at the floor and took a deep breath, but before she could say another word, Martin continued.

"I know it's not my place, and if I had been there I would have tanned his hide, but he needs your forgiveness. Sometimes a man does things he can't take back, and no matter how much he tries to make 'em right, his mistakes seem to come back to haunt him." He exhaled a long breath.

She had the distinct feeling the conversation had shifted to Martin. "Correct me if I'm wrong, but I don't think we're speaking of my father any longer."

"No, ma'am. I guess not." He set a plate filled with ham, eggs, and biscuits on the table, then placed a jar of strawberry jam next to the plate. Rosalind waited, certain he would say more, and after fixing two more plates with food, he did. "I know how your pa feels. Even though he can't change what he's done, forgiveness goes a long way, helps 'im be a better man. Heals the brokenness he's carried."

His piercing gaze begged her to understand, but why? God had revealed to her last night through the Scriptures that no one was righteous, not even one, but through Jesus. She was a recipient of forgiveness. Therefore, she should forgive others. "I believe you're right."

Surprise registered on Martin's weathered face.

"Forgetting isn't easy, and God will help me, but He wants me to forgive my father. I won't deny my father wounded me like no other, but I'm reminded of how I helped crucify Christ to the cross, and how He was wounded for my transgressions. I don't know why my mother's death or my father's betrayal had to happen, but I've learned a valuable lesson."

"And what is that, ma'am?"

"God never left me when I felt so alone. He was faithful to His promises."

Questions passed over Martin's face. His mouth opened as though to respond, but when Trent came through the kitchen door, Martin turned to the stove and began cleaning. If she had the chance later, she'd ask him what he had been about to say and thank him for his friendship. Trent slumped into a chair and began eating without a word. She poured him a cup of coffee and set it beside his plate. Martin left through the back door as she slipped into a chair alongside her husband.

Dark circles hung beneath his eyes. "Thank you," he said, scooping up his coffee cup. He took a sip. The scruff along his jaw seemed to have grown considerably since yesterday. Trent stabbed another clump of eggs. "I think when I'm finished I'll wash up and then go lie down." He covered her hand and met her gaze. "How's Lilly doing?"

"She's been asking questions about her mother and your horse. What's happened has opened up the floodgates, but I think she's fine now."

"I know she's all right. She has you." Trent squeezed her hand. "How are you holding up?"

"I'm exhausted physically and emotionally, but after comforting Lilly, I began to realize you were right."

"I like the sound of that." He smiled. "Right about what?"

His blue eyes held hers and reminded her how blessed she was. This man conveyed more devotion and love than any she'd known until now. "You told me God brought Lilly and me together. I believe you're right. Last night, I found healing. While I was talking with Lilly, she shared her fears about her mother and being alone. I understood the numbing fear she described and having no one to love you … but God led me to you. He led Lilly to me. To us.

"God truly loves me, Trent, as He does Lilly, as He loves us. I remember reading in the Bible somewhere that the Shepherd cares for His sheep and tends to them. I've seen Him in you. You never gave up on me. He never gave up on me. Never left me no matter what I went through." She cleared her throat, willing her tears to stay at bay as her heart was filled with joy. "Lilly misses you more than the horse."

"I'll try to stay up for her before I rest." Trent stood and pushed his chair back with his legs. "Washing up will help me stay awake." He yawned but drew her from her chair to his chest. "I'm thankful every day the Good Shepherd led me to you."

Thirty minutes later, Rosalind pulled the sheets to their bed back and fluffed Trent's pillow. He came into the bedroom, stretching and yawning. "I'm not sure how long I can stay awake."

She patted the bed. "You need your sleep. I'll wake you later so you and Lilly can spend some time together."

He slid into bed.

Rosalind drew the covers to his chest and bent down to kiss his cheek, but she was greeted with his lips—warm and inviting. She pulled away to stare into his eyes.

The corners of his mouth lifted. "I've missed you."

"It's early still."

"Does it matter?"

Trent awoke to his wife in his arms. A light snore vibrated from her mouth. How long had they been asleep? He traced the soft planes of her lips and cheek with his fingers, taken once again by the softness of her skin. "Rosalind."

She stirred and gave him a sleepy smile.

Oh, how he loved and treasured her. Trent kissed her brow and rose from the bed, letting Rosalind continue to rest. He'd spend some time with Lilly before he checked on Midnight. Pete said he'd keep him up to date if he didn't continue to improve.

After he dressed, Trent went down the stairs to find Lilly with Martin in the kitchen. "Well now, what do we have here?" Several pans, spoons, and a pot filled with a dark mixture sat on top of the table. He leaned over the pot and inhaled the sweet scent that would soon occupy the room.

Lilly ran to him and threw her arms around his waist. "We're making chocolate." She released him and rolled her finger for him to come down to her level. She spoke in his ear. "I don't know how to make chocolate. Do you?"

Trent laughed. "No, but Martin will teach us."

"Your horse better?"

"He seems to be."

She took his hand and pulled him to the table, where Martin worked.

Martin added some type of liquid to the mixture, then added butter. "Okay, Miss Lilly. Your turn to stir, but this is hot." He gave her a wooden spoon. "Don't touch the outside of the pot. I'll hold it."

She accepted the spoon, kneeled on a chair, and stirred.

Trent wanted nothing more than to make his girls happy. He glanced at Martin and was about to thank him for tending to Lilly, but something gave him pause. Martin's gaze darted from here to there. "Martin, got something on your mind?"

He looked slightly put out. "I wanted to go into town today to do a few things, but if I left now, I wouldn't be back for supper."

Trent grinned. "It won't be easy, but we'll manage without you for a night."

Martin set the pot on the table, stood, then placed a pan next to the pot. He poured the chocolate into the pan. "I'll leave this in the center of the table until it cools. But you'll need to put it in the icebox after a while." He took his hat from the hook by the door, looked back at Lilly, a wishful look flickering across his face.

"Bye, Martin." Lilly waved.

Martin seemed to force a smile, but it faded quickly when she turned away. He glanced at Trent as if on the verge of revealing something. Instead, he settled his hat on his head. "Tell Mrs. Easton bye for me." And with that, Martin left.

Lilly looked up at Trent from her chair. "Rose will be surprised. Chocolate is her favorite. When my papa gave Rose chocolate, she ate it *real* quick. Mama told her she'd get sick, but Rose laughed and told Mama she'd never live without chocolate again. Chocolate isn't my favorite, but I like it." She shrugged. "Since we're done, can I see your horse? Rose won't let me. Said I had to wait for you."

Trent's mind spun from the many directions Lilly's thoughts had traveled, but mostly there was concern for Martin. Something wasn't right, and he wished he knew what it was. "I'll take you."

Lilly shot out of her chair and skipped toward the door.

Glover rode over an hour from town. The sun penetrated his clothes and sweat rolled from every inch of him, and still no sign of Rosalind or the ranch. Did the woman at the general store tell him the correct information? He'd used his partner's name as an alias so as not to draw unnecessary attention to himself. Yes, he'd thrown money around—and that usually attracted attention—but it had been to secure men to help him with his plan, so that if by chance Rosalind disappeared, he wouldn't be blamed. His partner would take the fall.

He stopped his horse and glanced across the flat land. Several trees stood in the distance.

He spit dust from his mouth and snatched his canteen. How would he find Rosalind if Roger didn't show his face in town? Roger had been his only lead.

Glover swallowed the cool liquid, then wiped his face with his sleeve. Should he go back and wait for Roger or continue?

Wait. He harrumphed.

That was all he'd been doing with Rosalind. Why couldn't the woman get it through her head she belonged to him?

The sound of hoof beats rose in the distance. Glover wrapped his canteen strap around the horn of the saddle and wheeled his horse that direction, spurring it into a canter.

The horse and rider came up fast. Glover waved the older man down, tilting his hat as he brought his horse to a stop.

"Name's Williams," he lied. "I heard about a rancher by the name of Easton who sells horses. Could you tell me where he might live? I've been riding for some time, and I'm afraid I'm lost, being new to the area."

"And who told you they were selling horses?" The older man stared him straight in the eye.

"The woman in town. I can't think of her name, but her husband owns the general store. She sweeps a lot is all I can say."

The older man stayed silent and eyed him for a moment longer. "Mrs. Vines. She sent you out here for nothing. He doesn't sell horses. He sells longhorns."

"I'm in the need of a few longhorns too. You know, to start up a ranch myself. If you're gonna reach your dreams, you gotta start somewhere."

The older man relaxed. "I know what you mean." He turned in his saddle, one hand on the horn, the other close to his gun.

Did he suspect something? Glover moved his hand inches from his pistol.

But the man pointed in the distance. "See those trees over yonder? There's the beginnin' of Easton Ranch. Can't miss it."

Glover thanked him, then rode in the direction the man indicated. He sought shade under the tree that marked the beginning of Easton property, looking out toward several buildings. A man and a little child—girl, Glover thought—came from one of the buildings and walked toward a fence on the other side. The man picked the child up, and long red hair bounced. Definitely a girl.

Movement within the fence caught his eye. Glover shaded his face with his hand and squinted. His other hand balled into a fist. He'd know that man anywhere.

Roger.

Roger brought a horse to the fence, and the little girl petted the horse. He strained against the sun to see the man with the girl. Trent. He had a child?

Glover had sat for several minutes by the time Rosalind exited the home. Trent turned to her, and the child reached out her arms. Rosalind scooped the girl up and hugged her close.

Glover's face heated. His mind flashed back to the months shortly after Rosalind's mother's death, months that had drawn into an eternity, waiting for Rosalind to return. She'd been visiting Roger's mother … or so went the story.

Four months and three weeks were the number of days she'd been gone.

How many months would a woman need to hide a pregnancy, bear a child, and run from the shame? He clinched the reins as the stinging truth slapped his mind. "They had a child together. So Rosalind wasn't as innocent as she seemed." As Glover had believed. How could he have been so deceived?

Glover yanked the horse's reins toward town and kicked the animal into a gallop. His brain pounded against his skull. He'd come up with a plan. One that would take care of them all.

Rosalind closed the door to Lilly's room and entered her own. Candlelight flickered against the wall, casting shadows. Trent lay in bed with his Bible in hand, but he looked up as she reached him. "Do you want me to go with you to speak with your father?"

"I think I should go alone, but pray for me."

He clasped her hand and gave it a squeeze. "Of course."

She took a long breath and headed down the stairs to find her father. He sat at the kitchen table, hands wrapped around a cup. "Mind if I sit?"

He glanced up and shot to his feet. "Please. I didn't hear you come in. My mind must have wandered. Would you like some coffee?"

"No. Thank you." She sat, her stomach churning into knots, and folded her hands in front of her.

He watched her intently as he rested back against his own chair. "Whatever is on your mind, daughter, come out and say it. If you want me to leave—"

"No. Not yet … or ever. I don't know." *God, please give me the words.* She met his eyes. He was such a different man than she remembered. God had truly done a work in his life … and in hers. "I forgive you." The words came out easily and instantly. The burden of hurt, anger, and unforgiveness lifted from her, and peace settled.

His brows furrowed. "I was just sitting here thinking. How could you ever forgive me for what I've done?"

"God showed me how to forgive you. He reminded me of His forgiveness toward me, toward others."

"I'm ashamed, Rosalind. You don't know how sorry I am."

"I know, Papa … and I forgive you." Her father stood from his chair and came to her, holding out his hand. He assisted her up, and she fell into his arms. The warmth of his loving embrace brought unexpected tears. She inhaled a deep breath and held him tighter. How long she'd yearned for this, for him to love her again!

"I love you so much, daughter." He held her close and choked back a sob, tears not her own falling to her face. "Thank you."

Chapter Thirty

Trent stared back with eyes so intense, so dark, that Rosalind's heart raced. She could scarcely breathe. He loosened his hold around her and whispered close to her ear. "You could have been hurt. It's a good thing I was here. What were you doing on this ladder?" He unhooked the torn hem of her dress from where it had caught on a ridged section of the ladder and placed it over her calf and ankle, grazing her skin with his thumb in the process.

"I'm glad you were." She swallowed hard, trying to recall the question he had asked moments ago. "Your horse looks much better."

Smiling, Trent set her on her feet. "And you, my wife, need to change your dress. You are driving your husband mad with desire."

Her eyes widened. "Shhh. Someone will hear you."

"We are married. Two shall become one. And we are one."

She leaned into his chest. "Yes, but my father could walk in at any moment and hear you speak of … intimate things. He spends most of his time in this barn."

"Then he'll be gone today." Trent headed for the door.

She ran alongside him and grabbed his arm. "You can't ask him to leave. You can't."

He chuckled and collected her in an embrace. "I know."

"You're teasing me."

"Yes, for this." His lips glided along hers before parting them in a deep kiss.

Someone cleared his throat, and Rosalind jumped out of Trent's embrace.

Her father stood by the barn door, smiling. "Your mother and I loved each other deeply, and I can see the same love in both of you. I have been blessed coming and staying for a time, but I must leave."

Rosalind stepped forward, her neck burning. Had he heard their discussion? "Why? You've only been here a few weeks."

"Trent's horse is better. He plans to take Lilly for a ride today, so I'm no longer needed. It's time to begin my travel back to Boston." He walked to her and placed a hand on her cheek. "I'm so thankful for your forgiveness and your love."

She placed her arms around her father's neck. "I never stopped loving you."

"Thank you, my child. Your love means the world to me." He held her at arm's length. Tears glistened on his face. "I will be heading to Fort Worth and staying for a week. Maybe you both could stop by, and we could have dinner when Trent takes the herd to market." He looked over her shoulder, and she followed his gaze until it rested on Trent.

She awaited his answer. His handsome smile almost did her in. "Of course." Her chest swelled with love, more now than she ever thought possible.

Her father hugged and kissed her cheek a final time. "Let me say goodbye to Lilly, and then I'll be on my way." He strolled out of the barn.

Trent came to stand behind her and wrapped his arms around her waist. "He's a good man, Rosalind. He loves you."

She spun to face him. "*You're* a good man, Trenton." She gently pressed her lips against his, taking in his breath. "And you love me."

"Do you realize when we're intimate, you call me Trenton?"

She pulled her head back. "I do?"

He bent in, close to her face. "You do and I like it. As I call you—"

"Rose." She giggled with his lips slightly against hers. "I like it too."

"We should see your father off before we get into trouble."

She bit her lip.

He leaned back and searched her face. "What? You don't think we could get into trouble?"

"I'm afraid so." She released him, trying to recover her breath, and strolled out of the barn as casually as possible.

After Trent saddled her father's horse and pulled it out from the barn, Lilly and her father ambled down the porch steps. Lilly ran to Trent, and he scooped her up into his arms.

Trent held out his hand to her father. "We'll see you in Fort Worth."

"Thank you, Trent, for giving me a chance to make amends and for taking such good care of my daughter."

"Always." Trent met her gaze, his blue eyes sparkling.

Father climbed on his horse and smiled. "I look forward to our visit." He nudged his horse into a gallop.

"Horse ride?" Lilly grabbed Trent's face with both hands. "Yes?"

He pecked her nose with a kiss. "Only if you go with me."

Lilly released his face and wiggled her legs to get down. "I'll saddle," he said, placing her on her feet.

She strode to the barn, arms swinging side to side.

Rosalind tucked her hair behind her ear. "She's so relaxed here."

"What do you mean?"

"Lilly doesn't have to hide who she is behind propriety. She's running, jumping, expressive … able to be a six-year-old."

"And you?"

"I feel like I've belonged here all my life."

Lilly poked her head from the barn. "Are you coming? Or do you want me to saddle him by myself?"

They both chuckled, knowing she couldn't reach the saddle. "I'm coming," Trent said as Lilly disappeared into the barn.

Not long after they left, the blue skies gave way to dark gray. Rosalind went to the porch and studied the land surrounding the house. The clouds rolled straight toward her. She pushed worry from her mind, but her knees insisted on trembling.

Rosalind recalled the first week on the ranch and how the lightning storm caused her to pace all night. The wind had blown an eerie whistle past the window, and a branch had scratched against the glass like fingernails.

Trent and Lilly would get caught in the storm if they didn't hurry. She shot up a prayer for their safety when a wagon came down the path to the house. *Walt.* She waved as he stopped. Drizzling rain began to fall. "So what brings you by in this nasty weather?"

Walt joined her on the porch and propped himself against the side of the house. "There was a fight in town between two strangers and Martin at the saloon. I thought Blake should know since he's been lookin' for Martin. Is he 'round?" Lighting flashed in the distance.

Martin? She'd missed him these last two days and hoped

he'd return to them soon, but somehow she felt responsible. Did their talk drive him away? "Well, I'm sorry, but Trent took Lilly for a ride and I haven't seen Blake."

"Good to hear his horse is better. Too much ugly in the world."

"I know exactly what you mean." She herself was hidden away, protected from the ugly she'd known.

Walt looked up into the sky. "Well, I bes' be gettin'. I might make it back before the heavens pour down." He tilted his cowboy hat in her direction. "Ya take care."

"Thank you, Walt. Hope you stay dry."

"Yes, ma'am."

The wagon pulled down the path, but Rosalind's view focused beyond the direction Walt was heading. Her arms encircled her waist. "God, please bring them home quickly."

"See, I told you Midnight was better." Trent headed toward home. He'd seen the clouds rolling in, but Lilly and Rosalind so enjoyed the fresh wildflowers they collected every few days, he couldn't help searching out a bouquet. He loved seeing Rosalind happy. A surge of thankfulness filled his thoughts just as a flash of movement caught in the corner of his eye.

Trent slowed his horse and turned. Bile rose within his throat. In the distance, riders pushed his stock to the fence. He began to count. His men wouldn't … Blood pounding in his ears, he reached for his gun, then caught Lilly patting the horse's mane. There was nothing he could do. He couldn't endanger the child. If only she wasn't with him. Angry, he shook his head and turned his horse toward home.

A shot rang out, and Trent's body jolted forward in pain, the flowers in his hand scattering in the stiff wind.

Chapter Thirty-One

Where were they? Rosalind paced the porch as the rain fell in sheets, the wind howling past her face. She wished Martin were home. He'd help her look for Trent and Lilly.

She pushed her hair back from her cheek as odd thumping sounds hit the house. Pellets of ice fell to her feet. She looked toward the heavens. *God, please, bring them home.*

Within the wind, Rosalind thought she heard a child's cry. She squinted into the gloom past the outbuildings into the fields. Nothing. Then she heard it again, closer this time. *Lilly!* Ice pelted her as she ran into the rain. "Lilly! Where are you?" she screamed, her heart pounding.

A lone rider crossed the dirt path. Lilly screamed out in terror, her face red, "He's dead!"

Rosalind ran to her and grabbed the reins. Lilly's dress was soaked in crimson. Sharp, piercing fear stabbed her. She dragged Lilly from the saddle and searched for wounds. "Are you hurt? Where's Trent? Where is he?" She touched her hair and face, assuring she was unharmed. Rosalind squeezed her within her arms.

"Blood. I saw it. He told me the horse would take me home. Then he fell. He hit the ground. I tried to stop the horse. I couldn't. He's dead!"

"No, Lilly. He's not. Just like Trent's horse. Trent isn't dead either." She prayed for her words to be true. "Where did he fall?"

Sobs racked Lilly's small form.

"You have to tell me. Trent can't stay out in this weather. Where did he fall, Lilly? Please!"

She cried in gasping breaths. "By…the…beginning…of the…fence."

"Listen to me." She rushed on, mind swirling. "Go in the house. Change out of these wet clothes. I don't want you catching cold. I'll be right back."

"You promise?" Her teeth chattered.

"Yes, I promise. As soon as I find Trent. Now hurry and change." Rosalind kissed her cheek and sent her on her way.

Holding the horn of the saddle and slipping her foot in the stirrup, she pulled herself up onto the horse. She took the reins and let out a breath. "God, direct my path."

The rain poured harder as she rode toward the fence line. Lightning crashed and she jumped. "Lord," she whispered, holding the reins tighter, her nails digging into her palm. "Help me find him." The horse slowed to a walk. What was he doing? She remembered Trent telling her horses were directed by touch. She pushed her calves against the beast's body, but he didn't move in the direction she wanted and he didn't speed up.

Rosalind scanned the ground from left to right. Nothing. She wiped blinding rain from her eyes. She was at the fence. How could she have missed him? Turning around, she called out, "Trent!" They passed the fence once again before she saw a dark form on the ground.

Hopping down, Rosalind ran to his side and dropped to her

knees. Lilly had said there was blood. She'd seen the girl's dress, but there was none on him. "Trent." She rolled him over and saw it. Blood. Coming from his shoulder. "Trent, look at me. You have to wake up! I'm not going to let you die on me! I love you." Her breath caught.

A soft moan formed on Trent's lips as his horse sidled over to them.

"Help me get you onto Midnight. Hurry. You're not safe."

She glanced around quickly but saw nothing. Struggling to assist Trent stand, Rosalind found a strength that could have only come from above. Somehow, she managed to get him onto his horse. She stuck her foot in the stirrup and hoisted herself up behind him. He leaned against her. "Hang on."

Lilly had been right. Trent's horse did know where to go. As they entered the clearing, she felt Trent's weight shift. He was slipping. "Just a few more minutes! Hold on!" She tugged on him with all her might and managed to keep him upright until they reached the edge of the porch. Before she could formulate a plan to get him down, he slipped from her grasp, and her heart fell as his body hit the rain-slick dirt.

She didn't know how she did it, but she climbed down from the saddle and struggled to get Trent to the house. Once on the porch, her strength gave way under the weight of his body, and she stumbled, breaking his fall. She moaned as pain shot through her leg. She had to find help and quickly. Tears filled her eyes, though not from the pain. If something happened to Trent while she sought help … No, she wouldn't think such thoughts. The fear of death would not claim her as it once had. God was with her now. God was with Trent.

She struggled from under him and hobbled into the house. As she took the stairs, she bit her lip against the throb in her leg. Rosalind entered the room and found Lilly sitting on the floor, wearing dry clothes and rocking her stuffed rabbit. "Lilly, Trent's outside on the porch. I couldn't carry him inside." She ripped the blankets off the bed. "I'm covering him with these blankets since he's all wet, then I've got to find Matthew." She cringed as she knelt. "I'll be right back. Matthew can help. Stay inside. Will you do that for me?"

Lilly nodded.

She pressed a firm kiss on Lilly's forehead and turned to rush down the stairs. Once at his side, she covered him. "If you can hear me, I'm going for help."

The storm had begun to pass as Rosalind rode hard to the men's bunkhouse in the opposite direction of their home. Once there, she flung the door open. "Hello! Anyone here?"

Pete entered through the back door into the main room, eyes dark with concern. "What's happened? Are you bleeding?" The young man placed a hand on her arm.

She glanced down. Trent's blood stained her dress. "It's Trent. I need Matthew. Please, hurry!"

Pete stuck his head out the door and hollered, "Matthew!"

Matthew hurried into the bunkhouse, and when he saw her his eyes widened. "Rosalind, what's happened?"

Tears blurred her vision, and she wiped them away. "Oh, Matthew. Trent was shot while riding with Lilly. They were heading back from the direction of the stream. He needs the doctor." Rosalind glanced at her red-tinted fingers and feared she might swoon. She swallowed against the urge, following Matthew and Pete outside.

Pete's voice rose. "Matthew, there's something you should know. I didn't think much about it at the time."

"What is it?" Matthew asked as he leapt into the saddle.

"This might be nothing … but I saw Martin in the field the other day. The same spot where our other longhorns had gone missing."

"Stay with Rosalind. Keep her safe." Matthew yanked the reins and spurred his horse on.

As Rosalind and Pete rode back to the Eastons', Pete's words painted a picture she couldn't believe. Not Martin. Not her friend.

Near the house, Blake's horse stood by the spot where she'd left Trent, Matthew's alongside his.

Pistol drawn, Pete covered the barn while Rosalind entered the house and found Blake and Matthew hunched over Trent on the floor. Blake sliced Trent's shirt with his knife and dropped the wet garment next to him. "It looks deep. I need something to stop the bleeding."

Rosalind cringed. Pain pulsated up her leg as she rushed to their room and grabbed one of her old dresses, then dragged it back to the living room. Blake fisted his pocketknife, sliced the dress into strips, then placed a wad of cloth against his shoulder.

"Help me lift him to check the wound," Blake said to Matthew, as Rosalind placed a hand along Trent's clammy skin.

"He's soaked through." Rosalind moaned. "Shouldn't we change his clothes so he doesn't become ill?"

"It might be best." Matthew touched his skin and the hole on the opposite side of his shoulder. "There's no exit wound."

"Will he be all right?" she asked.

Regret shone in Matthew's brown eyes. "He's unconscious. I think he's lost a lot of blood."

They laid Trent back down. Blake finally said, "Pray there's no damage inside, but most importantly that no infection sets in. We need to try to keep that from happening."

What did that mean? Would her husband live? Rosalind's stomach heaved, and tears filled her eyes. She needed to check on Lilly. She pointed to the stairs. "I need to—"

Matthew placed a gentle hand on her shoulder. "We'll be fine."

Rosalind looked at her husband's pale face and swallowed, battling to compose her emotions before seeing Lilly. She took slow steps up the stairs where the child held Mr. Sanders in an embrace, rocking it much like Trent did when he held her.

Lord, please don't take him away. Her heart was breaking at the thought of a life without Trent. Once again someone she loved would die before her eyes. How could she endure losing him?

She was weary. But hadn't Trent told her she didn't have to be strong any longer, that she only needed to trust God? Hadn't she learned this lesson? She was weak, but through Christ she was strong, and He wouldn't leave her.

With a deep breath, Rosalind knelt at the rocker. "Lilly, you're a brave little girl."

"Is he dead?"

"No, sweetie. Trent's alive. I know this might be hard to understand, but when someone becomes sick or hurt, it doesn't mean they'll die. It just means they need extra help getting well. I know you're worried about your mama, but she had to go to the doctor to get well. That's why I mentioned Trent's horse earlier. You thought he was going to die, but he's healthy now, healthy enough for you to ride him today. He even helped me find Trent." Rosalind fingered Lilly's hair. "There's some pie left from yesterday. Would you like some?"

She nodded.

"All right. Let's go down to the kitchen, and I'll cut you a slice." Entering the kitchen, Lilly stared toward the living room. Blake and Matthew blocked their view, and Rosalind was thankful as she masked her worry. She pulled out the pie, cut a section, placed it on a plate, and set it in front of Lilly, who sat at the table. "Here you go, sweetie." Rosalind sunk into her own chair and closed her eyes for a second to focus a moment longer on the child instead of the man she loved in the next room. She took Lilly's small hands within hers, enjoying the warmth they provided.

"Rose, are you cold?"

"No, sweetie. Why?"

"You're shivering."

Rosalind looked at her hands, and they were indeed trembling. "Maybe I am a bit chilled since my dress is still wet from being caught in the rain earlier. Why don't we pray for Trent?"

Lilly nodded so Rosalind bowed her head. "Dear Lord, we come to You because you are the Good Shepherd who tends to Your sheep. We ask You to heal Trent and for his strength to return quickly. And Lord, we pray for Lilly's mama. Please heal her. Bring her parents to Graham safely. We thank You for Your tender care. Amen." Rosalind rose, placing a kiss on top of Lilly's head. "I'm going to check on Trent. I'll be back in a minute."

Rosalind walked into the living room and stood over Blake. He'd used her dress as a sling. Other strips wrapped around Trent's shoulder. "How is he?"

"He's in and out. His pulse is normal. It's the best we can hope for right now. I need to get the doctor. Where's Martin?"

I wish I knew. What Pete said had to be wrong. Martin would never be involved in anything like he suggested. "Haven't seen him since he left. Said he'd be back, but Walt came by and mentioned he was staying in town."

Blake took a heavy breath. "Do you know what happened here?"

"I don't. I was waiting for them on the porch during the

storm when I thought I heard a child's cry. Shortly after, Lilly came up on Trent's horse, alone. She'd left with Trent hours ago." She bit her lip as she stared down at Trent. His face looked so pale.

"We'll need to ask Lilly." Blake took a layer of bloodied fabric from Trent's chest.

"I know." She met his gaze. "I need to change out of these wet clothes. I'll be back."

Blake and Matthew both nodded.

Once in the bedroom, Rosalind fought back sobs as she dressed. How many times had she prayed a prayer for healing and God never answered? She shook the doubts from her head. "Please, Lord," she whispered. "Help me to trust You."

Minutes later she stood in the corner of the kitchen listening to Lilly tell Blake what she remembered of the shooting.

"Did you see anyone in the field while you were riding?" Blake asked.

"No," she said, pressing Mr. Sanders against her cheek. "But I know why Martin hasn't come back to cook."

Blake glanced at her quickly, then leaned closer to Lilly. The stilled silence in the room seemed to lengthen by the minute and drew their attention even more. "Lilly, why do you think Martin hasn't come back?"

"Because he doesn't have his horse. I saw it in the field."

Rosalind gasped as her hand flew to her lips. She hurried from the kitchen and stood in the middle of the living room. *Martin couldn't have done this. He wouldn't hurt us.*

"Rose … Rose …"

Rosalind sat up in her bed and touched Trent's skin. It

burned with fever. "I'm here."

"Rose ..."

She kissed his cheek. "I'll be right back with water and a towel." She hurried down to the kitchen and grabbed what she needed.

Matthew met her near the stairwell. "Is he all right?"

"He has a fever. The doctor said this might happen, but I'd hoped…"

"Thankfully the doc took the bullet out easily. If you get worn out, I can take over."

"Thank you." She climbed the steps and entered the bedroom. Soaking the small towel in water, Rosalind placed it over his face and eyes. She drew the covers back, releasing the heat captured within the quilt. Taking the other cloth she'd brought, she soaked it in the cool water before patting his chest.

"Rose."

"I'm here, Trenton. I love you."

Rosalind awoke with a start the next morning and sat upright. Glover had found her, shot Trent, and forced her to watch him die.

Her stomach tightened as she glanced at her sleeping husband. "It's only a dream," she reminded herself in a whisper, climbing out of bed. After getting dressed, she readied herself for whatever the day held and descended the stairs.

The day started early with Martin gone. Fixing breakfast was almost comforting as she remembered times she and her sister had cooked together with their mother. Oh, how she missed them both!

How were William and Anna? She tried to imagine how

they'd grown. How she missed holding them in her arms. Then Glover came to mind once again. Fear always seemed to rip her happiness from her. She closed her eyes. *Please, Lord, take it away. Help me to trust You.*

She opened her eyes to find Matthew staring at her. "Good morning," he said with a slight smile. "You're up early. I thought you'd be sleeping."

"Too much to do. Besides, I'm finishing up the biscuits, then I plan to head outside for some eggs."

"I'll get those before I do the milking." He grabbed a basket off a shelf. "How's Trent?"

"He still has a fever."

Matthew's face fell.

Rosalind continued slicing the dough, not wanting to think too hard on the fact that fever killed. Her mother included. She finally said, "Do you think Lilly could have been mistaken? It seems wrong, don't you think? Martin couldn't have done this." She placed the biscuits in the oven. Despite the radiating heat, she shuddered at the thought.

"I wish I knew where he was, but sometimes men have their own ideas. Sometimes their choices affect only themselves, but other times their choices affect those who love them. I've wrestled with telling you, but me and Blake think you need to be told. For your safety. Martin's been seen in town with two men. Last we heard a fight was involved, and I keep coming back to Trent getting shot. Martin is nowhere to be found, and those men have something to do with who's stealing the stock. Blake's out looking for him now."

"Is that why Pete and another cowhand are hanging around here?"

Matthew smiled. "Noticed, have you? It's for the best. Until Trent's healed."

"I appreciate you men looking out for us. So … does Blake have any other leads?"

Matthew went to the pegs by the door and snatched his coat. "Why don't I milk the cow and get you those eggs? We can talk more later."

Opening the icebox door, Rosalind nodded, not believing Martin could do this to her family. She chipped at the chunk of ice until her bowl was filled. If Trent's fever hadn't dropped by the time she got back upstairs, she'd rub the ice on his body to try to break the fever.

Trent called to her as she entered the bedroom.

"I'm here." She lifted from the floor a towel she'd placed on him earlier and laid it across part of the ice. With a spoon, she scooped a few ice chips from the bowl. "Open your mouth. Let the ice dissolve on your tongue."

His blue eyes showed through his heavy lashes as the cube touched his tongue. He let out a moan and shivered. She adjusted his covers and moved perspiration-matted hair off his forehead, then took the towel from the ice and placed it over his head.

"Are you trying to freeze me, woman?" His teeth chattered.

"I'm trying to make you well." Rosalind placed more ice into his mouth.

"Hmm … Ice feels good on my tongue though." His eyes closed.

She spent the next hour changing the bedding wet with fever and tending to him until he fell back to sleep and his body stopped shaking. He'd been awake most of the time they were together. Rosalind prayed that was a good sign. Her mother hadn't awakened before she'd died.

Rosalind stopped by Lilly's room to check on her before starting breakfast. She kissed Lilly's cheek as she continued to sleep, and on her way down the stairs, she almost stumbled when she heard Glover's name. Her body thumped against the wall, stopping her fall. She cocked her ear toward their conversation, seeing Blake standing before Matthew.

"He meets the same description Roger gave me when he came to the sheriff's office the other day. Dark hair. Dark eyes. Maybe your height. Usually rides alone. Very wealthy and likes people to know it. There's been talk about a businessman throwing his money around, asking for help."

"What type of help?" Matthew asked.

Blake paused. "Not sure."

"Did you speak with him?"

"I followed him into the saloon and introduced myself. I thought it was the best way, so I could find out his name without having to ask Rosalind."

"Did it match one of the names Thomas sent in the telegram?"

"It did. Richards. Glover Richards. He's here with two other men."

Rosalind covered her mouth. *No, God. Please, no.* She quietly headed back to her room, unable to stop the small whimper that escaped.

"Rosalind?" Trent's weak voice called to her twice.

"Yes." Fear made her voice shaky. She wiped her face and came to his side. His eyes struggled to open but failed. He lifted trembling fingers toward her. She clasped his hand as the wrinkles in his forehead relaxed. Fresh tears flowed down her face, and she could do nothing to stop them.

CHAPTER THIRTY-TWO

Saying a prayer of thanks for Trent's recovery, Rosalind bent and kissed his cool head. "Good night," she mouthed.

He stirred, but never woke.

Fear broke out on her like a hive. She had to do this. Not for herself but for Trent and Lilly. Saying the words in her mind several times steeled her nerves. She had to protect the ones she loved.

Glover came for me and me alone. Martin didn't try to kill Trent. It was Glover.

If Glover found where she was, Trent would give his life to protect her. She couldn't let that happen.

She almost stumbled sneaking down the stairs, but she caught herself against the wall. She'd need to be more careful. A snore came from the direction of the couch where Matthew slept. Rosalind shut the door behind her and headed to the barn.

Trent's horse was the only horse she'd ridden, so she chose and saddled him, repeating the steps she'd watched Trent and Blake do many times. Once she finished, she detached the left stirrup from the horn. With a deep breath, she stuck her foot in the stirrup and threw her leg over, only to slip and fall flat on her back. Pain shot up the leg she'd used to try to soften the blow. Now with an intense throb pounding in one leg, she used all her strength to hoist herself on top of the animal.

"God, please give me safe travel and success in my plan. I'm scared, but I have to do this."

Stay.

Rosalind shook the thought away and slowly exited the barn and rode down the path to town until she passed the boundary tree. Their tree. She didn't want to think of what they might have had.

Glover swung the saloon doors wide as his men and three others waited at a card game. Williams and Jones always rode with him, but the trick was to arrive in a town at different times so no one would suspect what they might be up to.

Glover had the other three men in his pocket. He'd found out they had been stealing longhorns and who they'd killed. Glover offered them a deal they couldn't refuse—either help him or Glover would go to the sheriff. They'd agreed without knowing the kind of help he required, but they would tonight. Yes, tonight would be the beginning of something beautiful. He'd take Rosalind for himself, and Trent would die.

Glover stood over the men. "Have room for one more?"

Williams shot him a glance, a smile lifting his lips. "As long as you're willin' to lose some money."

Jones chuckled. "Old man."

"You better watch it, or this will be the last card game you ever play." Glover pulled a chair from another table and slid into it. He plopped his money down. Cards were shuffled, dealt, bets placed. He spread his cards between his fingers like a fan.

"So what's the job?" The oldest man of the group stared at his hand before meeting Glover's gaze across the table.

"I heard someone did a job on the Eastons'. How would you feel about finishing it?"

The older man's gaze returned to his cards. "Not interested."

One of his men, a younger one, laughed. "He doesn't like to kill, but I don't have a problem if the price is right. What's the plan?" His focus landed on something behind Glover, and the others looked up. "Well, look who we have here. If it ain't the new Mrs. Easton herself." The young man stood with hunger in his eyes.

Glover turned in his chair and faced Rosalind for the first time since she'd left Boston. Heat ran up his neck as anger boiled, pulsating through him, until an image of the girl standing on her father's steps years ago came to mind. Innocence. Grace. A softness he wanted as his own. He stood. "I've traveled far for you, my dear."

"Mr. Richards." She curtsied as if they were at a soiree in Boston. "May I have a word with you in private?"

He stretched out his arms. "You may say what you need to in front of these men. They shall be my witnesses. Isn't that right, men?"

Lewd chuckles roared behind him. Fear flashed in her eyes, and he relished the knowledge that she hadn't forgotten him. Nor would she ever.

"I'm willing to leave with you tomorrow, if you'll still have me."

He took a step closer and ran his hand along her jaw and neck, grabbing her throat. His thumb found her rapid pulse. She swallowed hard. "And why would I want you after you betrayed me and married another man? I've seen the child. How old is she? How long have you and Trent been keeping her a secret? Tell me," he whispered.

"She isn't my child. She's six." Her voice quivered. "She's my charge."

"I see." The girl wasn't their child. Glover slowly released her, his hand running down her side and settling along her waist. "Why should I believe you?"

"I would never leave my own child."

His brow shot up. "But you would your husband?"

"Please, Glover, allow me to leave undiscovered. Tomorrow afternoon, I'll come to town for some baking goods. I'll meet you wherever you like."

Glover closed his eyes for a moment, enjoying the sound of her groveling. It was like music to his ears. Rosalind was smart. She knew it was better to plead than to speak of Trent. His grip tightened on her waist at the thought of how Trent stole Rosalind from him. But no longer. Soon she'd be in his possession. His mouth curved into a smile. "My room at the boardinghouse will suffice."

"If that is what you wish."

He ran his hand down her thigh. "You have no idea. But let me warn you, dear woman, if you double-cross me again, all that you love will not see the next sunrise."

Glover turned and pointed to the older man across the table from him. "I believe you know this fellow here. Martin, is it?"

Martin nodded, his eyes wary.

Yes, Martin would be useful. "He used to work for Trent, did he not?" Glover met Rosalind's gaze.

"He did, but he left unexpectedly. The child and I were worried, but it seems he's fine."

Glover pushed in his chair. "He's the one who shot Trenton."

Rosalind steadied a look in the older man's direction but remained motionless, expressionless.

He knew Martin's partner shot Trent, but the lie did nothing to find out her true feelings for the cook. "If you'd excuse me, gentlemen, I will escort my soon-to-be bride out of this unsuitable establishment." He held out his arm.

Rosalind paused for a moment, then slipped her arm through. They exited, and he led her to the waiting horse she indicated.

"What room shall I meet you in?" Her voice trembled.

"Room twelve. But remember my warning, Rosalind. Those men in the saloon will do my bidding."

"I won't forget."

She turned to the horse, but he wouldn't let her go so easily. He grabbed her and kissed her that she gasped for air and tried to pull away, but he held her tighter. She belonged to him and him alone. He fought against the hunger driving him, tasting the sweetness of her lips. Soon he'd have her, but not tonight. There were a few more details to take care of before tomorrow.

With a forced resolve, he pushed her away, causing her to stumble against the horse. "Tomorrow, Rosalind. Don't forget. You cannot escape me."

Rosalind thought she might swoon. She entered the ranch and dismounted as bile gurgled up her throat. Unwilling to think of what she'd done, she stumbled to the outdoor kitchen pump and scrubbed her lips with her sleeve.

She quietly skirted around Matthew's sleeping form on the couch and climbed the stairs. As she entered their room, her gaze fell on Trent as he lay fast asleep. Her leg rebelled against each movement, but what did it matter? The pain she'd soon endure with Glover would last a lifetime.

Rosalind bit her lip to keep from crying but lost the fight. She fled to Lilly's room, where the child slept peacefully, and knelt by the bed. "I'm going to miss you." Rosalind moaned and wiped her tears. "I've been blessed beyond measure, holding and loving you as my own. I never thought we'd part this way, but I must. Your safety is now a factor. I promised your mama and papa I'd keep you safe. And I will." Her forehead rested on the edge of the bed. "God, I'm scared. Give me the strength to keep my family safe."

Rosalind rose from the floor and entered her bedroom once again. She changed into a nightdress, then slid into bed next to her husband for the last time.

Chapter Thirty-Three

Rosalind dressed, thankful she didn't require buttoning help from her sleeping husband. She turned to see him sitting up in bed, tearing at his bandages. "Trent, leave them. I replaced those only last night." She touched his hand. "Are you hurting?"

"No."

She could tell he was, but she was about to hurt him far worse by leaving. *I'm sorry.* She blinked back the tears, helping to place his arm in the sling. "There. All set." She started to stand, but he held her hand, stopping her. Her leg rebelled at her awkward position and she winced.

"What's wrong? Are you hurt?" He pulled her to him, and she bit back her cry and managed to stay standing.

"I fell yesterday. My leg will be fine. No need to be concerned. You're the one who needs to heal. That's most important."

"What is it, Rosalind? What's troubling you? I can see it in your eyes."

"My leg hurts is all." She flashed him a weak smile and made her escape into the kitchen. Lilly sat at the table counting flowers. "Where did you find the beautiful wildflowers?"

Matthew searched the cupboards and brought out a glass vase. "We picked them after I milked the cows this morning." He filled it half full of water, then set it on the table. "We can put them in here, Miss Lilly."

"Like them, Rose?" Lilly smiled up at her, sending one stem at a time to the bottom of the glass jar.

"I do, sweetheart." She kissed the top of Lilly's head, then turned as her stomach rolled. She quickened her steps outside and swallowed the nausea coming in waves. She rounded the house and took deep breaths.

"Rosalind." Trent called to her, but she didn't move. "Please, tell me what it is that's upset you."

She turned to him. "Trent, you need to be inside. You don't need …"

He caressed her arms. Her face. Her hair. "Come back inside with me."

She shook her head. "I can't."

He ran a finger over her lips. "Tell me why?"

Tell him. Don't go.

She leaned into Trent's chest and kissed him, savoring him, allowing his touch, his mouth to brand her in every way. She would always be Mrs. Trenton Easton.

"I love you, Rosalind." He rested his head against hers. "I have this uneasy feeling as if God is trying to warn me, but I'm at a loss. I need to know you're all right."

"I'm all right." She moved from his arms and turned him toward the house. "Now go. I only need a few minutes to myself, while you on the other hand need your rest." She gave him a small shove.

Trent glanced over his shoulder and smiled in spite of the concern she witnessed on his face. She waited near the corner of the house, and once the door gave its normal creak and bang, she hurried into the barn.

At the sound of hoofbeats, Trent made his way outside in time to see Rosalind on Midnight, riding toward town. He stared after her, running his fingers through his hair. What was she up to?

He entered the barn and glanced at his horse's stall. She couldn't have saddled up that quickly. Had she planned to leave? There was no other explanation. Whatever the reason, he began saddling another horse, straining at the task while hot pain shot through his shoulder. Hoofbeats from several horses pounded the ground and stopped just outside the barn.

"Trent! Matthew! We need to talk!"

Trent recognized Martin's voice and exited the barn. He found Matthew's gun drawn to Martin's chest. Trent looked from Martin and to the other two mounted men and back to Matthew. "Matthew, what's going on?"

"What are you doing here, Martin?"

One of the riders with Martin pointed a finger at Trent. "I told ya I shot him in the shoulder."

It took only a moment for the fire in Trent's shoulder to fuel his anger. "You did this?" He didn't look to the man who'd spoken, but to Martin. "I had Lilly with me. She could have been killed! Did you kill Boyd as well?"

Pete came out from the side of the house. "I didn't want to believe it, Martin."

Martin turned to the man who spoke earlier. "I told you no more shootin'. If you'd killed that girl—"

"Ain't that why we're here? About his wife and that child?"

Rosalind? Trent's anger rose and he met Martin's gaze.

"So help me, Martin, if you so much as laid a hand on her, hurt her in any—"

Martin cleared his throat. "You need to listen, and listen good. There's a man named Glover in town. He planned to kill you and Lilly, but Rosalind stepped in. She made a deal with the devil."

"Glover's here?" Trent's chest constricted, and he swiveled toward the barn. "I have to go after her."

Matthew grabbed Trent's shoulder, stopping him cold. Pain shot down his arm, but it was nothing compared to the thought of losing the woman he loved. "How are we supposed to trust him after all he's done?" Matthew gave Trent a worried look.

Martin threw his guns down to the ground. "I was a black-hearted fool, but I'm a different man because of that little wife of yours and the child. They have a way of gettin' under a man's skin, of burrowing into his heart. When they came to the house, I finally felt like … part of a family, and all I wanted to do was protect them. I came because I want to help any way I can, and I thought you should know what Glover has planned. But there's somethin' Rosalind didn't know. Glover went back on his word. He sent us here to make sure no one lived, including Lilly."

Trent yanked his arm from Matthew's grasp, gritting his teeth against the pain. "Did you see Rosalind pass on your way here?"

"Nope. We came from Judd's place." Martin jabbed his thumb at the rider to his left.

Trent spun back toward the barn and closed his hands into fists. He had to get to Rosalind.

Matthew was right on his heels, slinging his horse's bridle off its peg.

Trent mounted, reining in his jittery horse. His eyes narrowed. "Martin …"

The man looked at him expectantly. Trent needed Matthew and Pete with him to find Rosalind. Could he trust Martin to care for Lilly when he just proved he wasn't trustworthy? But what choice did he have? "You need to stay with Lilly. If anything happens to her …"

Martin's jaw tightened, and tears glistened in the older man's eyes. "I'll protect her. Now hurry. Glover's waitin' for Rosalind in his room. Number twelve."

Rosalind stared out from the corner of Mr. and Mrs. Vine's general store window toward the boardinghouse undetected. Behind her, the storekeeper carried on a conversation, helping to cut several yards of fabric for a woman she'd seen last week, and she was thankful for the distraction.

"Rosalind! What are you doing here?"

She jumped at the sound of her father's voice. "What are *you* doing here?"

"Glover's here. Before heading to Fort Worth, I came to town for supper when I saw a man with a remarkable resemblance to Glover. Unfortunately, it was more than resemblance. I've been following him ever since."

Her pulse quickened. How long had he been here? "I know. Why didn't you tell me? If I had known—"

"What would you have done? Worry? I won't let anything happen to you. Not again." He took her arm, directing her out of the store.

Once outside, she halted. "It's too late. I saw Glover last night. He's promised me that if I go with him, Trent and Lilly will be safe."

Confusion and worry flitted across his features. "And all of a sudden you trust him?"

"I have little choice. Don't you see? My family's life is at stake, and I'll do anything to protect them."

He stared at her for a long minute. "You remember what I asked you a few weeks ago, about providing for your family? You are nothing like me, daughter. You're willing to give up your life for the ones you love." He cradled her face with his hand. "I'm so proud of you and the woman you've become."

Tears sprang to her eyes. These were the last moments she'd spend with her father, and she would always hold them close to her heart. "I love you, Papa."

"And I you." He hugged her tightly. "Let's go. I heard there's a telegram waiting for you. We can get it before we head back to the ranch." He took her arm before glancing back to Glover's room.

She followed along quickly, hoping she'd finally have a word on Catherine from Oliver. *Please, Lord, let today be the day.*

Rosalind entered the telegraph office, afraid to hope for a miracle.

The man behind the counter stood taller as they neared. "Mrs. Easton. How may I help you?"

"Do you have a telegram for me?"

"Let me check." He pushed his glasses to the bridge of his nose. "No, I don't see one, but you do have a letter. Came today." He held it out for her.

"Thank you." She took the envelope from his fingers and scanned it. *Oliver.* She tore into it.

Dear Mrs. Trenton Easton,
I've written to let you know Catherine is recover-
ing, and we will be on our way to Fort Worth soon. It

will take several weeks by train, but please tell Lilly we are coming. Oh, how we've missed her.

Catherine sends her regards, but honestly, she hasn't stopped talking about you. She has tried to convince me to move to Fort Worth for no other reason but for your friendship. And I happen to agree, but let's not tell her yet, shall we?

Please give your husband our regards as well and tell him how thankful we are to both of you for your kindness. You have our deepest gratitude.

Oliver Hadley

Her father came to her and stood at her elbow. "Is everything all right?"

She wiped her tears. "Everything is wonderful. Lilly's parents are coming. They should be here soon." Her father said he'd forgotten something at the general store, but she recalled little after. Catherine and Oliver were coming! How she wished to hurry home and witness the delight on Lilly's sweet face when she heard the news. She pictured how her green eyes would light up. The joy she felt moments ago vanished.

Rosalind had lied. She'd promised Trent she would never leave, and Lilly that she wouldn't leave without saying goodbye. But she'd done both.

Lord, please forgive me for not keeping my oath, but I have to protect them. Lilly will be with her family soon enough. She won't need me anymore, but Trent ... Please heal the pain I'm about to put him through. And Lord, thank you for answering my prayers.

Focusing on the here and now, she glanced around. Her father said something about the general store, but he was nowhere in sight. She stepped outside and glanced at the store, then at the boardinghouse. She knew what she must do.

Be still.

Yet the urging in her heart to do nothing didn't stop her as she hurried across the street. With a deep breath, she entered the boardinghouse. Stopping at room number twelve, Rosalind could scarcely breathe. She ran her sweaty hands down her dress and took another long breath. She had to protect her family at all costs. Thoughts of Trent skirted her mind, but she pushed them aside. Hardening her resolve, she knocked.

Glover answered right away. "Hello, my dear. I knew you'd come." He dragged a finger along her jaw, his dark eyes devouring her.

Her skin crawled.

"Come in, will you?"

She froze at the invitation. *What have I done? Lord, help me.*

He gripped her arm in a painful vice.

She gasped. "Glover, you're hurting me!"

"Am I?" His lip curled an instant before his maniacal laugh filled her ears and sent a chill skidding down her spine. "You have no idea what pain is." He wrenched her into the room and slammed the door behind her.

CHAPTER THIRTY-FOUR

Rosalind opened her eyes at the sound of someone pounding. It took her a moment to remember where she was, what had happened, and how Glover had knocked her unconscious. The pounding sounded again, and Glover yanked her from the floor. She stumbled but caught herself before falling.

"Don't say a word," he hissed.

"Glover! It's Roger. I need a word with you."

Glover chuckled. He swung the door and pointed a gun at her father's chest.

Her father drew his gun and reached for the hammer. His eyes shimmered with tears as his gaze roamed her ruffled clothes, settling on her face. "Let her go," he said, anguished.

Glover sneered. "I'm afraid not, Roger."

"Then you leave me no choice."

"But then again, you have two choices. Rescue Rosalind, or rescue her husband and that little girl. If you leave now, you might be able to save them. Oh, I think I've forgotten to mention … Three men are on their way to the ranch as we speak to do my bidding. One of the men you know. Martin."

Panic seized Rosalind. "No! You came for me. Me alone. You tricked me!"

"Of course. Why would I let the man you love live? So you can pine over him for the rest of your days? No, dear, you belong to me. I will share you with no one." Glover wrapped his arm around her neck.

Rosalind struggled. "Papa, please. I beg you. Save them. Please. Hurry!" She trembled as Glover's grip tightened.

A shadow fell over her father's eyes, and she saw indecision wrestling within him. Nauseating fear shook her to the core.

"What devotion. What love. Yes, hurry, Roger, before it's too late." Glover laughed as he hauled Rosalind from the room, using her as a shield as he exited the building.

Her father followed, gun still pointed. He was her only hope to save Trent and Lilly. "Please, Papa!" she begged as Glover carried her behind the boardinghouse.

Rosalind stumbled forward. Hard fingers gripped her arm, steadying her.

"Move it!" Glover barked, pushing her forward toward two men who waited on horses. Both seemed tall. Where one was lean, the other was large. She shivered. These were the same men Glover acquainted himself with in Boston.

Nearing the horses, she scanned the vacant area, her heart frantic. Anguish filled her as she sought for an escape. She would find it. She *had* to find it. God hadn't brought her this far only to abandon her now. *I was a fool, Lord, for trying to save my family alone. Please. Help me, Lord. Give me a way of escape.*

Glover's hold lightened on her arm as she reached the horses. The thin man leered down at her, then quickly glanced over her shoulder, eyes narrowing.

"You're a dead man."

Glover spun, releasing her.

Her father stood several feet away, his gun once again aimed at Glover. "Not another step, Richards." His voice demanded obedience.

Her pulse raced in her ears. This was it. Her chance. She lifted her skirt and ran.

"Don't shoot her!" Glover's voice rang out as she sprinted toward Main Street. Her breath came in ragged gasps.

Two shots vibrated in the air.

"Oh, Papa." Tears blurred her vision, but she couldn't stop. *Lord, save my father's life.*

"Rosalind!" Glover yelled, his obscenities catching up with her.

Only a few steps to Main Street.

When the general store came into view, she pushed harder.

Only a few more steps.

"Help!" she cried, running for the boardwalk. Hooves sounded in the distance and caught her attention. Trent galloped toward her, leading Matthew, Pete, and Blake. She blinked twice.

Trent was alive? Her breath caught as her mind spun. Did that mean Lilly was alive as well? She blinked away the moisture from her eyes.

"Rosalind, look out!" Trent's voice pierced her thoughts.

A hand clutched the back of her dress, halting her mid-stride. She fell hard against the dirt. Glover's haunting dark eyes loomed over her. His pistol pointed at her heart. "You will always be mine."

Save me, Lord!

A gun blasted.

Glover's face fell, and his body crumbled next to her on the ground.

The sky rumbled and a breeze brought in threatening clouds, and for the first time, Rosalind welcomed it. She released a heavy breath and inhaled the smell of rain. The nightmare was over. Glover was dead.

She shifted in Trent's arms as Blake exited the general store with a dark cloth and descended the boardwalk. He tossed it over Glover's body. "It's over. I'm finally free," she whispered.

Trent hugged her gently against his chest and kissed the top of her head.

"Are you sure Dr. Parker said my father will be all right?"

Trent intertwined his fingers with hers and brought them to his cheek, his lips, and kissed her hand, her knuckles. She relished the feel of him, his kisses, and thanked God for saving them. "The bullet only grazed him. The doctor said he'd be fine, and he'll bring him out to the ranch when he's finished."

Blake came to them and lifted his hat above his brows. "We'll find the man who got away. Don't you worry, Rosalind. Matthew and Pete are out lookin' for him now. Matthew is the best tracker I know, and Pete … Well, let's just say I'm glad he's on the law's side. Can't see anyone getting away from them." Blake glanced down the street and pointed at the sheriff's office. "The other man is locked up. I'll come out to the ranch for Martin when I've got everything wrapped up in town, but I don't expect him to run after what he did."

Rosalind had forgotten about Martin. She stood to her feet quickly, pulling Trent with her. "Martin, he's at the ranch? Lilly's in danger."

Trent was the first to answer. "It's all right. Martin warned me about Glover's plans. He cares for you and Lilly. It was because of you he became a changed man. He's watching Lilly now and will be at the ranch when we return."

Rosalind glanced at him, certain surprise registered on her face. It had pained her deeply to see Martin sitting with Glover, knowing he deceived them. On several occasions she had recalled their last conversation in the kitchen, but now it all made sense. He was sorry. He needed her forgiveness. He needed God's forgiveness. The first she could give easily, but the second was up to him.

"I'm ready to go home."

EPILOGUE

The following week, Rosalind and Lilly prepared to travel with Trent and the cowhands to Fort Worth. Their first stop after selling the herd was to visit Martin, who had turned himself in for the crimes he'd committed, then to rejoin Lilly with her parents.

Lilly came running from the house with Mr. Sanders tucked under her arm and a sheet of paper clenched in her hand. "I made this for Martin. Can I take it?" She held up a picture of herself and Martin stirring chocolate in a bowl.

"He will love it." Trent picked her up and kissed her cheek. He would miss this sweet girl, and the thought of her leaving them brought a deep heartache he and Rosalind rarely spoke of. "Is Rose almost ready?"

"She's coming, but I think there's something wrong with her. She keeps laughing."

He gave her a squeeze. "Do you think it's because she loves me?"

Lilly leaned into him and kissed his cheek, then pressed Mr. Sanders against the other. "We love you. Can I get in the carriage now? I can't wait to see Mama and Papa. Do you think they missed me?"

"Of course I do." He set her on her feet.

Rosalind came out of the house, her rich brown hair cascading down her back and her gray eyes finding his. She bit her lip.

He cocked his head and tipped his Stetson above his brow. "Hmmm, a kiss for your thoughts."

She blushed.

He drew her close, remembering the softness of her skin next to his and wishing they were alone now. "Are you passing up my kisses?"

"Never." She looked up at him through long lashes. "My mind is spinning. We're meeting Catherine and Oliver. I hoped and prayed this day would come. I just never thought it would be so hard. Do you think they will stay and make their home here as his letter mentioned?"

"That's my hope." Trent glanced at Lilly, who sat in the wagon and sang to Mr. Sanders.

"I'm looking forward to seeing my father off. I feel the need to thank him again for all that he's done, because if he hadn't interceded when he did …"

"It's over. They found the other man. You're safe." He touched her cheek.

"I know, but it's not only that… God never left me even when I was standing in that room with Glover. He was working to rescue me as He did before. He's been there this entire time… through it all. You leaving Boston, Glover, my father, this land, and now …" Moisture filled her eyes. "I've found my joy, Trent. That God is the same no matter what I go through, loving me, helping me."

"I'm sorry, Rosalind, but you lost me after you said, 'and

now.' What has God done?"

She smiled. "When we're in town, I'd like to see the doctor."

He pulled her back and searched her face. "What's the matter?"

She caressed his forehead with her fingers, as he would do to her. "No need to worry. God has blessed us with a child."

Trent lifted her in his arms and swirled her through the air. As he brought her back to his chest, he silenced her giggles with a kiss—one that contained all the love and hope he had for their future.

AUTHOR'S NOTE

I hope you enjoyed *The Rescue*. This story has always held my heart captive in the fact that it gives us a glimpse of how the Lord works behind-the-scenes in Rosalind and Trent's behalf, directing their paths. In many ways, our Lord does the same for us, even when we can't see Him move or act when we pray.

I'm reminded of scripture when Daniel prayed to the Lord, and He answered Daniel's prayer that same day, but evil hindered the answer from reaching him (Daniel 10). Even though *The Rescue* is a fictional story, it represents how we—as people of faith—may not see the Lord working on our behalf, but later receive blessings in the end result of His faithfulness and power to work in our circumstances.

Let us never forget that the Lord hears us when we pray. God's plans are to prosper us. Plans to give us a hope and a future.

Blessings, friends! Until we meet again.

Tanya

ACKNOWLEDGEMENTS

Heartfelt thanks to April Gardner for always being there. Whether it was a quick phone call in the carline, a million questions sent in texts, or countless rewrites, she never missed a beat. Even my spontaneous trip to Texas didn't faze her! Her endless support keeps me going. And where would I be without my dear friend, Mary Hamilton, my critique partner from the very first word, from the very first novel. Thank you for sticking around! I also want to give a special thanks to Carole Towriss and Laura Hilton for their belief in this story. Your support and friendship over the years is truly a blessing. Lastly, I want to thank my readers for their enthusiasm and support of my novels. I'm so glad we're on this journey together!

Read on for an
Excerpt of
Book Two
in the
All Roads
Lead to Texas
Series

The

PROPOSAL

BOOK 2

TANYA EAVENSON

CHAPTER ONE

B lake McKenny's hand rested on the butt of his holstered gun as he leaned against a tree. Sweat trickled down his back—the shade did little good—but he loved it here. Several hundred feet away the tree line stopped, and wide-open prairie stretched straight to the sheriff's office in Graham, Texas. God's country, he called it.

His office.

His land. Or it would be soon.

He inhaled and mouthed a prayer of thanksgiving. Seven years ago, he'd promised land to his wife—land he pictured them raising children on, land they'd work until they were old and gray. A promise he'd never been able to fulfill. At least not while she was alive.

He yanked off his Stetson and wiped his brow with his arm, thoughts shifting to the town meeting he left an hour ago in Fort Worth. Reports of men shot and killed while women and children were taken as hostages from stagecoaches to be sold to brothels.

He released a heavy breath. He had to find a way to keep the people in his town safe. But how could he stop outlaws or their schemes, or keep loved ones from dying at the hands of evil men when he couldn't prevent his own wife's murder? Images of so long ago flashed in his mind for what seemed like the thousandth time. If only …

He shook his head against memories and pain as oppressive as the Texas summer heat and tried to refocus on his personal Garden of Eden.

In the distance, a stagecoach rounded a bend at a hazardous pace. His eyes narrowed, tracking its movement. Dust billowed up from the ground around it, nearly obscuring the two horse riders approaching from behind the coach. The muscles in Blake's body tightened.

A light flashed in a rider's hand. A glint of sunlight off a pistol?

No. Just as he'd feared.

Shots sounded in the distance.

Blake ran for his horse. His fingers clinched the reins, and he leapt onto the saddle. Quickly he formulated a plan, and at this moment, anything would be better than letting those in the stage be taken. Or worse, killed. Blake rode hard toward the scene as more shots were fired.

Amid the dust, the driver of the stage lifted a rifle and fired back. The rider with a blue bandana jumped from his horse onto the driver's box. The two men fought, struggling to keep their balance as the horses pulled the coach off the road. When the driver fell to the ground, the other rider, still on his horse and with a red bandana covering most of his face, snatched the loose reins and brought the team to a halt.

Lord, help me keep a cool head and save these people. He pulled back a bit and slowed.

The man on the horse pointed his gun at Blake's chest as he approached. The other man on the stagecoach glared at him. His blue bandana had slipped to his neck, and Blake memorized the man's face. Crooked nose. Dark hair. Mole on the left side of his cheek.

Blake tipped his hat at the two. Their clothes were dirty and torn, but their guns, Smith & Wesson double-action, clean. He'd seen revolvers like these only twice before. Thankfully, he was wearing one on his hip. "Heard the shots. Thought you might need some help."

The man with the blue bandana secured his disguise. "I'm afraid your rescue attempt was in vain, mister. We ain't tryin' to help anyone but ourselves."

"Stealin' is more like it."

A hearty laugh came from the other robber. He kept his gun trained on Blake's chest.

Blake glanced at the stagecoach's door. If these men were the robbers who kidnapped women and children and sold them to brothels, he needed to do something and fast. He grunted and nodded at the stagecoach. "Take all you want. I'm here lookin' for a woman. When I saw you both comin' in after the stage, I knew this was my opportunity."

The man with the gun gawked. "Are you kiddin' me? Do you believe this, brother?"

Blake climbed off his horse.

Hard, dark eyes peered at him over the blue bandana. The robber had yet to jump down from the stage, and Blake strolled toward him like he had all the time on this side of heaven. Hopefully he did. "Let me take a look-see if there's a bride in here for me." He craned his neck to see inside the carriage.

Eyes the color of a raging storm glared back, brows knitted together. "Don't you dare touch me, or you'll regret it with your life," the woman asserted.

Blake blinked twice. *Great.* He had a fighter on his hands.

That's all he needed. "I'm in luck. I got me one *fine* filly in here." He turned back to the men.

"Brother, I thought you said there were no passengers?" The one on the horse glared. "Ain't that a woman's voice?"

The other threw the strongbox down with a thump. "He's lyin'." He jumped and landed a few feet from Blake. "Pull her out. I wanna see her."

The man on the horse chuckled, causing the gun still pointed at Blake's chest to shake. "If there's more, we could have a little fun."

So they knew this stage was carrying a strongbox, but not about the woman? Maybe Blake had a chance to save this from going bad.

A feminine but curt voice called out, "I'm not now, nor will I ever be his woman."

"She's the only one." Blake did as he was told, praying this woman wouldn't get him shot. He swung the door wide and waited, but no movement came. He'd apologize later, but he needed to play the part. Their lives depended on it.

Blake reached in and grabbed her wrist, then pulled her out the stage's door and yanked her to her feet. Brown hair like silk fell across her smooth cheeks. "You know what's expected. Do as you're told."

Sparks of lighting seemed to shoot from her eyes straight at him. He opened his mouth to speak and she spat into his face.

Red Bandana pointed his gun and snickered. "Well, I'll be. Look at who we have here."

Blake spun around, slipping a gun from his pocket and pointing it. Blue Bandana stepped toward them, and Blake growled, "She's mine. If you plan to die today, then take another step."

Something solid jammed between Blake's shoulder blades.

"Are you hard of hearing? I am not now, nor will I ever be yours."

Heat flowed through his veins. Here he was, trying to save this woman, and look where it got him. A gun in the back.

"Well, what a nice turn of events." The man with the red bandana chuckled. "C'mon, Brother, we got what we came for. She ain't worth it."

The man with the blue bandana set his sights on the woman yet again. When his gaze intensified, Blake was tempted to turn around to see why, but he held his stance. The robber took a step back, lifted the strong box, heaved it onto the horse, then swung into the saddle. With a wink for the woman, he unhitched the horses from the stage and shot into the air. The horses jolted into a full gallop, herding Blake's horse along with them.

Blake ground his teeth. It took all the patience he could muster to wait for the men to leave, especially the one with the blue bandana who lingered in the distance. He had to get his horse back, but first he'd have to deal with the metal digging into his flesh. "Put down your gun."

She hooted. "Not on your life."

"You're leaving me no choice."

"And if you move so much as an inch, I can promise it will be your last."

Time for a new strategy. "I must warn you, if you shoot me, you'll be hung for killing a sheriff."

She laughed again, distrust tainting her voice, threatening him all the while, but Blake had no choice. He wasn't ready to die today. He shifted his body weight to one side and caught a glimpse of her arm. He'd wait for the right moment.

"You're no lawman. Let me see your badge."

Of course, when he needed his badge, he didn't have it. If his deputy could see him now, Blake would never be able to live this down. "It's in my desk drawer. At the sheriff's office."

"Your first mistake, mister. A sheriff never forgets his badge. I've seen men like y—"

Blake twisted, grabbed her wrist, and yanked the gun from her as she flew past. She spun mid-flight and fell to the ground on her backside. He opened the revolver and dumped the bullets into his palm. "I'm sorry, but …" He looked down.

Those dark eyes sent daggers his way yet again, and he was sure one stabbed him in the heart. Never had he seen a woman with such fire, such … beauty. She jumped up, balled her fists, and held them up as if she planned to fight him.

He couldn't help laughing. No. Never had he seen a woman like her. "Ma'am, you have two choices. Ride back to town with me or walk, but I have a feeling I know which choice you'll take. However, if those men return, you won't be so lucky."

"Ride? On what horse?"

He drew his lips together, loosing a shrill whistle for Legend to return if he was still in earshot. "I need to look for the driver. You stay here." He pocketed the bullets and slid her revolver into the belt of his pants.

With that, her hands fell to her sides.

He walked toward the area where the driver had fallen.

"What's your name?" A softer, gentler voice sounded from behind him.

He didn't turn around. "Blake."

"Is that it? Just Blake?"

He couldn't understand this woman. One minute she was trying to kill him, and the next she acted like she cared. "Why do you want to know? To write it on my headstone?"

Legend trotted to him and stood like a soldier, waiting for his command. Blake ran his hand down his mane, collected the reins, and then continued his search for the driver.

"No. When I get to Graham, I'm going to find out who you really are."

"Blake McKenny." He spotted a crumpled body ahead. Dropping the reins, he ran to him and felt for a pulse. Weak. But at least there was one. He looked over his shoulder to find the woman holding his horse's reins. "He's alive but needs a doctor. I've got to get both of you to town." He rose to his feet. At least the man was alive and his horse had returned.

She climbed into his saddle, moving the horse farther from him. "I'll head into town and let the doctor know where to find you. It'll be quicker." She guided the horse into a canter, leaving him standing there.

Blake exhaled. Surely this woman would drive any man insane. Especially him. He had to get help, but there was no way he'd leave her alone with what had happened here or what he learned in Fort Worth. The idea of her riding off unaccompanied into dangerous country wasn't an option.

He allowed the woman her lead as he dragged the driver to partial shade under a mesquite tree, then drew his lips together and whistled. His horse circled and trotted straight for him. He didn't mask his smirk as she approached, or when one of her hands fisted as his horse stopped directly in front of him, or when he took the reins and climbed behind her.

It was the moment he realized how perfectly she fit against his chest that his smirk fell.

Jessica's blood boiled. Who did this man think he was, bossing her around like he did? If it wasn't for the driver needing help, she'd have the mind to … what? She was trapped, pressed against this strange man's chest, and every time she tried to break their contact, the movement of the horse brought her right back.

She glanced around at nothing but flat, destitute land as far as she could see. "How much farther?" She tossed the question over her shoulder, praying it wasn't much longer before she could be rid of him. He grated on her last nerve. But what choice did she have? Trust the men who were robbing the stage? No. She'd rather take her chances with this man—one who hadn't made any physical advances, although wedding bells seemed to be ringing in his brain, a loose bolt she'd fix once she got to town and found the sheriff. She'd see who this *Blake* really was. A bank robber, for all she knew. He'd be easy to describe with a scar that left bare lines running through his trimmed beard.

"Look ahead."

Jessica squinted against the blinding sun. A haze outlined several buildings. At least she thought they were buildings. It wasn't even July, but the heat played mind games with her vision.

She licked her lips. If she'd been smart, she'd have grabbed her hat and canteen from the stagecoach before trying to escape. *Impetuous,* her father had called her on more than one occasion, and now look where it had gotten her—all her belongings still in the stagecoach and her mouth bone dry.

Once again she leaned forward, anxious to escape her captor's presence. "Can't we ride any faster?"

"Suit yourself." Blake spurred the horse forward, and her back slammed against his hard chest. His arm came around her waist.

Her breath caught. She tried to struggle out of his embrace, but he only held her tighter.

"Let go of me!"

"We're almost there."

Her body tensed and her breath became labored as they

galloped into town and collected curious stares. She'd felt this way only once before, and terror caught in her throat. She fought against the memories of a man's hands on her waist as a knife dug into her flesh.

Blake halted his horse and swung off before she had time to blink, then ran into the building directly in front of her.

Her hand flew to her mouth, and she prayed to swallow the vile taste on her tongue. She gasped for air and squinted against the midday sun, craning her neck to read the metal sign above the door. *Doc Adams.*

Blake exited the office and another man rushed out gripping a black medical bag. Blake said something to him that she couldn't hear.

The doctor, she presumed, came her way, tipping his hat as he rushed past.

She followed his movements and noted the length of his stride, still able to feel Blake's presence at her side. "He's the doctor? He looks about … my age." With no response, she turned to Blake who stood there gazing at her. Questions seemed to run through his eyes. She hadn't noticed, until now, how blue they were, like the sky on a clear day.

He grabbed his horse's reins, breaking the trance. "He's new to town. And how old are you?"

She shook out of her thoughts and stood in the stirrups to dismount. "It's none of your concern." Strong hands took hold of her waist and lowered her to level ground. She was taken aback by his nearness and the pure size of him. He was a giant standing next to her, but she wasn't some helpless female. She'd have gotten off his horse without him. Jessica opened her mouth to give him a piece of her mind.

"Will you be all right?"

She stopped, surprised by his words. The genuine look of

concern on his face made her feel vulnerable. She hated it. Running her hands down her dress, she righted herself as much as possible and wished once again she had her hat. She fisted her hands to her side, then clasped them together. "Of course. Why wouldn't I be? I need to find the sheriff and tell him how you stole my pistol, and how you're trying to marry me against my will."

The softness of Blake's eyes hardened, and his jaw clenched. He pulled her pistol from his belt and handed it to her. Before she had the metal securely within her grasp, he brushed past her, climbed into the saddle, and mumbled something under his breath. "If I wasn't …" He yanked the reins hard in the opposite direction and rode off.

If he wasn't … what? One of the robbers? He wouldn't pin this on her. It was the life he chose, and there were consequences. Father always said everyone had a choice to do right or do wrong, and if you choose to go against the law, the law would find you.

She glanced around in search of the sheriff's office. What else could she tell the sheriff about the robbers? What had one of them said? *Come, Brother, we've got what we came for. She ain't worth it.* Her throat tightened at the memory, which led to another of the life she left behind in Oklahoma. Her hand flew to her neck. No, it wasn't Cliff's gang. It couldn't be them. Although she hadn't clearly seen the robber with Blake standing like a towering wall in front of her, but the other, the one with the red bandana covering his face, she hadn't recognized him. Surely it wasn't them.

Hoof beats broke into her thoughts as several men galloped out of town. With a deep breath, Jessica walked across the street, steeling her trembling hands at her sides. What she needed was a room at the boardinghouse while she stayed in town, not haunting memories.

She strolled past the seamstress shop before entering the livery, which also resembled a smithy. Two young boys ran in, came to an abrupt halt, and clapped their knees with their palms, panting for breath.

"I won."

"No. I did."

The tension in her body began to ease as she smiled at them, aged about eight or nine. "I'd say a tie."

The boys turned their mud-smeared faces to her. The one with dark hair shook his head, flinging sand in all directions. The reddish-haired one simply stared before saying, "Ma'am, ye sure? Me da said who ever won dinna be muckin' the stalls tonight."

"Oh, I see." She peered around the livery, her eyes adjusting to the difference in light. On the left, Blake's horse waited, tied up along one of the stalls. She'd know it anywhere. Her father taught her well.

A fire smoldered several yards away on her right. "It seems your dad is the liveryman but also the blacksmith. It'd take one person a *long time* to clean it by themselves, but if they had help, it'd take half the work, which meant more time for fun."

The dark-haired boy drew in a breath. "Nay, I can have fun all by meself." He reached over and smacked his brother on the shoulder. "You're it!" He took off running. His brother followed.

"Nice try, lass." A burly man the size of a mountain came out from the shadows. As he neared, a disabling limp to his right leg became apparent. He wiped his hands on his overalls. "Dinna pay me boys no mind. What can I do for ye?"

She straightened to her full height of five feet two inches but was still no match for the Irishman. The hard lines of his face smiled down at her. "I'm looking for a horse."

"Right now, I dinna have none to borrow."

"I'd like to buy one. That is, if you have any for sale."

"Aye, have one that's comin' in on the train in a few weeks."

"Three weeks?" She'd be stuck here till then? She couldn't let that happen. Too much time had already been wasted this morning. She had to be out of this town one way or the other.

"Lass?"

She took a steady breath and forced a smile. "Yes. I'm terribly sorry. My mind went elsewhere."

"There's a rancher who owns quite a few horses. You could see if he'll sell ye one, though I doubt it. Maybe if ye spoke to the sheriff—"

She perked up and clapped her hands together. "Oh, yes, thank you for reminding me. I need to speak with the sheriff. Where is his office?"

"Two shops down. Across the street from the boardin' house."

"Thank you, sir. I appreciate the help." She strolled out of the livery with purpose now. Who did this Blake think he was? Just wait! She'd knock him down a notch or two.

From the general store, Jessica could see the boardinghouse and the big, bold letters on the sign across the street: SHERIFF'S OFFICE. Unpleasant thoughts unraveled the nice little bow she tied to keep her emotions intact and hidden from the world, including herself.

It was the only way to deal with murder.

ABOUT THE AUTHOR

TANYA EAVENSON is an international bestselling and award-winning inspirational romance author. She enjoys spending time with her husband and their three children. Her favorite pastime is grabbing a cup of coffee, eating chocolate, and reading a good book. You can find her at her website www.tanyaeavenson.com/.

Undercover ICE agent Madi Reynolds has spent years infiltrating a human-trafficking ring, but when her life is threatened, she is forced to walk away and advised to leave the country. War Veteran and ICE agent Brice Johnson faces the biggest assignment of his life— protect the woman he loves.

Don't miss book 3 in the Gaining Love series—
To Gain a Bodyguard

BE THE FIRST TO HEAR ABOUT NEW BOOKS FROM TANYA EAVENSON!

Sign up for announcements about upcoming titles at www.tanyaeavenson.com/